P9-CEA-908

Save What's Left

Save What's Left

Elizabeth Castellano

ANCHOR BOOKS
A Division of Penguin Random House LLC
New York

AN ANCHOR BOOKS ORIGINAL 2023

The Cataloging-in-Publication Data
is available at the Library of Congress.

Anchor Books Hardcover ISBN: 978-0-593-46917-0
eBook ISBN: 978-0-593-46918-7

Book design by Nicholas Alguire

anchorbooks.com

Printed in the United States of America
10 9 8 7 6 5 4 3 2

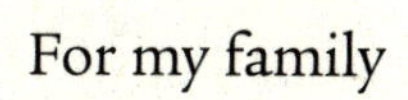
For my family

Save What's Left

1

NEVER BUY A BEACH HOUSE. Don't even dream about one. Don't save your money or call real estate agents or pick out a white couch. If you must do something, pray for the people who do own beach houses. Pity them. Certainly don't, under any circumstance, envy them.

Maybe it's too late for you. Maybe you've gone ahead and picked up some starfish tchotchkes and turquoise nonsense and you feel you're in too deep. Well, then let me tell you right now that those warm summer nights you're dreaming about will be spent arguing over parking restrictions and beach access. You won't paint or write or play tennis. You'll be too busy filing code enforcement complaints in the town attorney's office. You'll wake up to the sound of leaf blowers and you'll either spend half your life trying to protect a tree or cut one down. The village will be charming. The view will be beautiful. You'll attend countless meetings about how to keep them that way. Do yourself a favor and put a lawyer on retainer. Don't waste any time about that. You will, without question, not be on speaking terms with at least one of your neighbors in a year's time.

And, if you're like me, you'll eventually end up in a courthouse conference room in some godforsaken town, nervously clutching a tattered, overflowing, cardboard Christmas box with a picture of a dopey snowman and the words, "Bring on the Snow!" The box will be filled with letters and emails and blueprints and surveys and photos that began as minor grievances but are now exhibits in a money-laundering scheme. And what you'll think to yourself as you stare at that stupid snowman and search frantically for a tissue to wipe away the sweat which now routinely rockets from the top of your head is this: *Why did I ever buy that house?*

The worst part about all of this, I mean the really worst part—worse than the alleged wire fraud or the ruined view or the mounting therapy bills—is that now I am one of these people. I'm now the kind of horrible person who genuinely cares about what so-and-so had to say about the traffic from the chowder festival. I'm the kind of person who has an opinion about whether the beach sticker should be placed on the front or rear bumper of the car. I know more than one person named Bunny. I spend weekends reconstructing osprey nests. I carry around Freedom of Information forms in my purse. I fantasize about a tsunami sweeping away my neighbor's house and floating it out to sea (preferably with them in it). I, honest to God, look forward to town board work sessions airing on Channel 36. I'm the kind of person who has the town supervisor's cell phone number posted on my refrigerator and who has cried more than once in the town attorney's office. I'm that kind of person. The worst kind of person. I'm a beach person.

Three years ago, I didn't have a beach house. Three years ago, I was a normal person. I had a husband, a job, and a house with no view in Kansas City. Every Sunday, my husband and I would go to the same diner for breakfast. We'd order two omelets. We'd request the same waitress. We'd eat at the same table. We'd leave the same tip. We'd talk about work or we wouldn't talk at all. Then, one day, we went to a different diner and Tom ordered pancakes and he left me.

I don't know about you, but I'd like to think that if I were rotten enough to leave someone over pancakes after thirty years of marriage, I'd have the decency to have a good, juicy reason for it. I'd, at the very least, have the decency to make something up. You'd like to think there'd be some seedy affair or coming-out proclamation or witness protection situation. But, Tom didn't have any reason at all. He just looked up at me while he very casually poured his maple syrup and asked me, "So . . . do you think this is working?" I thought he meant the restaurant. I said I thought it was wonderful. I really did. I said, "I think it's wonderful."

I guess Tom hoped that I would say something like, "No, I see what you're saying. It's not working. Let's get a divorce." That would have been better. Then, we could have gone on enjoying our breakfast and possibly could have still made that stop at the estate sale on the way home to buy yet another old radio to add to Tom's collection. Instead, Tom launched into a twenty-minute monologue about feeling trapped and stuck and in a rut and weighed down and a few more metaphors meant to say, "I just can't stand you anymore."

Tom said he needed adventure. He said he felt suffocated. He wanted to "find himself," a phrase he no doubt picked up from one of his many self-help manuals about breathing and thinking and eating and general basic living. Whether Tom's "self" was lost or never found in the first place, I don't know. But, either way, he felt the most likely place to find it was on the *Queen Mary 2* ocean liner. So, he went ahead and booked a solo ticket for a four-month world cruise. It was setting sail from New York in a week. "It's the only way," he said. "I've had a paradigm shift." This was the man who needed the butcher to put pieces of paper in between each slice of American cheese—the one who had me ironing his boxer shorts for thirty years. It was the man who told me every summer that a beach vacation was not necessary because we belonged to the YMCA and that traveling to Europe would be nothing but a headache.

While Tom continued to walk me through all the reasons why he now considered our life to be unbearably dull, I started thinking about a pain in my rib that I had for about three years in the '90s. I started thinking about it because the pain came back right around the time Tom mentioned that he was planning to purchase a tiny home and trailer it across the country when he returned from his world cruise.

The pain first started in 1994 when my daughter was

six. I woke up with a lightning bolt feeling in my rib and like any good hypochondriac, I immediately consulted my 1978 copy of *The Merck Manual of Diagnosis and Therapy,* which I always keep on my nightstand in the event of such a situation. After a good deal of poking, I was able to identify the exact location of the pain—left side, fourth rib from the clavicle, smack-dab over my heart. If you're wondering how it is that I was able to poke a rib that was sitting directly over my heart, well, then you'll discover the reason why I married Tom in the first place. When I was twenty, I brought Tom home for Thanksgiving and my mother told me that if he ever asked me to marry him, I should accept because he was the best I would ever do considering my cup size, which was and remains nonexistent. This was bad advice. But, I took it. My mother also told me to never sign a prenup. This was good advice that I, of course, ignored.

Anyway, the pain in my rib lasted for about four days. On the fifth day, when it moved down my arm, I started writing my will. Lucky for me, my husband is a cardiologist. When he got home from work, he asked, "How was your day?"

"Pretty good," I said. "I think I'm having a heart attack." Something you should know about Tom is that he rides bicycles. Many people ride bicycles, but Tom has somehow managed to make it into a personality trait. It takes Tom at least fifteen minutes to enter or exit the house due to the amount of bicycle accouterments required for his everyday living. The news of my impending death did not interrupt this routine. When he finished clicking off his cleats and tucking them neatly into a basket beneath the bench by the door labeled *Cleats,* he asked, "Right now?"

"What?" I said.

"Right now you're having a heart attack?"

"Yes, Tom," I said. "Right now. Right now, I'm having a heart attack." He walked over to me and asked me where it hurt. I pointed to the spot–fourth rib down from the clavicle, left side. Then, without saying a word, he took his index finger and gave me a tremendous poke right in that very spot. I lurched backward.

"You're not having a heart attack," he said and casually opened the refrigerator to gather the ingredients for his midafternoon cool-down protein smoothie.

"Well, I'm having something," I said.

"It's muscular," he said. "Muscular or skeletal. Classic presentation. I see it all the time." Tom was always saying things were classic presentations. I hated that.

Over the course of the next few years, the pain would come and go. I went to at least eight doctors. I had x-rays and MRIs and EKGs and all kinds of acronyms, which all came back perfectly normal. I was sick over it, the not knowing, I mean. I was sure there was a tumor buried somewhere in there, too small to show up on any scan. Then, one day, I was at the gynecologist and I happened to mention, just for the hell of it, that I get a terrible pain in my rib that seems to come and go at random. She said it was anxiety. She said everyone in the office had had it. "You're hyperventilating," she said. "Stop doing that." And that was the end of my rib pain.

This is a long way of explaining why I was doing highly noticeable breathing exercises at breakfast. I resented Tom. God, did I resent him. Bad enough he was asking for a divorce, or a separation, or I don't even know what he was asking for. But, now, my rib pain was back and I would have to go around until the end of time practicing something called triangle breathing and chewing gum and sucking on mints, all while Tom gallivanted off into the sunset. That's the problem with a bad marriage. I don't mean a *bad* marriage. I mean, a just-okay marriage—one that isn't awful, but isn't quite good either. It's like a benign rib pain. It's not lethal. It's not causing excruciating pain. No one cares about it. You can still perform normal activities. It's just a worrisome annoyance that eats away at you until one day it decides to leave.

I'm sorry to admit that my first thought when Tom brought up the divorce was, *What will people say?* That's not true. My first thought was, *What the hell is a paradigm shift?* My second thought was, *What will people say?* I should be more evolved than this, but there you have it. Tom had thrown me a big surprise retirement party a few weeks before all of this. Everyone we knew was there. The decorations were still lying around. Balloons were still deflating in corners of rooms. I decided in the car ride home from breakfast that if people asked me what happened, I would tell them the only thing you could tell people in a situation like this—he left me for a younger woman. I would call her Jessica or Caitlin or Tiffany or something like that. I would say she had a degree in rhetoric from a liberal arts college on the Eastern Seaboard. I would say Tom is off playing shuffleboard in the Arabian Sea with her as we speak.

Good riddance, you're probably thinking. I thought that too. But, it was more complicated than that. It always is. When we bought our house in Kansas City, the old owners took the matching bedroom wall sconces and replaced them with two slightly different sconces—one clear glass, one frosted, both square. "Huh," we said, the day we moved in. They were almost right. They were just slightly wrong. We said we'd get them fixed. We said we'd find a matching pair. But, we didn't. We kept them. I slept on the clear side of the bed and Tom slept on the frosted. Thirty years and one terrible breakfast later, Tom and I had become the sconces. We were almost right. We were just slightly wrong. And no one had bothered to fix us. When we got home, I tore the sconces off the wall and fell into bed.

If I had a wedding ring, I might have very dramatically removed it and set it on the bathroom vanity or the nightstand or placed it in a little dish on the bureau and stared at it longingly for a while. But, I didn't have a wedding ring and neither did Tom. The night before leaving for our honeymoon in Saint Martin, I told Tom that I thought it would be best to leave our wedding rings in the safe in the closet of our cramped studio apartment on Seventy-Seventh Street. "We're going to be swimming," I believe was my argument. Tom agreed. A week later we returned to the apartment. Door open, safe empty, dirty dishes in the sink. "How did they get into the safe?" Tom asked.

"The key was in the lock," I said.

"Why?" Tom asked.

"I bought it for fire," I said.

We called the police, who confirmed that the robbers had more than likely lived in our apartment for the week. They ate our food. They slept in our bed. They watched our TV. They took our TV. "How did they know we'd be gone for the week?" Tom asked.

"I left a note on the door," I said.

"What?" Tom said.

"For the paperboy," I said.

"What did the note say?" a policeman asked me.

"It said: *Dear Rodney, We are going to Saint Martin for the week. Please do not deliver the paper.*" They never found the guys. We didn't get our rings back. We could have replaced them. But, we didn't. We didn't replace the sconces. We didn't replace the rings. And look what happened.

Before I told Tom to drop dead and get out of my sight, I had him set up the old VHS player that had been gathering dust at the bottom of our closet for the last twenty years. For the next week, while downstairs Tom excitedly packed for his cruise, I lay in bed upstairs and watched a tape of Carly Simon's 1987 concert on Martha's Vineyard. In 1988, my daughter was born premature and sick. During that time, I did a lot of weeping. I ate a lot of hospital cafeteria food and drank a lot of vending machine coffee. I did a fair amount of yelling, which was usually accompanied by more weeping. I did plenty of staring into space. But, I didn't do much sleeping—hardly any. Before this, I had been a world-class sleeper. I was one of those enviable people who could sleep on a bus or a train or any mode of transportation and wake up refreshed at my destination. And then, just like that, it was gone. I haven't slept well since 1988.

I found insomnia to be an excruciatingly lonely experience. Many nights, I remember feeling like I wanted to be anywhere or anyone else. I drank tea. I tried to meditate. I wrote down positive thoughts in a journal. I even prayed. Nothing helped, not even a little. Then, I found Carly Simon's concert on TV and for whatever reason, it made me feel just a little bit better. And that's really all you need when you're in a deep rut. You don't need a miracle or a cure. You just need something that will make you feel the slightest bit better. And at that time in my life, I thought nowhere looked as perfect as Martha's Vineyard and no one looked as effortlessly cool as Carly Simon.

But, I will tell you this, Carly Simon's music is a lot more uplifting when you're not facing a divorce and it's possible that I now harbor an unhealthy and unreasonable resentment toward James Taylor. The first time I watched the tape, I thought about Tom and I cried. I cried through the whole thing. The second time I watched it, I thought about my daughter, Hattie, so I called her and she cried. And by the end of the week, after about the fifteenth replay, I thought about myself. I thought about beach houses. I thought about ferry boats and sea breezes and pink sunsets. I thought about fresh starts and silver bangles and coral Keds and shoulder pads. I didn't think about Tom. All right, fine, I thought about "finding myself." I had a paradigm shift.

2

IN 1971, I met Josie Friedman from Levittown at Camp Laughing Waters. We were both eleven years old. For years, my parents had threatened to send me to sleep-away camp, and in the summer before sixth grade, they made good on that threat. I thought everyone who went to camp was being punished for something. I thought that was the whole point. Why else would summer camp have been invented if not to whip rotten children into shape? In my case, I was serving an eight-week sentence for smuggling a tribe of baby bunnies into my bedroom. For this and possible other infractions, I was forced to swim day in and day out in a leech-infested lake in New Hampshire.

It turned out, the only two girls who were at Camp Laughing Waters against their wills were me and Josie Friedman. Josie was in for running an illegal candy operation out of her locker at school. Not only did her business go belly-up in the spring semester, but her profits were ironically and unjustly used to pay her camp tuition. After being ruined financially, she spent the entire summer trying to get back in the black. She sold contraband nail polish and magazines. She charged a cool three dollars for forged letters home and started a hair-braiding operation from her bunk. It was not exactly difficult for Josie to run circles around our camp counselors who were a mere three years older than us, if that. I swear I never saw anyone older than fifteen at Camp Laughing Waters. For five decades, Josie has been a reliable storm that has blown through my life every few years. Josie was what my mother liked to call a "bad influence." Josie's mother called me a "godsend."

About ten years ago, I started receiving Christmas letters from Josie. These were not the usual yellow legal pad, ballpoint pen, mid-January letters that I had grown accustomed to receiving from her. These were proper Christmas letters—linen stationery, holly trimmed, antique typewriter-typed letters. No longer did the return address reference her much-beloved rent-controlled studio on West Sixty-Fourth Street. Josie was now living in a quaint, cozy, seaside town in a farmhouse with a vegetable garden somewhere east of Manhattan. She enthusiastically owned and operated a boutique gift shop while her husband farmed potatoes.

The Christmas letters read like tourism ad campaigns and I ate up every word. Josie described her new home as a bucolic paradise—a cornucopia of natural beauty and small-town charm. The effects of this beauty and tranquility were so powerful that they turned Josie's graying hair back to its brilliant red and had her unironically wearing things like overalls and aprons and bandannas in her hair. She talked about having picnics on the beach every Wednesday night with her girlfriends to watch the sailboat races. They would sip their favorite local wine and wave to the boats as they rounded the harbor. She said she picked up fresh fruits and vegetables every afternoon from a farm stand that ran on a cigar box honor system. Mind you, this was not one letter. These letters came every year, each one more saturated with words like *blessed,* and *lucky,* and *grateful,* which of course made me feel things like *annoyed,* and *infuriated,* and *enraged.*

The truth of the matter is, Christmas letters are the original social media, and by that, I mean full of lies and designed to make your friends and family feel bad. There is only one person on this planet, of whom I am aware, who writes an honest Christmas letter and that person is Cindy Schwartz, a real estate agent from Duluth, Minnesota. I do not know Cindy Schwartz. I have absolutely no idea who she is and yet, paradoxically, I know everything there is to know about her.

Neither Tom nor I have ever met anyone named Cindy Schwartz. We have never been to Minnesota. We never want to go to Minnesota. As far as we can recall, we have never even had a single conversation with anyone from Minnesota or about Minnesota. Cindy is a complete stranger and yet, somehow, our favorite person. Every Christmas, we treat her letter with reverence and give it the respect of any time-honored holiday tradition. We sit down. We all get comfortable. We wait until everyone is ready. The letter is read aloud—slowly and carefully. Enclosed pictures are passed around and studied. Now that I think about it, Cindy Schwartz is quite possibly the reason Tom and I stayed together as long as we did. Through the years, we have both thought, and even proclaimed out loud on multiple occasions, "What would Cindy do?"

About fifteen years ago, I received my first letter from Cindy. It was a long letter, about two pages, detailing every awful thing that had happened to her and her family that particular year. The fascinating thing about the letter was that Cindy did not seem to know that these were awful things that were happening to her. In it, she explained that she was fired from her job due to poor performance and use of foul language and sexist remarks in the office. Now, she was looking forward to "pounding the pavement," in the new year. She said her husband got a DUI and that he had been busy the last couple of months chipping away at his community service. He sure was getting his steps in! Her daughter was left back a year and was enjoying the opportunity to tackle fifth grade again. The Schwartzes' family dog sadly died after being hit by an ice cream truck. They had a beautiful ceremony for him in the park. It was well attended and featured in the local paper!

I thought the first letter was a mistake—an incredibly lucky mistake. But, for some miraculous reason, Tom and I have remained on Cindy Schwartz's Christmas letter list all this time. Around year five, I decided to send Cindy a Christmas card back. I thought it was only right. It had a picture of me and Tom and Hattie and our dog, Vivian, sitting on our front porch. It was risky. I knew it was more than likely that Cindy, upon inspection of our photo, would realize that she had been sending very personal Christmas letters to the wrong person for years. But, the next year, we received Cindy's letter right on time. At the bottom of it, she scribbled, "All my love to Tom and Hattie!" This is the true mystery of my life.

What I'm saying is, Josie Friedman is no Cindy Schwartz and I was well aware of that. But, I knew if Josie's beach town was half as nice as she said it was, it would be paradise and it would save me. Not to mention, I had been ready to leave Kansas City for thirty years. Something happens when you live in Kansas City for a while and that is you forget the fact that you are, as I was, actually living in Kansas. You think to yourself, *Well, this is a pretty cosmopolitan place and we have a newspaper and a football team and Fortune 500 companies and a fairly impressive hospital system and museums and a ballet company,* and you forget the fact that you are in Kansas. You're only reminded of this fact when you're away somewhere and someone asks, "So where's home for you?" And you start to say, "New York," but then you stop yourself and you say, "Kansas," and they look at you like you've just said, "The moon," and for the rest of the day you're depressed.

No one dreams of moving to Kansas City. It's just a place where people end up for one reason or another. My reason was an ultimatum disguised as a proposal, or maybe it was the other way around. I can't remember. When I was twenty-five years old, Tom asked me to marry him. It was so romantic. He took me out to our favorite German restaurant on Eighty-Sixth Street and told me he was going to do his residency in Kansas City. I said, "I don't want to go to Kansas City. I want to stay in New York."

He said, "Well, I'm going to Kansas City."

"Fine," I said.

"Good," he said and we ordered dessert. As we were leaving the restaurant, Tom said, "Listen, I think we should either get married and move to Kansas City or go our separate ways." So, we got married and we moved to Kansas City.

The deal was that we would spend four years in Kansas City—five, tops. Then, we would move back to New York. Tom would be a cardio attending at Mount Sinai or Columbia Presbyterian. I would get a job at the Metropolitan Museum of Art or the Whitney or MoMA. But, in the meantime, I got a job at Hallmark. I designed greeting cards for the B-holidays—Halloween, Saint Patrick's Day, Fourth of July, et cetera. . . .

Tom and I lived a whole life in the meantime. That's the other issue with Kansas City—when you get there you find out it's sort of pleasant. You find out you can get a decent enough job in a place that has nice enough people. You find out that that job comes with access to a cafeteria that makes the most delicious carrot cake you can ever imagine and that you can request that carrot cake be delivered upstairs to your office anytime you like. People say hello to you in the street. You hardly ever have to walk. You find out that you can afford a house, a big house, one with a playroom and an office and a den.

In Kansas City, even the laundry gets its own room! You find out that for the price of a one-room, fifth-floor, rat-infested walk-up apartment in New York, you can get a very nice four-bedroom home with a backyard and a garage and a tree with a swing. Life is so damn comfortable that you forget to leave! And before you know it, thirty years have gone by, and you find yourself sitting alone in your beautiful bedroom with the walk-in closet and the en suite bathroom, fighting the urge to remind your soon-to-be ex-husband to pack suntan lotion for his divorce cruise. But, I wasn't going to be left living in the meantime while Tom sailed off into the future. No way.

I could have had an exciting life. But, I blew it. I had a boyfriend in college who was smart and funny and could tell a story and he liked me. The only problem was that sometimes, not all the time, but sometimes, he'd tell me things like he was having thoughts about electrocuting me in the bathtub or pushing me off train platforms. He assured me that he did not want to do these things, just that he was thinking about them a lot. He once made me stop drinking a glass of wine because he was afraid he might have poisoned it while I wasn't looking. I found this a little off-putting. So, I broke it off. I have since found out that those thoughts are a fairly common manifestation of OCD. I know this because, coincidentally, my office mate at Hallmark suffered from the very same condition. For twenty years, whenever Angela had to take a pill, I would have to watch her take it. This way, I could reassure her for the rest of the day that I knew for an absolute fact that she did not accidentally lose control and overdose on aspirin or ibuprofen or gummy vitamins.

The point is, I could have married Patrick and we could have had an interesting, exciting life and I could have been living in Manhattan and vacationing in Paris. But, I married Tom, who pronounces the *t* in *exactly* and *often,* and who says things like *anyways.* I married the guy who collects old radios and who has a much too cozy relationship with his elderly optometrist. I decided to break up with Patrick—the cool, handsome intellectual who only needed a healthy dose of cognitive behavior therapy—and go with the man who keeps a journal detailing his experience with different brands of contact lenses. I went with that guy.

The hardest part about the separation was giving up my mother's giant, bulky, beautiful art deco furniture that I had spent decades preserving and protecting. I agonized over that. I don't even know if my mother really liked this furniture, but I know she always valued it. She was always very careful with it. It was routinely polished and dusted and repaired. By the time I was born, in 1960, this kind of furniture was completely out of fashion. And we had a lot of it—three full bedroom sets, a dining room table, six chairs, and two buffet tables. I think, at a certain point, my mother wanted to lean into the '60s style. Sometimes, when the two of us were out shopping, she'd peruse the minimalist Scandinavian-esque pieces that were all the rage at the time. But, we never bought any of it. As she said, "It wouldn't go." So, my mother stuck with the art deco style until she died and then I got it.

The only thing truly keeping me in the house in Kansas City was this furniture. There wasn't a time in my life when I wasn't surrounded by it and, although I didn't particularly love it, the thought of letting it go broke my heart. But, I did it. In the spirit of letting go and moving on, I sold it. The next day, I called a real estate agent from Josie's little seaside town and told her to find me the cheapest house with a water view.

The house was a little oyster shack. It was seven hundred square feet and had been recently fixed up, in that a bathroom had been added where there hadn't been one before. The most important thing was that it was waterfront. It was better than waterfront. It was practically floating. The second-most important thing was that it was cheap—cheap enough for me to afford on my own. I was told I needed to act fast. My agent said that the listing wouldn't last a week. She said it was a steal. She said she immediately thought of me when she saw it. I was getting the first look at the house because as my agent explained to me, her husband also left her for a younger woman. "Solidarity," she said.

Well, I took it. I looked at a couple of blurry photos and watched a shaky three-minute video and I signed the contract.

3

I HAVE A THERAPIST NOW. Well, I used to have a therapist. It's difficult to stick with a therapist after you've seen her arguing with a sixteen-year-old stock clerk about Greek yogurt flavors in the grocery store. It doesn't exactly inspire confidence when you see your well-dressed, mild-mannered, Harvard diploma–flaunting mental health professional stomping her feet and waving her fists in the dairy department.

So, I don't have a therapist anymore. Now, I have a man with absolutely no credentials who calls himself a life coach. I meet him once a week in his spectacular oceanfront ivy-covered Tudor home which I no doubt help pay for. Sebastian has a magnificently eccentric wardrobe. He is married to a famous person. I know this because he told me that he is married to a famous person. I don't know who, but I am determined to find out. His home is filled with all kinds of interesting knickknacks and art. There are photos of famous people hanging on the walls. He makes hors d'oeuvres and cocktails. Call me crazy, but at the end of the hour, I feel a great deal better.

Sebastian tells me that stealing Tom's thirty-seven antique radios and moving them to New York with me was a way of telling Tom that I still loved him. He says that by stealing the radios, I essentially sent a message to Tom that read, "I want you back." He is wrong. I stole them because I wanted to hurt Tom. I wanted him to lose something the way I lost something. It wasn't Tom I lost. It was my nerve. It was those years of my life when I wasn't afraid of every damn thing—the years when I wouldn't lay awake at night agonizing over whether or not I'd be able to successfully drive my car across the country alone.

That's the trouble with getting older. You get scared. You'd think it'd be the opposite. You'd think you'd have all this life experience and you'd know what's what and how things work and that would put your mind at ease. But it doesn't. Everything is infinitely more terrifying after you turn fifty. Suddenly stepping out of the shower could be fatal. Something like a fall, a thing you have been doing without serious injury for the entirety of your life, is now the most likely cause of your inevitable demise. When you're older, you know how things work, but you also know all the things that can go wrong and it is more than likely that things have gone wrong for you in the past. So, it is reasonable to think they could go wrong again. You can try and talk yourself out of this way of thinking. You can consult your optimistic young gay life coach. But, by now you're too smart and you've lived with yourself for too long to be able to trick yourself into thinking anything. So, there you go. You're scared. At least, I was.

If you want to know the real truth about the radios (and I don't know why you would, the metaphorical one is much better)—the real truth is that I didn't sell Tom's radios because I thought it would be a shame to break up the collection. That's all. It's as boring as that. I'm sorry I lied about it. But, that's it. I felt sorry for the radios. I looked at them with their little knob and button faces and I thought about all the years of estate sales and antique shops and eBay auctions. I thought about the hours of driving and researching and cleaning and repairing, and I just couldn't do it. If it were possible for radios to look sad, these did. So, I took them. I took them so that Tom couldn't have them and so that I could sleep at night and not be haunted by the faces of sad old lonely radios sitting in dusty antique shops in Kansas.

The irony in all of this is that the radios are the only thing that arrived in New York on time. I decided to FedEx them instead of having the moving company take them because the moving man told me that if it were him, he'd FedEx them. It took me three days to drive to Whitbey from Kansas. It took the radios one. They were accidentally delivered to my new neighbor—Rosemary Preston. She lived in the house directly across the street from mine.

I was feeling very good as I drove the last stretch of my long journey toward my new neighborhood. I had done it. It took three days, six states, two motels, a dozen doughnuts, three calls to AAA, a new tire, and ten boxes of tissues. But, I made it. I had used the interstate highway system to methodically knock out all the stages of grief. I was in denial in Missouri and angry in Illinois. I did a bit of bargaining in Indiana and was depressed from Ohio to New Jersey. I was the first person in history to reach acceptance on the Long Island Expressway. Three hours later, I took a narrow causeway that stretched for miles over a rising tide. I rolled down the windows and breathed in the salt air. I marveled at the tall dunes that caught the crashing waves. It was like I was on a road to paradise. There were bobbing sailboats and roadside farm stands. I even got stuck driving behind a red tractor.

Rosemary was the first person I met. She called down to me from her second-floor bedroom window exactly three seconds after I arrived. "Are you Kathleen Deane?" I looked up and saw a wild-haired woman looking through a pair of binoculars.

"Yes," I called up to her.

"The Kathleen Deane who FedExed thirty-seven boxes marked 'Fragile' from Kansas City?"

"Yes," I said, half-distracted now as I looked to the other side of the street.

"Nice, right?" Rosemary yelled as I stared up at a scene so jarring it's difficult to describe. Have you ever realized you've made a mistake one second after you've made it? One time, years ago, Tom and I thought about buying a little vacation home in Charleston, South Carolina. We read a few online articles that rated it number one prettiest city and number one small city and number one foodie city and we thought, *Well, what could be bad about that?* So, we booked a flight. Fifteen minutes before landing, Tom and I looked out the plane window. Tom looked at me and I looked at Tom and then he said, "Should we just see if we can get a flight home today?" Of course, we didn't do that. We spent four miserable days in Charleston and then we talked about what a miserable time we had in Charleston for ten years.

This was sort of like that, but worse. I couldn't fly home. I couldn't just wait three days for it to be over. I was here. I signed the contract. I packed up the house in Kansas City. I sold my mother's art deco furniture. I was alone. This was it. I was now the proud owner of a seven-hundred-square-foot, half-standing oyster shack with a hay bale foundation that sat beside what I could only assume was a McMansion in the making. But, I couldn't be sure. On this particular day, it was just a roof and a few walls balancing on stilts forty feet in the air.

Rosemary met me on the street. "Bastards," she said as we both looked up at the house. "Hope you're not the same," she said.

"What?"

"Thirty-seven boxes marked 'Fragile'? You're either some sort of criminal or rich," Rosemary said.

"They're old radios," I said.

"See, now, that doesn't sound normal," she said.

"I know," I said. "But I am," I said. "Normal."

"You know what I think when I hear thirty-seven radios?" she asked.

"No," I said.

"Extension," she said. "Excessive lot coverage. Zoning Board of Appeals. Watch, next week it'll be your house on stilts."

"I don't have any plans," I said.

"Yeah, well, we'll see. You'll be in for a fight, if you do. I'll tell you that much. I'm Rosemary, by the way," she said.

"Kathleen," I said, never taking my eyes off the teetering roof and the fleet of construction vehicles surrounding it. There was a gaping hole in the ground where I assumed the original house once stood. Twelve tall cement columns protruded from the hole, each surrounded by what looked like stacked milk crates. Swarms of pink insulation swirled through the air. Some of it coated the roof of my new house. A man standing on the roof catapulted solar panels into the pit below. They shattered as they hit the ground.

"The Sugar Cube," Rosemary said. "That's what they're calling it. Have you ever heard anything stupider?"

"No," I said and stumbled toward my shack. "Nice to meet you," I called back in a complete trance as I walked into my new house for the first time.

"My husband, Steve, will bring over the radios later!" Rosemary yelled as the screen door bumped behind me.

I only ordered one new thing in advance of my move—a white couch—an expensive, luxurious, made-in-America, white couch from a small local store called Turtle Cove. My real estate agent had, allegedly, signed for its delivery a week prior to my arrival. Her sister owned Turtle Cove. She said the couch was beautiful. She said it was worth the money. You get what you pay for. Shop local. Anyway, I found the couch on the back deck with three construction workers sitting on it having their lunch. When I asked them what they were doing, they told me they were almost finished.

So, I went for a drive. I dodged Rosemary, who was taking photos of a man placing orange cones in the middle of the street, and took off down Harbor Road. I drove east. I drove east until I ran out of land and found myself in a small village filled with historic Victorian houses with perfectly maintained lawns. Everywhere you looked there was a plaque that read, "Landmark." The only sound was that of birds chirping. It was much nicer there. There were no jackhammers or cement trucks or generators. There was a post office and a country store. That was it. I stopped in at the store and bought the local newspaper. On the counter, there was a stack of bumper stickers that said, *Save What's Left.*

"Help yourself," the young girl said. So, I did. As I walked around the village, I started to feel better. Things would sort themselves out. A bit of construction was not the end of the world. It would end. Suddenly, a woman pulled her car next to me. "I can't find a spot," she said. "I can't believe it! No spots!" She looked about ninety.

"I think there are some down this street," I said and pointed down the road.

"I live on that street," she said. "I just wanted to pick up my mail. It's my birthday. Eighty! I want to pick up my cards so I can call my family and say thank you." The post office was a few steps away. So, I asked if she would like me to get her mail for her.

"Would you?" she said and leaned out of her window to hand me a tiny silver key. "Box 954," she said.

Things like this happen to me. I think I have one of those trustworthy faces that says, *I'll listen to anything*, which is true, I will. One time, Tom and I were waiting for the crosstown bus on East Seventy-Ninth Street when a woman with a cast on her arm walked over to me and asked if I could please zip her fly. Tom was horrified when I kneeled down without hesitation. Over the years, Tom became the sort of person who wears headphones as a way of announcing to the general public that he is not interested in human interaction on public transit. He's not alone. You can spot these types everywhere. It's been my experience that these are the same people who have no stories. And what exactly is the point of a person without stories?

I was delighted to go pick up Barbara Time's mail that day. She told me that if the box was filled, which it probably would be, to ask the postman (Kenny) if he had any mail for her behind the counter. The post office was a little ramshackle building. Kenny flashed me a friendly, yet suspicious smile as I made my way to Box 954. A man with a standard poodle was also inside picking up his mail. The poodle, Teddy, received a treat from Kenny on his way out. It was picturesque. The whole thing was cute enough to seem made-up. I thought maybe Josie hadn't lied in her Christmas letters after all. Maybe this town was as charming and enchanting as she described. Maybe the air was cleaner. Life was simpler. Maybe people were better.

But, people are never better. People are the worst. People forget to send birthday cards. They forget to send birthday cards to Barbara Time on her eightieth birthday. And then what do you do? What do you do when a sweet old woman sends you into the post office to pick up a pile of birthday cards and the only thing in her box is a super saver circular? Then what? I'll tell you what you do . . . you ask Kenny if he sells birthday cards. But, he doesn't. So, you run and check the quaint little country store next door. But, they only have sympathy cards. So, you throw out the super saver circular and you go back to Barbara Time who is waiting anxiously in her car and you tell her that the mail truck is late. That's what you do.

"Really?" she said. "It's almost noon."

"Kenny's looking into it," I said and she shrugged. "Well, happy birthday," I said and took a few steps away from the car.

"That's my house there," she said and pointed down the road. "The blue one."

"Oh. It's pretty. You have a nice spot."

"Yeah, I was born in it. My friend used to live in the white one next door. She died last year. Now her grandson and his wife live in it. Not year-round. Weekends. The wife is expecting a baby girl this summer. That'll be nice."

"That will be nice," I said.

"Have you been to the state park?"

"No. Not yet."

"My husband was the groundskeeper there. After he retired, I mean. He was an accountant before that. He's dead now. He died five years ago. But, when he retired he used to go for walks in the park every day. He knew every species of plant in the whole park. One day, they offered him a job. What's your name?"

"Sorry," I said. "Kathleen."

"I'm Barbara Time. Did I tell you that already? Have you ever met another Time?"

"I haven't."

"Well, you won't. I'm the last of them. Want to know how we got that name? My grandfather came to Ellis Island from Germany. He couldn't speak a word of English. A man asked him for his name but, my grandfather thought he was asking for the time. So, he pointed to his watch. Eventually, he said his name was George and the man said, 'George what?' And my grandfather pointed to his watch again. So, the man said, 'Fine. George Time.' And that was that."

I talked to Barbara Time for about an hour that afternoon. She told me she needed to get back home because she didn't want to miss her daughter's phone call wishing her a happy birthday. On the way home, I stopped at a florist and had a bouquet of sunflowers delivered to her. I bought a bunch for myself as well. Then I called Hattie and told her that when I'm eighty, I expect her to mail me a damn card.

4

TO: Supervisor White (white@whitbey.gov)
FROM: Kathleen Deane (KDeane@gmail.com)
SUBJECT: The Sugar Cube

Dear Supervisor White,

I recently purchased a house on Harbor Road in West Creek and was surprised to see the massive construction project that is currently underway on my neighbor's property. I wanted to enclose the permit number in this email for your reference, but the only permit that I can find is in a Ziplock bag posted inside a second-floor window of the house, which, perhaps you know, is now forty feet in the air. I tried to read the permit using binoculars, but unfortunately it also appears to be ripped in half. It's orange, if that helps.

What I would like to know is if there was any kind of meeting or hearing in regard to this property, because if there had been I might have been interested in attending, or at the very least, submitting a letter of opposition. I bought my house (sight unseen) three months ago and was not informed by my real estate agent of any pending construction plans nearby. Could you tell me when the work began? As I am new to the area, I am not familiar with the laws or codes of the town, but never in my wildest dreams would I think something like this would be permitted to be built on such a small piece of property so close to the water.

My neighbor, Rosemary Preston, gave me your email address and encouraged me to write to you with this concern. Please let me know if there is a more specific department that I should contact. I was drawn to this town for its tranquility and beauty and I fear that I am not getting much of that at all on Harbor Road. Besides the overall scope of the project, here are some other issues that I was hoping you, or someone in town government, could address:

1. *Generators—There are five large generators set up in the middle of the street, blocking traffic. I grew up in a house that was smack-dab in LaGuardia's flight path. That pales in comparison. My house doesn't stop shaking until 6:00 p.m. when the construction crew packs up for the day.*

2. *Debris—Much of the debris from this construction is routinely launched from the roof of my neighbor's house into a dumpster beside my property. About half of that debris lands in the dumpster. The rest of it (glass, insulation, wood, nails, solar panels, etc. . . .) lands on my deck. Part of a kitchen cabinet nearly killed me yesterday.*

3. *Electricity—A week ago, I lost power for eighteen hours after a crane carrying a septic tank took out three power lines.*

4. *Dust—There is a lot of dust. I hope it's not asbestos.*

I would be very grateful if you could look into the permits for this property and perhaps ask an inspector to come and take a look at the construction site and ensure that everything is in order. I hate to make out like the sky is falling, but the sky is literally falling.

Thank you very much for your attention to this matter.

Sincerely,
Kathleen Deane

Every morning a group of ladies walk by my bedroom window. Five walk by at 7:16 and two more at 7:20. The first five stand on the beach next to my house and wait for the stragglers. While they do this, they ponder out loud who in their right mind would buy my house. After that's done, they all head off together until they eventually circle back at 7:38. They never take a day off and they're never late. When I thought about having a bedroom window that faced a white sandy beach, I didn't imagine people on it. I imagined crashing waves and pink sunrises and enjoying my morning coffee while listening to the calls of seagulls. That was dumb.

There is no such thing as a private beach. Did you know that? I didn't know that. I was certain there was such a thing. Apparently, it all has to do with tides. It doesn't really matter if you have a one-bedroom bungalow or a $28 million estate. It doesn't matter if your real estate agent said it was worth the price because it came with a totally and completely 100 percent private beach. It doesn't even matter if you stick cute little hand-painted signs in the sand that say, *Private beach.* You don't own anything below high tide. And thanks to global warming and rising sea levels, high tide is often the entire beach. So, you don't have a private beach. What you have is a public beach and all are welcome.

I'll say this, the seven women laughing their heads off every morning on the beach at 7:16 about God knows what were better than the jackhammers and generators and chain saws that started in at eight. My biggest worry about moving to a new place alone was that I'd have nothing to do and no one to talk to. What would my days look like? A lot of times, you think to yourself, *If I only had the time and if I could just be left alone for five minutes, I could do all of these fabulous things.* I'd do all of the things I always wanted to do. I would learn guitar and another language. Maybe I'd pick up sewing or cooking or join a club or try out for a community theater production. I would volunteer. I would definitely volunteer. I'd be at the soup kitchen at least twice a week. But, of course I knew, that in all likelihood, if left to my own devices, and in the deteriorating mental state I was in, I wouldn't end up doing any of those things. I knew that what I would probably do is sleep or try to sleep. I would sleep all the time and when I wasn't sleeping, I would be eating.

That didn't happen. All that worrying for nothing. First of all, I learned that it is physically impossible to sleep in a shaking house. Fight or flight really starts to kick in when your mind feels certain that your house will collapse at any moment. Second of all, one of the side effects of being riddled with newfound dread and anxiety is that you entirely stop caring about how much you weigh. And, lastly, most importantly, I did have something to do. I had a mission—a life calling, if you will. I had something to do that was so all-consuming that there was hardly any time at all to learn guitar or volunteer at the soup kitchen or even think about Tom. It was sawdust. It was piles and piles of sawdust that rained down on me every moment of every day and collected on every surface you can imagine.

I spent my first couple of weeks at my new dream beach house sweeping while wearing noise-canceling headphones. Instead of that chic new bar cart that I was eyeing, I went ahead and bought a super deluxe cordless vacuum. There was no keeping up with it. It didn't matter what I did. Everything was covered in dust—the table, the chairs, the birdhouse, even the ten-foot-tall wooden egret statue that came with the house that I specifically said I didn't want but still, to this day, can't figure out how to get rid of. I started tasting it in my food and feeling it in my sheets. It was in my hair and between my toes. It was caked on every window and plastered to every inch of my car. I found that if I swept the back deck every half hour, I could just about stay ahead of it. Then came the leaf blowers.

It was just an average day. There I was minding

my own business, sweeping away, when three workers with leaf-blower jetpacks strapped to their backs assembled on the property line and unleashed a storm that could have rivaled the Dust Bowl. All I could do in that moment was close my eyes and hope that death would come quickly. And don't think these guys didn't see me. They saw me. They looked right at me and fired. I'm guessing they got wind of my email to the supervisor.

Here's another fun fact: a leaf blower emits three hundred times more air pollutants than a pickup truck traveling from New York to San Francisco. I know that because Rosemary made it her business to remind me of that fact almost daily. She insisted that the pollutants from the leaf blowers alone would, without question, clog our lungs and kill us. So, with my eyes crusted closed and my hair now plastered to my head, I marched right over to the contractor and here's what I said: "Did you know that a leaf blower emits three hundred times more air pollutants than a pickup truck?" He looked me up and down and then this is what he said: "Where are you from . . . Albania?" Well, I wasn't expecting that. I don't know why this was the most hurtful and offensive thing I have ever heard, but it was and I still think about it all the time.

Before I could say anything, Rosemary opened her bedroom window across the street and shouted down to us. "Kathleen, I'm calling the police!"

"You don't have to call the police!" I yelled back.

"I'm on the phone with them right now!" she said. I didn't know what to do. The contractor didn't move. So, I didn't move. So, we just stood there in the middle of the street staring at each other and listening to Rosemary describing the scene to the police operator.

"That's right," Rosemary said. "He called her an Albanian. Al-ban-ian! Well, it's harassment, for one thing. . . . I understand that, but it's the way he said it. Threatening. That's what it was. No. I know it's not a threat. But, it was implied. I'm the next-door neighbor. It's intimidation and it's not the first time. Do you know what this same man said to me last week when I stepped out to hang my clothes on the line? 'Nice muumuu.' No, it was not a compliment. Would you take that as a compliment if someone said that to you?" The contractor and I stood there and listened to the whole conversation.

Finally, I broke my silence. "I'm from Kansas, just so you know." At first, he didn't say anything. Then, Rosemary called down—"Forget it! They're not sending anyone!"

The contractor raised his eyebrows and smirked as he prepared to say what I could see brought him tremendous joy. There was a little sparkle in his eye as he leaned in closer to me and said, "Looks like you're not in Kansas anymore!" And if you think my first thought at that moment wasn't "I'm getting my husband!" you're crazy. I don't know why I thought that because all Tom would have said was, "What do you want me to do?"

The contractor decided to leave on a high note. He hopped in his truck and drove off, giving me an enthusiastic wave as he turned the corner. "You made that worse," I said to Rosemary when she joined me moments later in the street.

"Oh, so, we should just let him get away with that?"

"I was handling it."

"Let me tell you something," she said as she followed me into my house. "These people only understand consequences. Don't you think I already tried the whole 'reason with them' thing? You think I started out this way?" She took a seat on my now very off-white couch and made herself comfortable.

"Tea?" I said as I made my way into the kitchen. Rosemary routinely invited herself over to talk strategy and she was constantly disappointed in my lack of enthusiasm for the cause.

"Sure," she said and leafed through my library books that were sitting on the coffee table.

"You actually read these things?" she said, picking up one of the three romance beach reads with matching azure-blue covers.

"Yes, I actually read them," I said as I ran a paper towel under the faucet and worked to remove the now hardened layer of spackle affixed to my eyelids.

"Phooey," she said and tossed it back on the table. "Did you write a letter to the supervisor yet?"

"I did," I said.

"And?" she asked.

"No answer," I said.

"Right," she said. "You know how this whole thing started? A goddamn jar of honey. That was the beginning of the end." I handed her the tea and took a seat. "I used to be friends with them—pretty good friends. They'd come over for dinner all the time and we'd go to their New Year's Eve party every year. Then, a few months ago I got home from the supermarket and there was a jar of honey on the bench on the front porch. It was from Ivy Orchards so, you know, it was expensive. I looked at the little card that was in the shape of a bumblebee and it said, 'Just because. Love, Jack and Sarah.'"

"And then what?" I asked.

"I haven't seen them since before the honey. I went over the next day to thank them and no one was home. They've been gone ever since."

"Where are they?"

"Last I heard, Montana. But, that's just what Owen told me. Have you met Owen?"

"No," I said.

"President of the civic association," she said. "He's fifth generation."

"La-di-da," I said.

"La-di-da indeed," she said. "I think he has your door knocker, by the way. I saw it his store window the other day."

"Oh my God," I said. "I was wondering where that went."

"You shouldn't leave these things lying around."

"Lying around, as in secured to my front door?"

"Well, let's be honest, it was hardly secured," Rosemary said. "Besides it has an *H* on it. What good is that to you?" I threw my hands in the air, which Rosemary ignored. Instead, she took a long look around my minimally furnished and half-heartedly decorated cottage with its uneven wood floors and old bowling alley ambiance. Everything in the house was just slightly off-kilter. None of the doors closed properly. They had mismatched doorknobs. The kitchen window wouldn't open. The splintered shelves in the bedroom sloped in a downward trajectory and the new bathroom came complete with a crooked almond toilet that required a very specific sideways straddle. The refrigerator, one end of which was propped up on a series of matchbooks from a restaurant called Captain Jerry's, had six old radios stacked on top of it. There were four radios on the kitchen counter. Ten in the closet. Two were on the floor being used as doorstops. One was on the coffee table and three were in the crawl space. Five were under my bed and the remaining six were precariously stashed on a rotting beam above the wood-burning stove. I had meant to hire painters and a handyman to spruce up the place. But, it didn't seem worth the trouble, at least not until things calmed down next door. Plus, the lack of furniture made for easier vacuuming.

Rosemary's face turned to disgust as she flicked at the peeling paint beside the couch. "You should get a dog," she said.

"I don't want a dog," I said.

"Well, you should get something. It's like death in here. I didn't think anyone would be dumb enough to buy this place. You know it was on the market for over a year, right?"

"I got a good price," I said.

"Who was your agent? Stacy Peters?"

"You know her?"

"Everyone knows her. She's also a lawyer. Ambulance chaser. Did she tell you that?"

"No," I said.

"Well, she wouldn't, would she? She represents the gruesome twosome next door. Her ex-husband is the ex-supervisor. That certainly helps things. She's got her nose in everything out here." I guess Rosemary saw the sheer look of rage on my face because she said, "If you're thinking of suing her . . . forget it. You won't get anywhere. She's a shark."

"Well, that's great," I said. "That's just great."

Rosemary took a long sip of her tea. She winced at the sound of a large crash next door.

"Wood delivery," I said and she nodded.

"Did I see a *Save What's Left* bumper sticker on your car?" she asked.

"Oh yeah," I said. "I got it at that cute little store in Chester."

"Yeah, well, people noticed," Rosemary said and raised her eyebrows.

"What?"

"So, you just slapped a bumper sticker on your car and you don't even know what it means?"

"I figured it meant what it says—save what's left—like of the environment."

"Well, it did. Sort of. Until a few ladies decided it meant save what's left by fundraising to buy what's left and then build on what's left and then profit from what's left until nothing's left."

"Which ladies?"

"The Birch Street Bitches," she said casually. "Or the Bay Mission Mainstays, if you like. Depends on who you ask."

"Who?" I said.

"You don't hear them every morning—7:16 on the dot?"

"Oh my God," I said.

"What?"

"I gave them a thousand dollars last week."

"I know," Rosemary said.

"What do you mean, you know?"

"Well, everyone was talking about it," Rosemary said. "What were you thinking?"

"I was thinking here's a group of nice eighty-year-olds knocking on the door asking for a donation for a community fund."

"Ruffled quite a few feathers," Rosemary said. "Did you at least get something out of it? Usually, they throw in a little prize."

"That," I said and pointed to a pitiful painting leaning on a windowsill. "They said it was a silent auction." Rosemary shook her head. "I may have signed a petition too. I don't know. I signed something. It was 7:16 in the morning!"

"Well done," Rosemary said.

"I'll take the sticker off," I said.

Rosemary nodded her head, took a last slug of her tea, and set it down on the table. "All right, I gotta go," she said. "I'll see you later." She took one last look at me as she reached the door. "Buck up!" she said as she stumbled down the shaky steps.

So, I did. I bucked up. I went to visit Josie. I promised Josie that I would stop into her little boutique for a visit once I settled in. But, I never got around to it. I planned on waiting until I felt, I don't know, not terrible, to go. But, I wasn't confident that day would ever come and the idea of ever settling in seemed far-fetched. So, I drove over.

The shop was called the Cultured Pearl. From what I could tell upon first inspection, Josie, at some point, had gotten her hands on a can of white paint and said to herself, *This is a business.* She ran with it. She bought a little brick building on the main road and painted it white. She topped it with a white roof. She didn't stop there. The door was white. The windows were white. There were white flower boxes filled with white daisies and a whitewashed driftwood welcome sign hanging on the door.

I spotted Josie in the alley beside the building furiously painting a blue chair, white. I wasn't surprised. Nothing ever surprised me about Josie. Fifty years of friendship had numbed me to her shape-shifting nature and I learned, over time, to overlook a lot. I didn't pay attention when she started speaking with a Southern twang in the '80s. I completely missed her bookish phase when she dated that professor. I ignored the midlife crisis triathlon obsession. I had no comment when she mused about joining a convent and I certainly didn't raise an eyebrow when she opened a hip lesbian bar in Chelsea years later. Josie fell into lifestyles the way some people fall in love. Each new identity was "the one," until it wasn't. She went all in, and then without any warning, she went all out.

I chalked the whole thing up to what I like to call Josie's Levittown complex. Josie grew up in a house that was identical to the seventeen thousand other houses in her neighborhood with a TV in the staircase and a white picket fence. Her mother stayed home and made ambrosia salad. Her father worked for the railroad. They had a baby-blue 1966 Chevy Bel Air station wagon with a hula girl on the dashboard that Josie's father picked up while stationed in Hawaii. I loved Josie's house. I loved the ambrosia salad and the Chevy Bel Air. But, I mostly loved the hula girl. On any given day, if you asked Josie where she was from, she would tell you something different. She'd say, "Exit 44," or "The South Shore," or "Thirty miles east of Manhattan." Today, she says, "Up-island," or if she's being especially evasive, just, "West." Anyway, this is all to say, that Josie's ever-changing persona is fueled by her incessant need to sparkle and stand out and be different and I think it's because there was a TV in her staircase.

In her latest reincarnation, Josie made her living scavenging around the neighborhood looking for discarded wooden furniture and odds and ends and bits and bobs that she could pass off as shabby chic with just one coat of white paint. Inside the store, I felt like I had stepped into some sort of Martha Stewart–inspired fever dream where people really did have button cabinets and everything was neat and tidy and fresh. Only where Martha Stewart might have arranged wildflowers in antique glass bottles, Josie opted for spray-painted dandelions stuffed into thimbles. There were hundreds, maybe thousands, of mason jars that were painted white and organized according to size. "Look at these!" Josie said as she walked me around a leaning stack of freshly painted old doors and toward a pile of sticks that she had painted white and propped up in an old milk jug.

"You have to come for dinner," Josie said and gave me

another hug. Just then, a woman in a linen jumpsuit stepped through the door.

"Hi, Josie!" the woman said cheerfully, her golden retriever tied to a flagpole outside.

"Hi, Carol!" Josie beamed. "I've got those teacups for you!"

"Oh, great," Carol said and Josie heaved a wooden milk crate full of mismatched chipped teacups onto the counter. Carol picked one up to admire it. "They're fabulous," she said. *This,* I thought, *is what I want.* I want to think twenty chipped teacups are fabulous. I want to think anything is fabulous.

Ten years in Whitbey had made Josie downright wholesome. My mother would have been thrilled with the transformation. Even Josie's voice had developed a softer, wispier, more elegant tone. I watched as she floated around her perfectly curated shop, twirling antique doorknobs and rearranging hand-cut bars of herb-infused soap as she passed. "I can't believe you're here!" she said for the fifth time. "Take anything you want! My treat! It can be my housewarming present."

"Oh, no. You don't have to do that," I said as I thumbed through a stack of framed black-and-white photographs that were neatly placed between two baskets overflowing with white teddy bears that Josie informed me were actually lavender sachets in disguise.

"This looks like my house," I said about one of the photographs.

"It probably is your house." Josie laughed. "I picked it up in a dumpster a few weeks ago not far from your house. I snagged it before Owen got his hands on it. Have you met Owen?"

"Not yet," I said.

"Oh," Josie said, surprised. "Well, that photo had the frame on it and everything. But, it was red. . . ."

"Well, we can't have that," I said.

"Certainly not," Josie said with a laugh. "It's a special paint I use," she said. "It gives it that quality. See?" And she held the frame closer to my face.

I looked at what could only be described as a poorly painted frame and said, "Yes. I see. It's beautiful."

"It's yours," Josie said and peeled off the handwritten *$45* sticker. "So, are you coming to dinner?"

"I don't know," I said.

"Oh, come on. Dan will want to see you. Are you busy? You're not busy! What are you doing? Come for dinner! What will you do instead?"

"Probably mindlessly walk on my beach and look for tiny orange shells like I do every other night," I said.

"They're jingle shells," Josie said and pulled out a drawer filled with shell necklaces. "Want one?" she said and held it up.

"That's okay," I said. I didn't mention the fact that I had amassed an embarrassingly large hoard of jingle shells in record time and for absolutely no reason in particular. I just kept picking them up. I kept walking and thinking and stewing and triangle breathing until my entire house was filled with bowls and jars and cups and vases and buckets of orange shells. I've since sold them to Josie for a cool twenty bucks. And now, thanks to my near nervous breakdown, a woman named Debbie is able to set her morning coffee on a one-of-a-kind jingle-shell-adorned coffee table that she bought for $600. Everything works out for the best.

"But you'll come for dinner," Josie said.

"I'll come for dinner," I said.

Josie lived on a farm in Fleet Bay. She had chickens and goats and pigs. But, those were not considered the farm. The farm was potatoes—fields and fields of potatoes. The chickens and goats and pigs were an investment for what Josie ominously referred to as an "expansion plan." I followed Josie's red truck down a winding wooded road that bore no resemblance to my corner of Whitbey. Here, there were hills and towering trees. Houses were tucked away out of sight, perched on tall cliffs overlooking rocky shores. Besides a handful of deer and what Josie later described as a confusion of guinea hens, the streets were lifeless. No one was out going for a stroll or stopping for a chat or popping in or swinging by. There weren't any restaurants or shops or community gardens. Beaches were distant visions, only accessible by way of hundred-step stairs.

Then, there was Josie's farm—a fifty-acre Brigadoon, complete with a charming, historic, only slightly crumbling 1800s farmhouse. We walked on a stone path, past a field of lavender and a sprawling vegetable garden dutifully marked *Certified Organic.* "Dan's picking up Chinese," Josie said. "Best place in town."

"Oh, what's the name?" I asked.

"Chinese Food," Josie said with a laugh and creaked open the front door. Inside the white farmhouse was a world of color—pink walls and orange chairs, a cheetah-printed couch, and a Navajo-inspired rug. "What?" Josie said when I smirked at the purple-painted mantel.

"Nothing," I said. "I love it."

Josie's husband was Dan, formerly Daniel, a stagehand, turned bar owner, turned potato farmer with a love of ballroom dancing. He inherited the farm from his uncle Jim back in the days when Whitbey was still just a wrong turn on the way to the Hamptons. Josie likes to use this fact as evidence that she discovered Whitbey.

"So, have you heard from Tom?" Dan asked over wonton soup.

"Don't ask her that," Josie said.

"I can't ask that?" Dan said.

"No," Josie said. She passed out the egg rolls and then we talked about Tom. We only talked about Tom.

The unfortunate thing about moving to a new place is that you realize that you are still yourself. You still have all your bad habits. You're not suddenly happier or more productive. A cool sea breeze does nothing to extinguish the bitterness from your impending divorce nor does it stop you from checking your soon-to-be former spouse's cruise itinerary every morning. *Where in the world is Tom today?* I liked to imagine him catching dysentery in India or being kidnapped while having lunch on his shore excursion in Abu Dhabi. I wondered if cholera was still around as he floated down the Nile. Perhaps, a very poisonous jellyfish would sting him in Australia or better yet, he could be eaten by a shark. I don't want to sound unkind, but, if a man leaves you in search of adventure, you want that man to choke to death on a deep-fried cricket in Beijing. You just do.

It's not like I wasn't having an adventure of my own. It's just that my adventure was less globe-trotting and more asking construction workers to please stop dropping solar panels on my house. It's a terrible thing to feel sorry for yourself, but I found that I had a true talent for it. And it's always a shame to waste one's talent. I just felt awful for myself. For a while, maybe a couple of weeks, I really embraced a "woe is me" philosophy. Almost overnight, I developed a sincere skepticism toward anyone who looked or seemed to suggest that they were mildly happy. I'd like to say that at the first sign of trouble, I committed myself to making the best of things. But, for at least two months, I left voice mails for my real estate agent begging her to find me a buyer.

This is not to say that my new town was nothing but a string of nuisances. It was, I'll admit, as beautiful as Josie said it was. Everything looked like it belonged on a postcard. On the southern edge of town, soft white sand blanketed the beaches and to the north tall cliffs and rocky beaches made way for hidden coves. Every day, the bay was bustling with activity and teeming with wildlife. Sailboats with giant colorful spinnakers soared past my kitchen window every Wednesday evening for the weekly race. The narrow winding roads throughout town were lined with darling farm stands with hand-painted signs. Everyone had a red wagon on their porch and a *Meet us at the beach* sign hanging on their front door.

Still, when I saw a "Depression Quiz" advertised on the cover of the AARP magazine that was shoved in my post office box, I decided to partake. I stopped in at the little café on the corner, picked up a coffee, and settled into the quiz at one of the many picnic tables on the hotly contested vacant lot. Scattered around the lot were posters and signs. A banner with the words *Save What's Left* was draped across a chain-link fence and a man at the edge of the property was hammering wooden posts into the ground.

The quiz had nine statements and you were meant to decipher on a scale of one to three how accurately those statements described your current state of mind. Those scoring between nine and fourteen could consider themselves mildly depressed; fifteen to twenty-one, moderately depressed; twenty-two and higher, severely depressed. There was no scenario for those who were not depressed. AARP assumed that those people would skip the depression quiz and move straight to the sexy summer reads.

The truth is, the quiz wasn't really necessary. I was sitting alone in a vacant lot, drinking stale coffee at a half-rotted picnic table on a patch of dirt and the first thought that came to me as I fished through my bag to find a pen to fill out the depression quiz in AARP magazine was *This will be a fun little treat!* I dove straight in. . . .

I feel sorry for myself and/or I feel I've let myself and others down. *3*

Poor appetite. *1*

I speak slowly enough for people to notice—This one stumped me. I sat for a while and considered it. Was I speaking slowly? Slowly enough for people to notice? What does that mean? Would someone have to point it out to you? Who? What if you were alone and there was no one around to tell you, *Hey, you're speaking slowly.*

I was interrupted by a voice calling out from the

street. "Anything good?" Rosemary said as she made her way toward the post office.

"Depression quiz," I said and held up the magazine.

"Right-o," Rosemary said and gave a wave.

I caught up with Rosemary back at home. She was violently plucking weeds from her oyster shell driveway. "Well?" she said. "What's the verdict?"

"Moderately depressed," I said.

"Well, there's still time," she said and hoisted a bucket over her shoulder.

5

TO: Supervisor White (white@whitbey.gov)
FROM: Kathleen Deane (KDeane@gmail.com)
SUBJECT: Bay Mission Mainstays

Dear Supervisor White,

A few weeks ago, I threw my support behind the Bay Mission and its goal to preserve the vacant waterfront property located at 1127 Main Road. I signed a petition in favor of the Mission and contributed $1,000 to the cause by way of a regrettable silent auction bid for a small, plagiarized painting of a seashell. I'm writing to you today to rescind my support for the Bay Mission and to ask you to please remove my name from the petition that was submitted to the town board.

After attending at least three very tense community meetings held by the Bay Mission, I am doubtful that this group, well-meaning as they may be, are qualified to handle a project of this scale. To say these meetings are chaotic is putting it mildly. There is often yelling, insults, and by the end of the night, usually tears. The Bay Mission claims to be saving the community from large-scale development, but in the meantime it is pitting neighbor against neighbor. Now that all this money has been raised and the property has been purchased, the question of what to do with the vacant lot is tearing the community apart. I, of course, am new to this discussion, but from what I can see a consensus is not likely anytime soon. And yet, the Bay Mission continues to hold large-scale events. It continues to fundraise to reach a goal that as of today does not yet exist.

Unbeknownst to me, my $1,000 contribution to this organization landed me on an exclusive email list for the "Mainstays" of the Mission. These emails are sent to the supposed "unwavering supporters of the cause." They read like cult newsletters and it would appear that Patty Tilley, self-appointed Bay Mission president, fancies herself the Grand High Witch. Each time one of these emails arrives in my in-box, I half expect it to include a recipe for turning all the children of Whitbey into mice.

I attended the last informational community meeting held by the Bay Mission on Wednesday in the schoolhouse. There was talk of a beach cleanup, a plant sale, and a possible beautification committee for a proposed Zen garden. Patty Tilley assured the audience that the Mission's "Save What's Left" mantra was very much alive and well. The next day, Thursday, I received a "Mainstay" email that painted a vastly different picture. As usual, the email had top-secret undertones with one sentence reading, "Use discretion when speaking on matters of the Mission." More alarming were the plans detailed in the email—hotels, yacht clubs, wedding venues, etc. . . . The third paragraph begins: "Large-scale concerts could be accommodated." It seems the Mission Board Members envision this property as a "destination" of sorts.

It is not for me to say whether these ladies have good intentions or not (it is very possible they do). But, I would like to say on the record that I do not support any development on this property. For one thing, it will damage our quality of life and for another thing, it will be extremely detrimental to the surrounding wetlands. You have no doubt received a flurry of angry emails this morning, and I'm sorry to say, you have me to thank for that. Despite Ms. Tilley's warning "DO NOT FORWARD," I did forward Thursday's "Mainstay" email to my neighbor Rosemary Preston, who went ahead and circulated it to presumably the rest of Whitbey.

Thank you for your attention to this matter. Attached are three "Mainstay" emails.

Sincerely,
Kathleen Deane

I have one sister. Lilly. About four times a year, she calls me to tell me I'm a socialist. We reminisce about old times. We make plans to see each other. We promise they won't fall through. She tells me she loves me. I tell her I love her. The plans fall through.

I didn't tell Lilly about Tom, at least not right away, because Lilly has opinions. When you have a sibling who is twelve years older than you, they either have a lot of opinions about your life or they have none. Lilly had a lot. In her own life, Lilly was free. She took chances. She made mistakes. She dropped out of high school. She married three men. She married one man twice. When Lilly was twenty-seven years old, she lived in Italy for a year for no particular reason. While she was there she read a book about neurology. The next week she came home and finished high school. Eight years later, she had her PhD.

Lilly saved all her planning and sensible ideas for me. She took it upon herself to chart the course of my life and she was determined to make it perfect. When it was time for me to go to kindergarten, Lilly personally toured the schools. Saint Teresa's was the best school in our neighborhood. But, Saint Teresa's had bad landscaping. The purple flowers in front were dead. The hallways were dark. It would require a bus. Sacred Heart, which was just down the road, had better flowers. There were more windows. The kindergarten classrooms had play kitchens and new dollhouses. And, most importantly, Sacred Heart was down the block from Howard Johnson's. So, I went to Sacred Heart and whenever Lilly picked me up, we'd stop at Howard Johnson's and have fried clam rolls.

Lilly's best friend was Louise Deane. Louise had a very nice family. They lived in an apartment underneath an elevated train and above a diner. The mother and father both worked for Elizabeth Arden and their entire apartment smelled like Blue Grass perfume. There were five children. Louise was the oldest. The youngest was Tom. I met him once when I was five. He was loud. I didn't like him. I met him again at a Harvard football game and I married him. The story goes that when Lilly and Louise were fifteen years old, they decided that Tom and I would grow up and get married and that they would wear pink bridesmaids' dresses at the wedding. And that's exactly what happened.

But, then, Tom was gone and I was alone in an oyster shack and for whatever reason, it smelled like Blue Grass and every day it made me sad. Lilly wasn't sad. She was furious. Louise Deane, now Louise Kaminski, decided to give Lilly a ring to tell her that I had broken it off with Tom which apparently had led him to a nervous breakdown, because why else would someone go on a world cruise alone.

"Well, I hope you're happy," Lilly called to say. "Louise is just about ready to fly to Asia to meet Tom. Asia, Kathleen."

"Why?" I said.

"Why? She's afraid Tom's going to kill himself. Why else?"

"He's not going to kill himself," I said.

"Are you?" she asked.

"Not today," I said.

"All right, then. How's the house?"

"Bad," I said and paused. "Do not tell Louise."

"Louise wants you to call her."

"I'm not calling Louise."

"So, what's wrong with the house?"

"It's this town," I said. "I have this nightmare construction site next to me. You know, McMansion."

"Mm-hmm," Lilly said, unfazed.

"You know, I keep emailing the supervisor. He never writes me back. I call code enforcement, they don't come. I have this insane neighbor, Rosemary, who has been on a crusade about this for I think years. She's not getting anywhere." I could practically hear the wheels turning over the phone.

"Do you want me to call the supervisor?" Lilly asked in an *I'm calling his mother* sort of way.

"I'm not even going to answer that."

"You know what you should do?"

"What?" I said.

"Letter to the editor. Is there a local newspaper?"

"No," I said. "Yes. I don't know. I think so."

"Okay, so write a letter to the editor. Or guest column. Do you think they'd let you do a guest column? Our paper down here has a guest column almost every week and you know what? It makes a difference. People read those things. I always read them."

"How is Florida?" I asked.

"The same."

"Get out of there," I said. "I don't know why you ever moved there."

"You know," she said. "Maureen's sister . . ."

"I know Maureen's sister said it was nice. But, it isn't."

"It is nice," Lilly said.

"Move here," I said. "We can live in the oyster shack together. I'll pick up a few cats from the animal shelter."

"There's an idea," Lilly said with a laugh.

"Well, are you going to come visit at least?" I asked.

"Of course I will," she said.

"When?" I said.

"When Tom comes back," she said. "He's a better cook."

"That ship has sailed," I said. "Literally. As of this morning it's pulling into Sydney Harbor."

"You should get a therapist," she said.

"I'll talk to you soon," I said. Outside, I heard the Bay Mission ladies walking by—bad press had inspired the addition of an afternoon constitutional. They stopped in front of the Sugar Cube.

"Isn't this nice," I heard one of them say to a construction worker. "It's going to be beautiful when it's all finished! Is this all teak here in the front?"

"No English," the man said.

"Well, it's gorgeous," she said. "It's just gorgeous. Are you available in the spring because I was thinking of extending my sunroom?" No response. "I'll give you a call then. Is this the company? This name on the truck?" No response. "Do you do bulkheads too? My bulkhead is starting to rot. Would I need a wetland permit for that?" I wondered how long it would take Rosemary to storm out of her house and bonk Bunny on the head. When she didn't, I assumed she was under the weather.

Out on my deck, I found another surprise. I have read enough books to know that when you buy or rent a beach cottage in a trendy beach town, it is only a matter of time before a young handsome "local" man shows up at your door. It took a month for mine to show up. I found him lounging in an Adirondack chair on my deck flipping through his phone and sitting beside what looked to me like a surfboard made for a giant. "Hi," I said to him as I kept one eye on the falling glass shards from the construction site next door.

"Oh, hello," he said and only briefly looked up from his phone. I didn't know what to do. I just stood there and sort of looked at him blankly and took him in for a moment. "I'm waiting for someone," he said, when he felt my eyes beaming through the back of his head.

"Oh," I said. "Okay."

"She said she knows you," he said. "She said it'd be

okay if I sit and wait here. But I can wait in the water if you want."

"No," I said. "You don't have to wait in the water. . . ." Just then, the cowbell attached to the gate clanged and Josie popped through.

"Oh, good," Josie said as she shimmied past some fallen debris. "You met."

"Well, not exactly," I said.

"This is Henri," she said. "He's French. He's giving me a paddleboard lesson."

"Is paddleboarding a thing you need lessons for?" I asked.

"If you want to do it right," Henri said as he buckled his life jacket and fished a pair of paddles out from underneath the bulkhead. "Are we ready?" he said to Josie.

"Ready!" Josie beamed.

"Well, maybe I could join the two of you one day," I said.

"Definitely," Henri said. "Someday."

"Next time," Josie said and she awkwardly flung her sport tankini-clad self over the edge of the bulkhead.

While Josie and Henri giggled and splashed in the bay, I sequestered myself in my tiny bedroom and began work on my guest column. *I'll just do it as an act of catharsis,* I told myself. I wrote it in a flurry. I began with my plane crash story. I don't know if I've mentioned this yet, but I am a survivor of the world's smallest and least exciting plane crash. In 2006, my mother died and I flew to New York to sort out her affairs. The day I was set to leave, Tom was pulled into emergency surgery. So,

I went alone. Everything went fine. I packed up the house. I arranged the memorial date. I put Mom's sapphire ring in a box and mailed it to Lilly. I got the pearls. Three days later, I boarded a flight back to Kansas City. It was a clear sunny day. No wind. We taxied for a long time. Then we took off. The plane lifted approximately three inches off the ground, crashed back onto the tarmac, and then slammed through a fence and into what looked like a very big puddle.

The worst part of any plane ride is the last ten minutes when everyone kills each other to get their stuff out of the overhead compartments. Everyone knows that. What everyone doesn't know is that even when the plane crashes, and part of the wing catches on fire and the giant yellow emergency slides inflate, people still do this. I think it took an hour for all of us to slide down the slides. We were told to leave our things, but nearly everyone disregarded that advice and instead went bouncing down the slide clutching their Samsonites. When it was my turn to go down the slide, I was clunked on the head by a paisley Vera Bradley that was desperately flung from a woman still on the plane. By the way, I left my luggage on the flight and I never saw it again. So, joke's on me.

Anyway, the plane crashed and there was a very small fire and everyone was fine. But, it was a slow news day, so the press showed up—hundreds of them. They swarmed the passengers and for the most part, everyone was more than willing to detail the trauma that they had just experienced. I did my best to avoid the cameras and headed back into the terminal where I hoped to get the sandwich that I didn't have time to get before we took off. At the sandwich shop, I bumped into a reporter late to the scene. He said he was new at the job. He said if he didn't get an interview with one of the passengers he was going to be fired. So, I let him ask me a few questions while I waited for my turkey club.

"Okay," he began and waved over another man with a camera who was lurking at one of the big windows. "So, we heard that the airline is handing out vouchers," he said.

"Yep," I said and held them up.

"Okay, so, you got the vouchers. And we also heard that there are water and snacks being passed out to the survivors. . . ."

"We're hardly survivors," I said.

"But, you got the snacks?"

"Granola bar," I said. "Yeah."

"And the water?" he asked.

"And the water."

"Okay, just a few more things here," he said and anxiously searched through his tiny notepad. "Did the airline provide you with maps and contact information?"

"They did," I said.

"Okay, okay . . . And . . . um . . ." He took a long pause before saying, "And were you comforted?"

I turned to give him my full attention.

"No," I said, outraged.

"No?"

"I didn't get any comforting," I said. "Where are they comforting people?"

"I just know that people were comforted," he said.

"Well, I could use some comforting," I said. "And if they're going to hand out comforting, then they should tell people."

"Right," the reporter said. "I understand. This must be very hard for you." At this point, I started weeping.

"It is," I said as I thought about my mother and her house and all the things I never told her.

The reporter didn't lose his job. He was promoted. The three-minute clip of me standing in front of a case of giant salami while crying my eyes out over a lack of comforting by an airline ran on loop for two days. I was mocked relentlessly at work and at home the phrase *I need comforting* became a common punch line.

It was a stretch, but I needed something for the guest column—something punchy, something clever, something to keep them reading. So, I tied the plane story into my run-ins with local government and called it a day. Supervisor White didn't call. He didn't write. The few people in town hall that I could get on the phone told me to file a complaint. Fill out a FOIL. Submit a letter to the file. Nobody cared. The house was being built. It was a bell that couldn't be unrung. I knew that. I got my granola bar. I had my map. Where was the comforting? Where was the *This will never happen again*? How about a *It was a mistake,* or better yet, *I'm sorry*? I explained that town government needs transparency. I said emails should not go unanswered and that mistakes or loopholes in the town code needed to be corrected.

The editor of the paper said he'd run it. He said it was great. They'd edit it for grammar. He took my picture.

The following week it was in the paper. Before I could pick up a copy of it, I got a call from Josie.

"What did you do?" she said.

"What?" I said. "Did you see the column? Is the picture okay?"

"The picture's okay. The column, however, reads like a snippet from *Fatal Attraction.* Were you drunk?" I hung up with Josie and raced to the coffee shop down the street. My heart just about stopped when I saw the words CAN YOU HEAR ME, SUPERVISOR WHITE? splashed across page 2. The column had been rewritten. The first sentence read: "I am a survivor."

6

TO: Supervisor White (white@whitbey.gov)
FROM: Kathleen Deane (KDeane@gmail.com)
SUBJECT: Sorry

Dear Supervisor White,

I am mortified. I assume that you have seen my guest column in this week's Whitbey Weekly *and I can understand if that makes me the last person you want to hear from. Actually, I debated for quite a while about whether or not to send this email. On the one hand, I want to explain myself. On the other hand, I'm worried you will see my name flash in your in-box and immediately call Chief Henderson to request a restraining order. I did consider writing a letter to the editor to clear the air, but unfortunately, in this case, the editor is a lunatic with a vivid imagination and a subscription to Grammarly. So, I'm just going to tell you what happened and hope that you understand.*

First of all, let me assure you that the column that ran in the newspaper on Wednesday was not the column I wrote. I never said you were "attractive." I said you were experienced and capable. I did make a reference to Norma Rae, but I have no plans to "sit outside your office all night" nor am I going to "assemble an army." Mr. Price, editor of the Whitbey Weekly, *clearly does not understand sarcasm. The column I wrote was lighthearted. It was tongue-in-cheek. I thought that bringing a bit of humor to the piece would help land the message. Obviously, I was wrong. I am not a writer. Lesson learned.*

Mr. Price has painted me as a delusional, lovestruck nut. And, he did it in my own words! He didn't write an article ABOUT me. He wrote it AS me. And then he had the nerve to drag David Bowie into it. Were "Space Oddity" parody lyrics necessary? He took my silly story about a very minor plane incident and made it out as if I were currently suffering from PTSD. Just because I expect answers to emails regarding building code violations doesn't mean I was in any way suggesting that I consider you a "knight in shining armor." I can't tell you why Mr. Price said that I was "spending all of my time alone in my house perfecting my Tinder profile." I'm not. All I said was that I was recently separated and new to the area. And, by the way, I have not considered online dating as the edited column suggests and even if I did I certainly wouldn't be "looking for a Supervisor White–type."

Again, please accept my sincere apologies. I called Mr. Price to give him a piece of my mind and request a correction/apology. But, he took the opportunity to remind me that he was married. So, I doubt I will see much in the way of restitution. Also, if your secretary tells you that I was outside your office this morning, know that I was merely passing by on my way to the clerk's desk to get a beach sticker.

In other news, the house next door has climbed a few more

feet overnight. The chain-link fence has encroached so far into the street that it now regularly impedes traffic and the entirety of the roof, which was said to be preserved, was demolished a few days ago. If something could be done about the falling debris, I would really appreciate it.

Sincerely,
Kathleen Deane

P.S. Attached is the original column.

Here's something new I learned about myself: I can't eat in a restaurant alone. I thought I could. But, I can't. There is a little maritime village a few miles away from my house. The streets are lined with restaurants and cafés and bakeries and cheese shops and sweet shops and ice cream parlors and of course the obligatory empty art galleries in between. There's always a new restaurant opening up. It's always said to offer "farm-fresh ingredients." The chefs are always "world-class." The desserts are "to die for." There are lines out the door. Cocktails cost fifteen dollars. And while I hate the phrase *foodie destination* almost as much as I hate the foodies themselves, I wanted to go. I really wanted to go.

"So go," Sebastian the life coach said one rainy afternoon.

"I know," I said. "I will. I'm going to."

"Go with Josie," he said rather indifferently.

"Well, shouldn't I go alone? Shouldn't I be able to go alone at my age?"

"It's not mandatory," he said and passed me a bruschetta. "What else? Are you keeping a routine like we talked about?"

"Tom contacted me," I said.

Sebastian gasped. "He called? Or a letter. Did he write you a letter?"

"Close," I said and reached in my bag to produce a small plastic bottle. I handed it to Sebastian.

"What is it?" he asked, inspecting the bottle and the Saint Bernadette sticker crookedly affixed to its side.

"Holy water," I said.

" 'I prayed for you at the shrine,' " Sebastian read the sticker aloud. "Well, that's . . ." He paused.

"Right," I said, shaking my head. "It's not good."

"No," Sebastian said. "It's . . ." He struggled to find the word. "It's sweet. It's sort of sweet."

"Well, then you'll like this," I said. "This came with it." I reached to give Sebastian a gold mass card.

"Okay," Sebastian said. " 'A prayer will be offered for KATHLEEN DEANE for ONE year at TWO masses each day at the Lourdes Shrine,' " he read.

"Mm-hmm," I said.

"That's a lot of prayers," Sebastian said.

"That's right that's a lot of prayers," I said. "He thinks I need two prayers a day for a year? How many prayers did he get for himself?"

"Maybe it's his way of apologizing," Sebastian said.

"Via Saint Bernadette," I said.

"What do you think it means?" Sebastian asked.

"Well, he's in France," I said. "We know that much."

"It's not even full," Sebastian said and tilted the bottle from side to side.

"No, well, I've been using it," I said.

"I didn't know you were religious," Sebastian said.

"I'm not," I said. "I just put a dab of it on my forehead every morning. A little holy water and a little Estée Lauder's Pleasures and I'm ready to go."

"Uh-huh," Sebastian said, writing in his notebook.

"And I sprinkle it around the house every once in a while," I said. "I think it's helping."

Sebastian continued to study the bottle and the card. "Says it's fresh holy water from the grotto," he said.

"Well, good," I said. "I hate stale holy water."

"Nothing worse," Sebastian said.

"So what do you make of it?" I asked.

"Well, I think it's all very positive," Sebastian said.

"Is it?" I said.

"Yes," Sebastian said.

"I don't know," I said.

"Don't always think the worst," Sebastian said.

"I'll go to a restaurant," I said.

"Go to a restaurant," Sebastian said.

So, I asked Josie, who in true form took a simple thing about me and made it difficult and all about her. "How about Friday?" she said when I proposed the idea.

"Perfect," I said. "My treat."

"Okay," she said. "Meet me at nine in front of the supermarket on Prince Street and we'll walk from there."

"Why nine?" I asked.

"Oh, I signed up to man the campaign table for the town board election," she said. "My friend Susan was going to do it with me, but her son has chicken pox. So, you can keep me company and then after we'll get lunch."

"For how long?" I asked.

"What?" she said.

"For how long do we have to man the table?"

"Just four hours," she said.

"Forget it," I said. "I'll go alone."

"Kathleen, this is a great way to meet people. Weren't you just saying you need to meet people?"

"I don't even know the candidate," I said.

"It's Dan's friend. Another farmer. Good guy. Nice family. Democrat. What else do you want to know?"

"Fine," I said. "But, I'm also getting dessert, then."

"Okay, good. I'll drop off your T-shirt tomorrow."

"You don't have to," I said.

"It's no trouble," she said. "I'm meeting Henri anyway."

"Is that a good idea?" I said.

"Listen," she said. "He's no Supervisor White, but . . ."

"All right, goodbye," I said and hung up.

That week, I got a call from Louise–Tom's sister. Well, I got several calls. I got about two calls a day for two weeks. And I didn't answer. I let each one go to voice mail. I had no interest in hearing about how Louise wanted me to get back together with Tom or how Tom was devastated or how I made a mess of things or anything else. I knew what she was going to say. "Forgive him." She was going to make a whole case for him. She'd reminisce about our wedding day. She was going to say that Tom's selfishness was only secondary to his kindness. She'd remind me that he was an excellent father. Then she'd ask about my new house and even if I said it was great, she would hear in my voice that it was terrible and she'd report back to Tom.

But, Louise was persistent. She kept calling. So, eventually, I picked up. She didn't ask about my new house. She didn't say anything about Tom.

"Do you remember the figurine Michael and I gave you as a wedding present?" Louise said.

"Yes," I said and eyed the closet where I had it Bubble Wrapped and sealed in a cardboard box with my never-used Limoges dishes.

"Well, Emily is getting married."

"Oh, I didn't know," I said. "Congratulations. To Stephen?"

"Mm-hmm," she said. "Ten years they've been together."

"Well, that's great," I said. "Stephen's great."

"He is great. And we get along with his parents. So . . ."

"Makes wedding planning easier," I said as I waited for the other shoe to drop.

"That's right. And how's Hattie?" Louise said.

"Good. She's good."

"Still with Andrew?"

"Still with Andrew. They're in Seattle now."

"So, you know Emily was an art history major," Louise said.

"Right. I remember," I said.

"She did her thesis in sculpture."

"Right," I said.

"So, I'd like to give her a piece of art as a wedding present. And I thought the figurine we gave you and Tom would be perfect."

"Except you gave it to me and Tom," I said.

"Yes, well, I didn't think you'd mind. I mean don't you think it should stay in the family?"

"You're kidding," I said.

"Kathleen, I'm not kidding. That was an expensive figurine. I think Emily should have it."

"Hold on a second, Louise," I said and walked into the kitchen. I grabbed a coffee mug from the cabinet. "Louise, are you still there?" I asked.

"Yes," she said. "I'm still here. I don't know why you're getting so upset about this. . . ."

"Okay, are you listening, Louise? Because I've got the figurine right here. I'm holding it." I held the phone out as I threw the coffee mug onto the tile floor. It shattered. "Do you hear that? That's what I think of the figurine," and I hung up.

This is not something I would have done in the past. Years ago, I would have mailed the figurine. I would have rolled my eyes and moved on. Because, no matter which way you look at it, no one wins in a fight over a figurine. Right or wrong, there is just no chance of you walking away from a figurine fight looking like a confident, respectable, self-assured woman. If you even say the word *figurine* more than twice, as I have done here, you feel embarrassed.

But, I can't tell you how much joy it brought me to hear Louise's small yelp when she heard the crash. And I know that that probably makes me a bad person. Still, it felt good. It felt really good. For most of my life, whenever some sort of argument or disagreement cropped up, I would ask myself, *Is it worth it? Is it worth fighting about?* And in almost all cases, the answer was no. I felt that confrontation should be reserved for the big moments, the big offenses. The little things should be let go. Then, I moved to a beach town where they only fight about the little things and I happily joined right in.

In a beach town, all the big fights are about little things. People are parking on corners. They're stepping in piping plover habitats. The pumpkins are bringing traffic. The $85,000 taxpayer-funded pumpkin trolley is never used. The dogs aren't on leashes. The ice cream truck music plays too loudly. Household garbage is being put in the cans at the beach.

No one in Whitbey ever asked themselves if a fight was worth it. It always was. To its credit, the Bay Mission inspired a level of fighting so intense that it warranted an article in *The New York Times.* After the community banded together to raise the funds to purchase the land, the issue of what to do with it ignited a civil war of sorts. In the meantime, they kept raising money. A lot of it. Every other weekend, there was a fundraiser. There was an art auction, a chowder festival, a harvest meal, a winter wonderland light display, and so on. The money was going into an account, tucked away until the day the residents came to a consensus.

People couldn't stop talking about it. They stood in groups in the street and argued over gardens and community centers and snack bars. Where was the money going? How much did we need? Could we just do nothing? Can we get our money back? I don't even like chowder! Everything else fell by the wayside. Any topic of discussion, personal, local, national, international could be tied to the Bay Mission.

"My daughter just had a baby girl. The hospital

charged her thirty-five dollars to hold the baby in the delivery room."

"It's greed. Well, just look at what's happening at the Bay Mission!"

"Did you hear about the conflict in the South China Sea?"

"Unbelievable. But then again, just look at what's happening at the Bay Mission!"

"Did you see the piece last night about the conditions in the Amazon warehouse?"

"I did. I'm not surprised. Just look at what's happening at the Bay Mission!"

"Disney World was so crowded this Christmas. We hardly got on any rides."

"You think that's bad? Just wait and see what happens with the Bay Mission!"

"They think I have cancer."

"Will you still make it to the Bay Mission meeting tonight?"

On Friday, I met Josie at Mermaid Foods on Prince Street. She was there, as promised, in her bright blue T-shirt and her card table filled with lawn signs and pens and magnets. Like any good Whitbey resident, I immediately brought up the Bay Mission. But, Josie, having recently climbed the ranks of the Mainstays, didn't want to discuss it. "Henri heard what you wrote to the supervisor about his mother," she said.

"What?" I said.

"Patty Tilley? The Grand High Witch? Really, Kathleen? Is that nice?"

"I didn't know she was his mother. And how did he see that email?"

"Forget it," Josie said. "Henri has let it go and so will I."

"Well, I don't know what you're letting go," I said.

"All I know is, Henri and his mother are nice enough to volunteer their time for this and they get a lot of crap for it. I mean, they're doing a lot of work, Kathleen. We're all doing a lot of work."

"What is Henri doing?"

"He writes the newsletters," she said and started rearranging the lawn signs and posters. "He went to Cornell. He's very smart. People don't realize that, you know, because he's so laid-back."

"And what's your title again?" I asked.

"Treasurer," she said.

For about an hour, Josie and I sat near the automatic doors of Mermaid Foods and successfully annoyed nearly every customer. "Look at these two," Josie whispered to me as two gray-haired women in white capris approached us. "Republicans," she said and made a face.

"They look exactly like us," I said.

"Oh, please, Kathleen," Josie said and ran her fingers through her freshly touched-up auburn locks.

One of the women picked up a pamphlet from our table and studied it. "A farmer, huh?" she finally said.

"That's right," Josie said. "He owns—"

"I know what he owns," the woman interrupted. "Shame on you," she said and tossed the pamphlet back on the table. "Shame on the both of you."

It was around hour two when I realized that Hank Brown, our candidate, was somehow both hated by the Republicans and loathed by the Democrats. This made for a morning of insults, dirty looks, and a heavy dose of inappropriate language. Many of the Mermaid

Foods shoppers were happy to delay their weekly shopping trips to explain in vivid detail how exactly Hank Brown had singlehandedly ruined their lives with fruit pies and pumpkins. More than one person told us to go to hell. One woman recognized me from my photo in the paper. She looked me up and down with a puzzled expression and then said, "Well, I guess you're very photogenic." Josie didn't understand why I didn't take that as a compliment.

After one man told us that he sat in three hours of pumpkin traffic last Saturday thanks to Hank Brown, he kicked the leg in of our card table, sending its contents flying across the parking lot. "I think I'm going to get us some coffees," Josie said after we finished chasing flyers and posters around the lot.

"You're leaving me here?" I said.

"Five minutes," Josie said. "It's just around the corner. Latte?" she said and I nodded. I wasn't surprised when she didn't return. Josie was not reliable. She just wasn't. She never was. Josie could never be the designated driver. You couldn't count on her to return a borrowed dress. When Josie was twenty, she went to Australia for a two-week trip. She was deported from the country six months later. She just forgot to leave. When we were young, I would find myself searching through a sea of people at concerts looking for Josie only to find out the next day that she had hitched a ride home with someone else. I once waited four hours in the Antwerp train station for Josie to disembark from a train she never got on.

So, I campaigned alone for the candidate that I didn't

support. I agreed with everyone who said he was a bum. "The traffic is horrendous," I said. I told them to write in their own names on the ballot. I said that's what I was going to do. "You can't even get any of these politicians to answer an email," I said to one woman, who feigned an interest in the subject.

"You know who you should talk to?" the woman said. "I don't know her name. But there's some nut who wrote a guest column in the newspaper a couple of weeks ago. She was saying the same thing."

I tried to change subjects and tell people about the Sugar Cube, but no one wanted to hear it. I envied all of the people whose biggest problem was pumpkin traffic. Let them try living near the great glass wonder. Let them spend a few mornings waking up to jackhammers and falling glass. Pumpkin traffic? Please. Finally, I saw a familiar face.

"What in God's name are you doing?" Rosemary said. "Hank Brown?"

"I know," I said.

"You know he's the one who–"

"I know, caused all of the pumpkin traffic," I said.

"I was going to say was arrested for tax fraud," Rosemary said. "But yeah, the pumpkin thing too."

"Oh my God," I said.

"If I were you, I would pack up this crap and pretend this never happened," Rosemary said and started collecting the yard signs into a neat pile. She looked around to check for witnesses.

"Right," I said and angrily scooped up the pens and magnets. "All I wanted was to go have lunch," I said.

"I'm going to have lunch," Rosemary said. "Oyster House. Have you tried it yet?" She pointed up the road.

"With who?" I said and piled the posters and signs into the nearby garbage can.

"What?"

"Who are you going with?"

"Nobody," she said. "Did you see the latest addition to the house?"

"No," I said.

"That's something for you to look forward to when you get home. Good luck getting into your driveway. They planted about ten trees in the street this morning."

"Great," I said.

"I filed a complaint already," Rosemary said. "I signed both of our names. Let's go," she said and waved me in the direction of the Oyster House.

We had lunch and it was delicious. We tucked ourselves away in a trendy, twenty-seat speakeasy and talked about nothing but the Sugar Cube. It was divine. Each of us had found a captive audience in the other. Rosemary and I were the only two people on earth who were genuinely interested in variances and wetland permits and health department certificates. We traded information. We drank wine. We listened to Elton John's "Rocket Man." We listened to it six more times. We ordered mussels. We laughed. We plotted next moves. We made fun of town officials. We complained about "Rocket Man." We were asked to leave. We apologized. We laughed some more. We sang along. We had dessert.

Back home, a special surprise was waiting for me in my post office box—"Greetings from Venice." I walked out of the post office in a stupor and leaned against the flagpole to examine the postcard. I stared into an image of a gondola floating down a Venetian canal while I weighed my options. To flip or not to flip. To read or not to read.

Dear Kathleen,

You can't believe how delicious the pizza is in Italy. We're going on a bus tour to Florence tomorrow.

Love,
Tom

I walked home and threw it out. About two hours later, I fished it out of the kitchen garbage. I scraped off the coffee grounds and stuck it on the fridge. He did say *love.*

7

TO: Supervisor White (white@whitbey.gov)
FROM: Kathleen Deane (KDeane@gmail.com)
SUBJECT: Demolition vs. renovation

Dear Supervisor White,

Two weeks ago, the West Creek Civic Association held a special meeting in the schoolhouse. I bumped into the vice president of the WCCA, Bunny Williams, at the post office the other day and she asked that I attend. Unbeknownst to me, the one and only item on the agenda for the meeting was my neighbor's house construction. I now understand that the civic association meetings are extremely well attended. As I'm sure you can imagine, it was a full house and there were many questions raised about the size and scale of this project and the ongoing noise and traffic problems. I was asked to come to the podium and give an update on the town's response, where I had no choice but to report that I had received no communication from your office.

Things took a turn for the worse when the subject of demolition came up. It was a rather heated debate, to put it mildly. (See attached police report.) There is another meeting scheduled for tomorrow and in the hopes of avoiding more police involvement, I was hoping you could bring some clarity to this subject. Perhaps you could settle the argument regarding the definition of a demolition vs. a renovation. I have read and reread Section 78 of the town code and, as I understand it, a project is considered a demolition if less than 20 percent of the original structure remains. The day after the meeting, I called the Building Department and spoke to Trish, who told me that the chief building inspector, Mr. Fredrickson, was out on assignment and was not available to speak. So, I told Trish about the meeting and also that there seemed to be a general consensus in the community that more than 80 percent of my neighbor's house had been demolished. She said she would pass along the message to Mr. Fredrickson.

I did not receive a call back and, in the meantime, more of the house was demolished. Last Thursday, I called the Building Department again. I was told Mr. Fredrickson was at an HVAC conference in Syracuse. That weekend, the remainder of the second floor was torn down. Today, I received a call from Mr. Fredrickson, who informed me that he had visited my neighbor's property and, as far as he was concerned, everything was perfectly proper. It is his belief that the 20 percent rule outlined in the town code is a guideline and that "things happen" in construction. But, either way, he was certain that at least 20 percent of the original structure remains.

I, of course, have not done an inspection of the property and I am not an engineer. But, from where I'm sitting, a mere ten feet to the north, the only original thing left of this house is a pile of bricks where the chimney once stood. I asked Mr. Fred-

rickson to attend tomorrow's meeting and explain his position, but he declined. After our conversation reached an impasse, he advised me to contact you. So, here I am. How am I supposed to stand up at the meeting tomorrow and tell these people that according to the chief building inspector five bricks equal 20 percent of a house? Any assistance you could provide in this matter would be greatly appreciated. Thank you very much.

Sincerely,
Kathleen Deane

Someday, I'd like to be the kind of person who gets joy from the little things. I'd like to be the person who can be in a book club and not want to strangle the other members when it's clear they didn't read the book. I want to be the person who doesn't mind when someone doesn't speak one word at a dinner party, or worse, only talks about the food. I'd like to be able to smile and nod and be perfectly happy chitchatting about blooming petunias. Maybe one day when I'm ninety, all the cynicism will melt away and I'll make a friend who says things like, "Cute top," and we'll go for daily walks around the neighborhood and talk about absolutely nothing and we'll do that every day and I'll be happy until I'm dead.

But, until then, I'm me. And, as of today, I am still the person who only makes friends with people who have nothing nice to say. I don't think I've ever had a nice friend. In fact, I'm certain of it. I've had good friends—loyal friends. I've had friends who make me laugh. I've had friends who are smart and tough and successful. I've had friends I've admired. But, I've never had a nice friend. Because here's the terrible truth about me: I would rather have a clever person insult me for an hour than spend a minute with a dull person doling out compliments.

This is not the easiest way to march through life and I'm not exactly proud of it. But, it's a fact either way. I wouldn't even bring it up, but I've come to the point in the story where you'll start to wonder why I've become such good friends with Rosemary and you'll wish we could go back and spend more time with Josie, who is a far less prickly person. But, if you knew me, you'd know that it was inevitable that I would befriend the curmudgeon across the street and that's what I did.

The thing is, we had a common enemy. It started out as mostly Rosemary's enemy, but the bigger and higher the house grew next door and the more emails I sent that went unanswered, the more it became my enemy too. For a long time, I basically accepted the construction and the noise and the workers peeing on my deck and the generators in the street and the debris falling from the sky. I accepted the fact that I had to walk down to Owen's little store and buy back my door knocker that he had reappropriated. I accepted the ladies waking me up every morning at 7:16. But, eventually, there comes a time, when enough is enough.

When I was in college, I used to park my car on a street widely accepted as awash with crime. About once a month, I would return to my car only to find that its battery had been stolen. The good news was, the gentleman who stole my battery worked out of a mechanic shop just at the end of the block. So, I would walk to the shop and say, "It seems my car battery has been stolen."

And the man would say, "You're kidding. What kind of car do you have?"

And I'd say, "A Ford Fiesta."

And he'd say, "Let me see if I have something that will work." Then, he'd return, moments later, with my car battery and hold it above his head and say, "Today's your lucky day!"

I'd say, "How much?"

He'd say, "Fifty."

I'd say, "Ten."

He'd say, "Fine," and that was it. No hard feelings. It was the cost of doing business. He understood that. I understood that. It, honestly, wasn't a problem.

But, this house—this monstrosity next door—this was something else. This wasn't a once-in-a-while problem and it couldn't be solved with a ten-dollar bill. This was unsolvable and it was every day. I tried to rise above it. Trust me, I did. I hardly said anything when the construction crew ruined my expensive white couch. I ignored the ground shaking beneath me and the fact that I needed to ask someone to move their truck every time I wanted to pull out of my driveway. I accepted these things. I let it go when the contractor told me to go back to Albania. I decided to look the other way when he would call over the fence and say, "Good morning, Dorothy!" I was too good, too mature, to fall into that trap.

You can accept a lot until you can't. You can accept

someone stealing your car battery every once in a while, until the day he steals the whole car. And when thirty-five years later, you find yourself living in a dream beach house that is actually a nightmare, you tell yourself it will get better and while you wait for it to get better you collect shells. And you accept the fact that a porta-potty has been placed practically in your backyard. You accept that due to the level of debris on the construction site and the poor positioning of a chain-link fence, the porta-potty is only reachable by way of your deck. You can even accept it when that porta-potty becomes the go-to pit stop for every truck that happens to drive through the neighborhood. But, you cannot accept it when, due to popular demand, a second porta-potty is delivered. That's when you say, "I've had enough." That's when you go to the lady who had had enough long before you had had enough.

But first, you wait until after the holidays. Rosemary was away in Green Bay, Wisconsin, visiting her son and daughter-in-law when this whole porta-potty fiasco happened. Hattie offered to fly out for Christmas to see me, but I told her to wait until the summer to visit. Whatever I said to Hattie inevitably got back to Tom. So, when she asked me about all the construction noise on my end of the phone, I told her that I was putting in a new kitchen. Most years, Hattie spent Christmas with her California in-laws who liked to rendezvous in Hawaii for the holidays. Who could blame her? Tom and I gave up the in-law competition years ago. We forfeited early on. They were too good. They were too nice. They didn't fight. They didn't yell. They didn't judge. The mother called everyone she met a "doll" and the father thought everything was "terrific." So, at the wedding they got the buffet when we wanted a sit-down. They picked the favors and the flowers and the shape of the tables. They got Christmas. We got Thanksgiving. It is what it is.

I did get a tree. I was alone and miserable, but I got a tree. I said to myself, *I'll either get a tree or I'll go on medication.* This town is filled with farms—they stretch out for miles. In the summer they sell corn. In the fall, pumpkins. And, in the winter, not two months after the last pumpkin is picked, those empty patches magically sprout homegrown seven-foot-tall Fraser firs out of thin air. I couldn't justify a $200 Fraser fir. So, I bought a four-foot balsam for $125 and was happy to do it. I sent out Christmas cards. I sent one to Cindy Schwartz in the hope that she would choose me over Tom in the separation and she did. Her letter revealed that in one year's time, Cindy had gotten a divorce from her "no-good cheating husband" and remarried a hedge funder with only the "slightest facial deformity." Her daughter was getting married to a felon. But, they were having the wedding at the Plaza. They also got a new dog. He was blind.

I didn't exactly knock myself out with the decorating. Tom always insisted on white lights. So, I bought multicolor. I did the tree and then drooped the rest of the lights haphazardly around the house, coiling them around beams and winding them across doorframes and windows. I hung what ornaments I could fit. Hattie's third-grade handprint and hot-glued felt reindeer ornaments nearly had me calling to say, "Cancel the flight to Honolulu." But, I resisted. I hung a wreath on the front door and two on the doors of the porta-potties. I hooked a handful of candy canes to the construction site's chain-link fence and swirled some lights around the towering egret statue forever nesting on my deck. Before remembering that I had no furniture, I unboxed the sprawling Christmas village, unwrapping each glittery building and snowcapped tree from last year's wadded-up newspapers. I set it up on the floor in the corner of the room and then put on a Joni Mitchell album to make myself feel even worse.

Two weeks before Christmas, I heard footsteps on my roof. Away to the window, I flew like a flash and found Jim from Public Works securing a twinkly light-covered sailboat medallion to my cupola. The six-foot-tall medallion was draped across Harbor Road and powered by a series of extension cords that gathered in my gutters and dangled against my windows. "Hey," I said to Jim as he admired his work.

"Ho, ho, ho," he called down with a chuckle.

"Is that safe?" I asked.

"This is the way we always do it," he said.

"Don't you think someone should have asked me?" I said.

"We do it every year," he said.

The owners of the Sugar Cube also made a special holiday visit. They pulled up in a Porsche on Christmas Eve and marveled at their geometric wonder. They were an attractive couple. Clean, very clean. The woman was holding a cup of coffee as if it were an accessory. I watched them through a slit in the shutters that covered my bedroom window. In just a few months, I had become Rosemary. I hadn't showered in at least three days. My hair was wild and I wore a giant red robe twenty-four hours a day. Spying on neighbors through shutters made the resemblance almost uncanny.

The contractor joined them and waved a big roll of blueprints in the air, pointing to different corners of the house. When he was finished doing that, he spread the blueprints out on the hood of my station wagon to get a better look. I threw my winter coat over my robe and marched outside. "What are you doing?" I said.

"Oh, hello," the contractor said. "This is Dorothy," he said to his clients.

"Kathleen," I said and they gave me a confused look.

"We needed the flat surface," the woman said. "I'm so sorry." Her voice was soft and angelic. Her hair was perfectly swooped in a clip. She smiled an unsettling sweet smile and offered a sympathetic look.

"Oh. That's fine. No problem. Nice to meet you," I said and quickly retreated back into my house. The next morning there was a jar of honey on my doorstep.

On Christmas Day, I opened the present Hattie mailed me—a set of beautiful new paintbrushes. Some people find painting relaxing. I don't. For the most part, I find it unbelievably irritating. But, it's something I can do and I can do well and there's nothing quite like the satisfaction that comes when a big mess finally turns into something worthwhile. I don't like painting. I like having painted. Rarely, will I ever paint for no reason at all. I require a task, an assignment. I would have done well in the Italian Renaissance. Commissions only. This personality trait doesn't go over well with other artistic types, who are under the assumption that talent is always married to passion. Anyway, I gave myself an assignment—a painting for Rosemary.

I assembled the easel that, during the move, had been dismantled into a pile of paint chip-covered wood. I fished the pieces out from the attic crawl space that was only accessible by way of the antique rolling library ladder that inexplicably stretched from one end of my house to the other. I kept my paints and brushes and miscellaneous art supplies in a fifteen-year-old pink plastic Tupperware tub that once belonged to my mother. A crinkled masking tape label slapped on its side read *Memories* in my mother's loopy handwriting.

I thought about painting a sailboat or a few sailboats or a beach or a barn or a bird. But, in the end, I painted what I always paint—a sad rainy city scene featuring a woman holding an umbrella, usually a red one. Feel free to psychoanalyze this. If you visit Josie's house, you'll find the original sad lonely red umbrella woman and about five later iterations of her. The woman seems to age as I do. This is not intentional.

Rosemary returned home from Wisconsin in rare form. I found her in her garden planting tulip bulbs on New Year's Eve. She was dressed in an ankle-length down coat, snow boots, and a straw hat. I watched as she furiously cleared the snow from a flower bed near her back patio. She tossed a purple pool kickboard at her feet and fell to her knees.

"Don't you have to plant those in the fall?" I asked.

"That's a myth," she said, nearly out of breath from

chipping away at the frozen ground. "It's just harder this way." She didn't look up at me.

"How was your Christmas?" I asked.

"Good. Good. Everyone's good. I asked Steve to plant these in the fall," she said, pulling a basket of bulbs nearer to her. "But did he? No. So, here I am." She used her shovel like an axe, smashing it violently into the ground. "So, what's new?" she asked, still focusing only on the dirt in front of her.

"Well, they delivered a second porta-potty," I said and pointed to the house across the street.

"And you want me to do something?" she said as she plopped a bulb into the jagged hole she had just finished digging.

"Well, no," I said. "I just . . ."

"Listen," she said. "Are you ready to fight? Or are you just bullshitting?"

I hesitated and she looked at me. "Bullshitting, I guess," I said.

"Okay, then." And she went back to her digging.

"And I met them—Sarah and Jack. I got a jar of honey and everything."

"Well, you know what that means?"

"What?" I asked.

"They're about to break another law. How big was the jar of honey?" she asked. I held out my hands to indicate a sizable jar.

"Yep," she said. "I bet they break ground for the pool." She continued digging. "Pool or roof deck," she said. "One of those. Do you hear that?" Rosemary said as she lifted herself from the ground. There was an engine rumbling on the street.

"I think it's just the food truck," I said.

About three times a week, a purple-haired woman would park a food truck on Rosemary's grass. She'd park, crank out an awning, fire up the grill, and serve sandwiches and hot dogs and hamburgers and panini to the entire construction crew. Before I could say another word, Rosemary was trudging across her yard, through the gate, and out into the street. She cut in front of the line of construction workers and confronted the woman—"You took my stick," she said. "I'd like it back."

"What stick?" the woman said. At this point, I was standing beside Rosemary at the food truck window. The woman looked at me puzzled and repeated, "What stick? What stick?"

"It was the stick from your grass, right, Rosemary?" I said. Rosemary didn't answer. So, I addressed the woman. "There were orange sticks here in the grass . . . ," I said and pointed to the ground below us.

"You know what stick!" Rosemary suddenly shouted as she reached a finger into the window and pointed it at the woman. "The stick that was right here in my grass to stop you from parking here!"

"I don't know about any stick," the woman said.

"Okay," I said. "Well, maybe if you could park your truck on the street instead of the grass . . ."

"I watched you," Rosemary interrupted again. "You parked here. You ran over my stick and you drove off with it stuck in your fender." The woman stared blankly with her eyes fixed on Rosemary's hat.

"Oh, forget it!" Rosemary said. "I'm going to take a nap."

"Okay," I said.

"I'll come by later," Rosemary said as she walked away. "We'll talk strategy."

"Hold on," I said to Rosemary and ran inside my house to grab the painting. "Made you this," I said and handed it to her. The construction workers looked on while they waited for their food.

"You did?" Rosemary said and took it gingerly.

"Merry Christmas," I said. Rosemary studied the painting for a moment.

"It's me," she said finally, smiling as she stared at the woman with the red umbrella. "Thank you."

"Sure," I said.

"I'm going to take that nap now," she said.

"Okay," I said.

"I'll come over later," she said.

"Okay," I said. But, she never came over. On that particular day, she didn't have any fight left. Sometimes, the only thing left to do when nothing goes your way is sleep.

In her junior year of college, my daughter, Hattie, studied abroad in Vienna. She was going to spend six months studying music and art and history and theater. Hattie and I spent the whole summer before her trip shopping for clothes and supplies and giant suitcases and power adapters. We bought the deluxe Eurostar train package. Tom and I bought plane tickets to France, where we planned to meet her for Thanksgiving. We switched phone plans. We ordered a six-month supply of everything she could possibly need. We paid for extra luggage.

Then she got there and her apartment was in the attic of a brothel in the red-light district. On her first day, she called to tell me she was using the new sundresses we had bought that summer as bed linens. The next day, she said her "university" was in a community center and her classmates were cab drivers. So, she didn't go to class or meet people. She just slept. That's what Hattie does when she's stressed or nervous. She sleeps. Two weeks later, she was back on campus in Massachusetts. We like to call this time in Hattie's life her Vienna nap.

Tom and I ended up paying for the entire six months in Vienna as well as the full fall tuition. I always regretted not making a bigger stink about that. I regretted not flying to the college to give that study-abroad dean a piece of my mind. But, I was afraid they'd take it out on Hattie. As it was, Hattie decided to recover from her Vienna nap by drowning her sorrows in pistachio nuts in her dorm room. So, I let it go. I didn't fight. I didn't write a letter. I didn't throw a fit.

So, when Rosemary's prediction proved correct and our neighbors began construction on an illegal pool, I decided to fight. I decided to throw a fit. I went to town hall and walked straight into the office of the Water Conservation Committee. I was very confident. I knew just what I was going to say. I had my facts ready to go. Then, I met Virginia Bittner, the WCC secretary, who fancied herself the warden of wetland permits. The office is big, but it is impenetrable. There is a long counter inches from the door that blocks anyone from entering. The space between the wall and the counter is only suitable for the very slimmest among us. So, most opt to stand in the doorway itself. I waited at the counter for about five minutes before saying, "Excuse me," to the secretary who was staring at a stapler.

"Sign in!" she shouted and pointed to a tattered spiral notebook sitting on the counter. I printed my name and waited some more. I perused the other names in the notebook briefly before it was snatched away from me. "That's private," the secretary said. "You can't read that. If you want to read that, you have to FOIL it. Do you want to FOIL the sign-in list?"

"No," I said.

Ms. Bittner was wearing a polka-dot sweatshirt, and a pair of rhinestone flip-flops. Her hair was tied back in a long braid that nearly scraped the office floor. I told her, very politely and calmly, that my neighbors were currently rebuilding their house and that they had an open permit with the Water Conservation Committee.

"Okay?" she said.

"So, I was trying to read the permit. But, it's posted inside the second-floor window of the house–"

"That's where it needs to be posted," she interrupted. "Permits go in the second-floor window." She spoke in a monotone voice. Her face was expressionless. She continued, "When a builder is granted a permit, they get instructions to post the permit in the second-floor window."

"Right," I said. "But, the problem is that the house has been raised and put on stilts. So, the second-floor window is now forty feet in the air. So, I can't read the permit and I wanted to find out–"

"Well, that's where the permit goes–in the second-floor window."

"But, it's on stilts," I argued.

"Doesn't matter. Doesn't matter where the second-floor

window is as long as it's in the second-floor window. It doesn't matter if the house is raised or lowered."

"How could a house be lowered?" I asked.

"Sometimes a house is raised and then an owner changes their mind and then they come to us and they fill out an application and they ask to lower the house."

"Okay," I said. "Maybe I could just look at the permit here if you have a copy of it." She grunted and headed to the file cabinet against the wall. I had never so thoroughly annoyed someone with so little effort. She, honest to God, seemed like she wanted to jump across the counter and slap me. Her eyebrows furrowed and her eyes squinted with each question I asked.

"It's in storage," she said with a slam of the file cabinet drawer.

"The permit's in storage?" I asked.

"That's what I said. It's in storage. I thought maybe it'd still be here. But, it's not. Technically, once a permit is issued, it goes in storage. So, that's what happened. It was put in storage."

"Okay," I said. "Well, do you remember if there was a pool included in the permit?"

"No. No pool," she said.

"So, they don't have a permit for a pool," I said.

"Right!" she barked. "There's no pool in the permit."

"Okay. So, I believe they are building a pool."

"How do you know?" she asked.

"Well, they're digging a giant hole in the backyard. We share a bulkhead and I can see that the hole is very deep."

"How do you know the hole is for a pool?"

"I don't," I said. "I'm assuming."

"Ah," she said.

"What else would they be digging a hole that deep for?" I asked.

"Trees?" she said, confidently.

"No," I said. "I'm certain they're building a pool. There was a cement truck there this morning."

"Well, there's nothing we can do until they actually build a pool. I can't send out the Marine Police because they're digging a big hole. They can dig a big hole if they want to dig a big hole. Besides, it all depends on the phragmites," she said as she walked to the other side of the office. "You see this?" she said and held up a long reed-like plant. "This is a phragmite. If an applicant plants enough of these, it counteracts the building." She handed the phragmite to me. "You can keep that."

"Thank you," I said.

"Have a nice day," she said and I left.

Highway hypnosis kicked in on the drive home. I started to ask myself things like, *Who am I? Where am I? What does it all mean?* I used to think that I had met every kind of person you could meet. I thought I had reached the age when I had essentially seen it all. I walked into the Water Conservation Committee office thinking I knew a lot about life. I walked out, certain I knew nothing.

"I see you've met the Queen of Phragmites," Rosemary said when I got out of the car with my drooping plant.

"I have met her and she has won," I said.

8

TO: Supervisor White (white@whitbey.gov)
FROM: Kathleen Deane (KDeane@gmail.com)
SUBJECT: Beach overcrowding / pickleball

Dear Supervisor White,

The secretary of the civic association has encouraged all residents of West Creek to write to you about our concerns regarding beach overcrowding. I believe there is a petition circulating as well. The hope is to enact regulations in time for the summer season. I moved into my house in September, so I have not yet experienced this alleged overcrowding. But, I have seen the photos and they are frightening. Please add my name to the list in support of parking restrictions in the hamlet.

There is also much talk in the community about the recent pickleball court installed two weeks ago next to the ball field. Everyone is wondering where it came from. It seems to have appeared out of thin air overnight. Someone heard from the town clerk that it was a gift from the town. Let me assure you, this is not a gift. This is a curse. I have been told that the Whitbey Pickleball Association carries a lot of weight in this town, but the crowds that this court attracts are unacceptable and the community should have been consulted before such a heavy burden was placed on its shoulders. We now have hundreds of pickleballers invading our streets every Tuesday and Thursday evening. The WPBA has a section on their website devoted to fundraising for the addition of more courts to accommodate tournaments! Something needs to be done.

Lastly, I wanted to bring the lack of transparency in the Water Conservation Committee to your attention. After not receiving a response from you regarding my neighbor's house construction, I decided to attend last week's WCC work session in the town hall basement to get some answers. I understand that these meetings are open to the public. They are noticed in the local paper with the words "Community input welcome." So, I was taken aback when I, the only member of the public in attendance, was greeted with the words, "I don't know why you're here."

I was then told by Ms. Bittner, the Water Conservation Committee secretary, that the room was too small to accommodate another chair and directed me to either stand in the corner, or better yet, leave. One of the members, I believe Mr. Smith, suggested that they could make room for another chair. But, Ms. Bittner quickly informed him that, even if there were room, there was not a chair to spare in the entirety of the building. So, I stood in the corner.

I was not offered an agenda, but I know that there were fifteen items on the agenda because that's what the chairman said and also I had to stand through all fifteen of them. Luckily, it did not take the members long to whiz through each application. I don't think one file was even opened. When I tried to ask a question, I was informed that there was no speaking or comment allowed at work sessions. I have not been able to review my neighbor's file, because it is supposedly in "storage" and it is apparently not subject to FOIL because it is "pending." Perhaps the Water Conservation Committee office could be forwarded a copy of the Open Meeting and Freedom of Information Laws.

Thank you very much for your attention to these matters.

Sincerely,
Kathleen Deane

There are plenty of movies and documentaries about people who live in areas where the air is polluted or the water is contaminated. It's always the same story. There's a big, greedy, horrible corporation that makes something that everybody needs. They do a really great job making that thing. They do such a great job that they are hired by the government to write the laws regulating that thing . . . blah blah blah . . . there's no regulation . . . everyone gets poisoned . . . the end.

In each one of these films, you are certain to find an interview with a concerned citizen. The interview will most definitely take place in a dimly lit living room. There will be a table in the living room and it will be filled with maps and diagrams and binders and paper clips and Post-its. There will be highlighters and scribbled notes in margins. The concerned citizen will look frazzled. You'll watch and you'll say to yourself, *Didn't they know the camera crew was coming that day? Couldn't they have put on a nice pair of slacks?*

The film crew will ask the citizen a question and he will desperately shuffle papers on the table searching for the answer, or, rather the evidence that supports his answer. He will be able to tell you without hesitation the magnitude of the earthquake to the decimal and the water contaminant percentages by order of contaminant. He will know the date of every meeting and the contents of every email. It is always clear that there is no life for this person outside of this issue. There is no time to put on clean slacks. There is no time for anything. It has swallowed him up.

The question everyone always has is, how did this start? The camera will pan around the living room and you'll see pictures of this man at his wedding and fishing with his grandson and you'll think, *He looks like a normal person.* But, normal people don't stay up all night to track earthquakes. They don't test water quality in their backyard and store test tube samples in their basement. They don't write letters to their congressional representative every week. So, you'll ask yourself, *How? How did this person get here?* Sometimes, the filmmaker will ask. Almost always, the answer is, they asked a question. They asked one simple question and they were told a lie and they knew it was a lie. So, they looked something up to prove it was a lie and they found some more lies and the next thing they knew they were elbow-deep in it.

So, why do they stay? I presume many of them don't have enough money to leave. Others, do. But, I think it's mostly a reluctance to give up the fight. After you've dedicated years to the cause, how do you pack away all of your papers and test tubes and evidence and forget the whole thing? How do you skip the meeting and let them tell their lies unchallenged? How do you let them win when you know that they're wrong?

I never understood these people until I became one of them. The only problem was, in my case, no one was killed. There weren't any earthquakes. There was no water to sample or air quality to monitor. It's one thing to lose your mind when lives are on the line or the environment is threatened; it's an entirely other thing to lose it over a house that is being built beyond the scope of its permit. It's certainly not a good way to make new friends.

It didn't take long for everyone in town government to hate me. I found that the more I threw around the word *corruption,* the less people wanted to talk. Rosemary and I did everything we could. We really did. We read the applications. We spoke up at the meetings. We sent the emails. We reviewed the code. We filed appeals and petitions. Nothing worked. She started to lose hope. But, not me. I doubled down. For whatever reason, probably boredom, I decided I'm in this. I'm all in this.

When it became abundantly clear that I would lose, I shifted my efforts away from making rational arguments and more toward annoying the town board with my mere presence. If I were going to be annoyed, well, then, so were they. I sat front row at every town board work session and meeting. I printed out the agenda at home and sat with it in my lap. I listened attentively to their discussions. I wrote notes on my agenda. I never said a word. This drove them nuts.

The meetings were televised. My maneuver inspired another concerned citizen to regularly attend—Jeff Finster, my unexpected partner in crime. Where I was, for the most part, a one-issue attendee, Jeff was a real renaissance man. He saw what was clearly an underutilized opportunity for local fame and he seized it. Every meeting, Jeff took to the podium to perform his one-hour set. He never came prepared with a statement. He was more of an improvisational speaker.

Jeff spent most of his time debating himself. A leash law came up for discussion in February. Jeff loved dogs—loved them. He hated to see dogs cooped up and leashed and forbidden from the beach. It wasn't right. They should be able to run free. But, on the other hand, they barked, they pooped, they were a nuisance. Get them the hell off the beach. In March, Jeff reported that he saw three youths destroying freshly planted beach grass during a game of what appeared to be Ultimate Frisbee. He was confident that the alleged offenders were unaware of the severity of their crimes. Still, he believed, it was only right that they receive a summons and, at the very least, be required to replant the destroyed habitat. Jeff concluded every speech with the words, "Am I right, Kathleen?" to which I always nodded in full agreement.

This worked. We wore them down. Jeff didn't know he was a participant in my master plan. But, he was, without question, the most valuable player. After a couple of months of Jeff-led town board meetings, the construction site next door fell quiet. Workers didn't show up on Monday. They weren't there on Tuesday. Their little trucks and miniature plows all sat motionless for the first time. On Wednesday, magically, miraculously a small piece of orange paper was pinned to the chain-link fence. Rosemary spotted it first. "Go see what that says," she said over the phone. *Stop Work Order,* the paper read. Rosemary watched me from her bedroom window. "Stop work order!" I yelled up and she shook her fists in the air with glee. It was the first time I had seen Rosemary truly smile. This was an ear-to-ear, pure-joy, smile. I felt a wave of relief. The truth did prevail. It took time, but it prevailed.

Now, I thought, *I will make friends. I will have time to make friends. I will put on a nice pair of slacks. I will go to the pancake breakfast for the Bay Mission. I will bid on the terrible local art. I will hang that terrible art on my wall. First, I will paint the wall. I will paint and then I will hang the terrible art. I will play pickleball in the field with the other ladies on Tuesday and Thursday evenings. We'll wear matching T-shirts. I will invite them over to my house to watch the Wednesday night sailboat races from my deck. I'll buy bottles of local wine and I won't mention that the grapes are grown in California. I'll learn how to cook, how to really cook and entertain. I'll be Ina Garten. I'll be fabulous.*

I was still standing in the street admiring the little orange note and dreaming of future dinner parties, when a jeep towing a thirty-foot Airstream pulled into my driveway. "Jesus Christ!" Rosemary yelled from her window. I was momentarily blinded by the sun hitting the wall of aluminum in front of me. I cupped my hands over my eyes and waited for the blindness to subside. In the meantime, I heard a very familiar voice say, "Did you take my radios?"

It turned out the *Queen Mary* was not all Tom had hoped it would be. "It's just eating," he said. "Just old people eating and going to lectures. Anyway, I'm fat now," he said and poked his stomach. I didn't say anything. What was there to say? I just looked at him and looked at the Airstream and looked back at the little orange note that had brought me such joy a few seconds earlier. I used to think the worst thing that could happen to someone is for their husband to leave them for a six-month floating all-you-can-eat buffet. But, it isn't the worst thing. The worst thing is when that husband leaves his cruise early, gets on a plane, flies from New Zealand to New York, buys an Airstream, drives it two hours to his soon-to-be ex-wife's new house and complains about that buffet. That's the worst thing.

"You wouldn't believe it," Tom said as if nothing had happened between us, as if he weren't standing in the driveway of my new house that was 1,300 miles away from our old house. He leaned his back against the trailer and said, "I mean, half of them were on oxygen tanks, Kathleen. It was depressing. I got so depressed, I thought about jumping, for God's sake." Then, that made me think about him jumping. For a few minutes as he rambled on about how there were only so many crab cakes someone could eat, I thought about Tom bobbing in the middle of the Atlantic or drifting out to a deserted island in the South Pacific. "How's things with you?" he said casually.

"I mean. Not good, Tom," I said and threw my arms in the air.

"Yeah, what's happening here?" he said and looked up at the glass tower that cast a tremendous shadow over my house and the beach beside it.

"What are you doing here?" I said.

"Who's that?" Tom said and pointed to Rosemary, who was leaning out her window.

"Okay," I said. "You need to go."

Tom's face crinkled. His face always crinkled when he was pretending to be confused.

"Where am I supposed to go?" he said.

"I don't care," I said. "Go anywhere."

"I've been everywhere. I didn't like it. I told you. And you sold the house in Kansas, thanks for telling me."

"I did tell you I was selling the house in Kansas," I said.

"All right," he said. "Okay. I'll only stay a few days. Who am I bothering? I'm not bothering you."

Tom must have told me that he wasn't bothering me about ten thousand times over the course of our marriage. And in 100 percent of those times, he was in fact bothering me. Tom once told me that he thought that a good marriage or a good relationship did not depend on two people liking the same things. "You have to hate the same things," he said. "That's the ticket." At the time, I thought this was very wise. Tom and I didn't like the same things. I didn't like golf. He didn't like travel. And yet we both hated cilantro. We hated flip-flops. We hated phoniness. We were the perfect pair.

About ten years into our marriage, I realized that what I really hated was not being able to make a sandwich in the kitchen without Tom following me and starting some kitchen-related project of his own. I'm not even going to explain this further. If you know what I'm talking about, then you know. And if you don't know what I'm talking about, well, then you'll never see my side of it. The point is, whenever I told Tom that I would be out of the kitchen in five minutes and could he wait until then to bone out a chicken or whip up a smoothie, he would say, "I'm not bothering you," and proceed to do whatever it was he was planning to do.

Anyway, Tom started living in the Airstream in my driveway and it bothered me, but he said it didn't. So, there you go, we were right back where we started. He only came in the house once to get his radios. He could only fit fifteen of them in the Airstream. So, the other twenty-two stayed with me. Other than that, I banned him from the house. For one thing, I didn't want to deal with him and for another thing, I knew he wouldn't last long living in the driveway. But, he lasted. He did more than last. He thrived.

He plugged the Airstream into the side of my little house, so that he could literally suck the energy right out of me. Once he got the power and water going, he got a dog. He rescued a depressed senior German shepherd named Roger. Roger spent most of his time lying in the driveway with his head partially in the street. People would pass and pat him on the head. Some checked to see if he was alive. I told Tom that Roger shouldn't be lying in the street like that. I said, "Roger is allowed in the house." But, Roger didn't want to come in the house or the Airstream. He just wanted to lie in the street and wait to die and frankly, so did I.

But, we didn't. Roger and I both decided to live. I

started meditating and Roger started taking walks. Tom and Roger took so many walks that they started making friends. Suddenly, Tom knew everyone in the neighborhood. People would stop and knock on the Airstream door to invite him for coffee or fishing or tennis. Rosemary was the only person who knocked on my door and it was almost always to tell me a piece of bad news.

One morning, I saw smoke coming from the Airstream window and out of concern for Roger, I went to investigate. "There's smoke," I said to Tom, who was wearing a navy-blue Whitbey Pickleball Association apron.

"I'm making soup," he said and pointed to a big pot boiling on the stove. "It's for Robert," he said.

"Who's Robert?" I asked.

"You don't know Robert?"

"I guess not," I said.

"Kathleen, you know Robert. He lives right down the street." I looked at him blankly. "His birthday was last week. He turned ninety-two. We all signed the card."

"I didn't sign a card."

"Oh," Tom said and went back to stir the soup.

"Well, why does he need soup?"

"For his anxiety," Tom said. "He gets anxiety headaches."

"Where's Roger?" I asked and Tom pointed to the street.

"He shouldn't be lying in the street like that," I said.

"He's not bothering anyone," Tom said.

"Okay. See ya later," I said and took three steps back into my own house.

"See ya!" I heard Tom call out.

Tom started walking Robert's miniature poodle with Roger every morning. He volunteered to emcee the Bay Mission auction. He started playing pickleball with the ladies and he made friends with a man named Freddy Bandana. He joined the pickleball association. Suddenly, people knew me as Tom's wife. I couldn't describe to you in better terms the people of my new community than to tell you that Tom living in an Airstream in the driveway didn't intrigue anyone. "I'm not allowed in the house," Tom would tell one of the ladies and she would say, "Oh, that's all right." Anywhere else, it would be the talk of the town. But, not here. I soon found out that Tom and I probably had the most normal arrangement of anyone in a five-mile radius.

I learned that there was a man on Queen Street who proclaimed to be a professional harmonica player, though his truck indicated that he did "Roofing and Siding." Tom went over to his house every Thursday afternoon to "jam." They made a YouTube channel. On Gull Road there was a seventy-year-old man with a twenty-year-old girlfriend and on Hamilton Street there was a seventy-year-old woman with a twenty-year-old boyfriend. A boyfriend and girlfriend were living together in a converted barn on Fourth Street. She was eighty. He was ninety-seven. They bred corgis.

Rosemary was the only person who didn't like Tom, which made me like her even more. Her husband, however, was solidly Team Tom. They bicycled together and would come home to brag about their mileage for the day. Rosemary said that Tom was costing her a fortune.

Her husband bought a $3,000 bicycle to better compete with Tom, who had spent decades cultivating his knowledge and possession of professional bike equipment. But, I think it was the *Save What's Left* sticker on the side of the Airstream that really sealed the deal for Rosemary. That or the *I Love My Rescue* sticker next to it.

A few weeks after the stop work order was posted, I got a call from Rosemary. "Can you come over?" she said. Rosemary never said things like, "Can you come over?" She said things like, "Where are you?" Or "Get over here!"

Rosemary felt like an old friend from the moment I met her. There was a sort of unspoken understanding between us that we would look out for each other. I had burned all my bridges and, for the most part, so had she. We never bothered with pleasantries. It didn't feel necessary. Almost everyone in the neighborhood was afraid of Rosemary, but I felt such comfort in the fact that she lived across the street.

"Better bring Tom," she said on the phone that day. Then, she hung up. I slammed my fist on the Airstream to get Tom. That was one good thing about him. Tom was good in an emergency. He didn't ask questions. I always appreciated that about him. "I need you to come over to Rosemary's with me," I said. He didn't say, "Why?" Or "How come?" Or "I don't like Rosemary," which he certainly didn't.

He said, "Okay," and scrambled to put on his shoes. This didn't make him any less of a thorn in my side, but I took note of it.

We let ourselves into the house and found Rosemary

lying on her back in the upstairs hallway. "What happened?" I asked.

"What do you think?" she said.

"Are you hurt?" Tom asked.

"Steve is out fishing," she said. "He usually picks me up."

"Are you sure we should move you?" I asked. "Maybe we should call an ambulance."

"Oh, for the love of God," Rosemary said. "Grab my arm and help me up!"

"I don't know," Tom said and began squeezing her ankles. Rosemary stared up at the ceiling.

"Or leave me," she said. "I don't care. Steve will be home soon."

"You've got to get rid of these throw rugs," I said and ran my foot under a curled corner.

"Oysters Rockefeller," Rosemary said.

"What?" I said.

"That's what Linda said she's making for dinner on Saturday. I couldn't remember. I've been trying to think of it all day."

Tom looked at me and raised his eyebrows.

"Rosemary," Tom said gingerly as he crouched on the floor beside her. "I want you to spell the word *world* backward for me."

"Are you nuts?" she said, turning her head slightly to face him.

"Can you do that for me? *World,*" he repeated. I nodded my head encouragingly as I struggled to perform the exercise in my own head.

"D-L-R-O-W," Rosemary said confidently.

"Okay, good," Tom said softly. "Now, I'd like you to—"

"Oh, get out of here," Rosemary said. "Kathleen, give me a hand."

"Just a few more," Tom said. "I want you to point to the window after you point to the door." I looked at the window. Rosemary pointed to the window.

"Try again," Tom said.

"Stop messing me up," Rosemary said to me and she pointed to the door and then the window.

"Good," Tom said. "Now count backward from one hundred by sevens." Rosemary sighed and closed her eyes. Tom and I waited for her response.

"Are you thinking?" I asked after about a minute passed.

"I'm thinking why the hell did I ask you to bring Tom," she said.

"He's a doctor," I said.

"Bully for him," Rosemary said. "I'm fine. I'm just fine," she said and lifted her head. She pushed Tom's hand away from hers.

"By sevens," Tom said.

"One hundred," Rosemary began, "ninety-three, eighty-six, seventy-nine, seventy-two . . . What, do I have to go the whole way?"

"No, that's good," Tom said. "I think we can skip the finger and toe taps."

"Super," Rosemary said and Tom and I hoisted her from the floor and guided her over to the window seat. I took a seat on the floor and Tom went to the kitchen to get some water. There was a long pause and then Rosemary said, "Who's that?" She repositioned to look closer out the window. "What are they doing?" she yelled. "Hey!" she yelled and slapped the glass. "What are you doing?"

We both watched as a man with a white mustache and a red polo shirt removed the little orange stop work order from the fence. Rosemary fished for the phone on the floor. She dialed a number that she knew by heart. "Yes," she said. "I'd like to speak to Andy Wexler—Zoning Board of Appeals. You can't do that," Rosemary said.

"What?" I whispered and she waved her hand in my face.

"Well, we're coming. What time does it start? We'll be there," she said and threw the phone back on the floor. "Let's go," she said and started marching downstairs. The public hearing about the stop work order that was due to take place in one month's time had been rescheduled.

The Zoning Board of Appeals holds their public hearings in the town meeting hall that seats fifty. They hold their special meetings, where all the real work is done, in a glorified storage closet. "You can't talk," the ZBA secretary told us as we arrived. Rosemary and I sat on two folding chairs against the wall with our noses inches from the backs of the board members' heads. We could smell their shampoo. We sat and listened to Andy Wexler, the ZBA chairman, explain that the lawyer representing the Sugar Cube (my old real estate agent) had submitted a new engineer's report. It stated that they had only demolished 5 percent of the original structure and that no work had been done within eighty-five feet of the water that wasn't already permitted.

"Five percent!" Rosemary said. "They demolished the whole thing!"

"Ma'am, you can't speak at this meeting," the chairman said.

"Hold on," Rosemary said. "Just hold on. I have a picture here," she said and started furiously rummaging through her bag.

"I'm sorry," Mr. Wexler said. "This is a meeting for deliberation of the board only. Unfortunately, there is no public comment permitted at these meetings. You may sit and listen and that's it."

"Here!" Rosemary said and ripped a stack of photocopies out of her bag. "I had these made at the library last week," she said and started passing them out around the table, "because I knew you people would pull something like this. I knew it!" Rosemary kept one copy for herself. She held it in the air à la Norma Rae and marched it around the room. "Does this look like five percent to you?" she said as each of the board members tried desperately to avert their eyes.

"I think we should move on," one of the board members said.

"Agreed," Mr. Wexler said. "Do I have a motion?" he asked.

"Motion to lift the stop work order for application number five-three-eight-four," a woman said.

"Second," said another.

"All in favor?" Mr. Wexler asked.

"Aye," said the group and Rosemary took her seat and buried her head in her hands.

Just as they ruled that the stop work order be immediately lifted, an older man in overalls entered the room and sat in the folding chair next to mine. He was tall—well over six feet. He took off his hat and tried with great difficulty to squeeze his legs behind the chair in front of him. "Tight in here," he whispered to us and gave a small smile, not knowing what he had walked into. I nodded and smiled back.

"I can't take any more of this," Rosemary said. "I have to go."

"I'll go with you," I said.

"No talking," the secretary barked.

"No," Rosemary whispered. "I'll wait outside. You stay." She shimmied carefully past the man. "Sorry," Rosemary said as her bag clunked his knee.

"No problem," he said. "Take care."

Rosemary carefully closed the office door behind her and the board moved on to the next application.

"Did they talk about O'Reilly yet?" the man whispered to me.

"I don't think so," I whispered back. "But, I got here late."

"Excuse me," the man said to the board. "Did I miss the O'Reilly case?"

"No," Mr. Wexler said without turning to look back at the man.

"Oh, good," the man said. "Thank you."

"We're not discussing it," Mr. Wexler said. "It's a permitted use. It's not a ZBA matter."

"No, it is," the man said. "It is a ZBA matter. I sent an email. I don't know if you—"

"We got the email," Mr. Wexler said.

"Okay," the man said, nervous now. "I just have a statement here that I wanted to read. I don't know if you could just indulge me for a minute. You know this guy next door to me, he's building . . . Well, you wouldn't believe what he's building. It looks like a lookout tower. And, he's got about a hundred wind chimes on it. I, well, I was looking at the town code and, here, I have it here," he said and unfolded a piece of paper. "It says in, let's see, in article twenty-three, section—"

"We've received your comments," Mr. Wexler said. "And the board has decided that it is not in our purview. You may take it up with the town board."

"Oh," the man said and refolded the paper. "I just feel—" he began.

"Motion to go into executive session?" Mr. Wexler announced.

"Second," said the man at the head of the table.

"All in favor?" Mr. Wexler asked.

"Aye," said the board.

"What does that mean?" the man whispered to me.

"It means we're kicked out," I said and the two of us clumsily headed for the door.

"What happened?" Rosemary said when we reached the parking lot.

"Executive session," I said.

"Well, they're consistent," Rosemary said. "What are you in for?" she asked the man.

"Wind chimes," he said.

"God help us," Rosemary said and got in her car.

9

TO: Supervisor White (white@whitbey.gov)
FROM: Kathleen Deane (KDeane@gmail.com)
SUBJECT: Boil water advisory

Dear Supervisor White,

Last year, my neighbors received a variance to exceed the town code's height requirement. They also received a special exception to build four stories, where only two are permitted. I believe the roof deck application was denied. Yet, it is coming along nicely and nearly completed from what I can see. These variances and exceptions were granted with the condition that the owners install a sprinkler system, because, as I understand it, the local fire department is not equipped to handle a building of this height. And if, God forbid, a fire did break out at the property, there would be no means to put it out. This is of particular interest to me because this house sits four feet from my house, which has a hay bale foundation that I suspect would not fare well in a fire.

I'm sure you are aware that the short-lived stop work order at this property was lifted last week and, as of this morning, construction has started in once again. Despite the fact that the house is almost entirely finished, today was the day that the construction crew tested to see if it was even feasible to install a sprinkler system using the town water supply. In case you haven't already heard, it is not. There is currently about three feet of water flooding Harbor Road. My neighbor went to get his mail at the post office in a canoe. This afternoon, I received a call from Mr. Barth at the county health department. He was calling to inform me that a mandatory boil water advisory had been activated for my street. This was not surprising because all the water coming from the tap in my house is a muddy brown color with an extremely foul odor. Mr. Barth said that he did not know what was causing the color or odor of the water, but hoped things would get back to normal in a week or two. A week or two!

While all of this was going on, a landscaping company arrived and installed massive metal cages along my property line. There are fifteen in total and they are at least eight feet tall. I do not know what these cages are and I shudder to think what will go inside of them. One of my neighbors guessed it was for a collection of exotic birds. But, these cages look to be designed for a much more formidable animal. Any information you could provide on this subject would be much appreciated.

Unfortunately, I will not be able to attend this evening's parking meeting because I have an appointment with the ENT for what my primary physician suspects is stress-related TMJ. If it's possible, could the meeting be recorded and uploaded to the town website? Thank you very much.

Sincerely,
Kathleen Deane

That week, spring officially arrived. The last of the snow melted and the sun finally broke through beyond the dark cloud that seemed to hang over the town for months. The Sugar Cube was nearly complete. A team of window washers spent an entire weekend polishing every surface of the glass façade until it sparkled and cast tiny rainbow flashes in every direction.

"Well, it is nice," Josie said when she saw the finished product. "I mean, you have to admit that."

"Do I?" I said. As the construction died down next door and the sunny days became more plentiful, Josie and Dan made a regular habit of popping over to my deck with sandwiches and wine around lunchtime. Tom and I were, of course, invited to these soirées, but our attendance was certainly not expected.

"Oh, so you wouldn't like to live in a house like that?" Josie went on. "If someone offered it to you for free, you'd say, 'No thank you'?"

"I might," I said.

"Yeah, right," Josie said. "Says the woman who wouldn't pierce her ears until she could afford two-carat diamonds."

"That's true," Tom chirped in.

"All right," I said.

"Well, at least the construction part's over," Dan said, sipping his wine.

"Right," I said.

"And now we can enjoy your deck, finally," Josie said. "You're not going to be able to get rid of us this summer."

"How's life in the Airstream?" Dan said, turning to Tom.

"Don't ask him that," Josie said.

"I can't ask that?" Dan said.

"No," Josie said.

"Well, it's a beauty," Dan said, tilting his chair to admire the Airstream glistening in the driveway. "If you ever want to sell it . . ." he said.

"You know what you should do with it?" Josie said. "Food truck."

"Food truck! Exactly! Exactly what I was thinking," Dan said, pointing at Josie. "Pizza truck at the wineries? You'd make a killing."

"No. Not pizza," Josie said. "People don't want pizza at their weddings. It'd have to be upscale. French."

"No, no," Dan said. "Forget the weddings. Just do the tastings. How many wineries could you hit on a Saturday. Six? Seven?"

"Oh, just the tastings," Josie said. "Now, that's interesting." She took a bite of her sandwich while she considered the possibilities. "Are you thinking about selling it?" she asked Tom, finally.

He looked to me for guidance.

"Not at the moment," Tom said.

"I thought kitchens weren't allowed at the wineries," I said, further dampening the mood.

"Food trucks are," Josie said. "But, you have to move it a half mile every thirty minutes."

"Since when?" I asked.

"Last month," Dan said.

"Peddler's license," Josie added, crunching into a pickle. "Hank Brown pushed it through."

"After some arm-twisting," Dan added. Hank Brown, having run the worst campaign in history, secured his spot on the town board, winning the election by a healthy margin after his opponent was caught on tape disparaging local corn at a fundraiser.

"Doesn't matter," Josie said. "It's not like we're in a position to buy it." She looked at Dan.

"Don't say it," Dan said.

"Fine. I don't have to. They know," Josie said.

Dan famously gave up a union stagehand job at the Metropolitan Opera in 1982 and Josie never got over it. "They're making five hundred thousand a year now," Josie said. "Pension, benefits, everything."

"That can't be right," Tom said.

"I'm not discussing it," Dan said and returned to his sandwich. For a few moments, there was silence.

"I picked up a pie at Bauer's yesterday. Peach cherry. If anyone's interested . . ."

"On a Tuesday?" Josie asked. "Hope you got it for half-price."

"What?" I said. "No. Thirty-eight dollars."

"Kathleen, you have to ask for the list," Josie said.

"What list?"

"The half-price list. It's behind the counter. All the locals know that."

"This is all I'm going to say," Dan said, in a sort of burst. "I'm going to say this and then I'm not going to say another word about it. I would still be a stagehand if it hadn't been for—"

"Oh God," Josie said. "Here we go. . . ."

"*La Bohème,*" they said, almost in unison.

Tom and I had heard the story about a dozen times. A young, edgy set designer from Sweden flew into New York and pitched a setless version of *La Bohème*—no walls, no doors, no Paris streets. Dan said it was stupid. All the stagehands said it was stupid. The actors said it was stupid. The musicians said it was stupid. The technical director called it a nightmare. Then, gradually, over time, everyone changed their minds, except Dan, who quickly became persona non grata. The day before opening night, he walked out and leased a small restaurant in Chelsea. It started as a French bistro in the '80s, transitioned into a barbecue joint in the '90s, and hit its stride as a lesbian bar in the early 2000s. It's a Petco now.

"How are things on the farm?" I asked.

"Coming along," Josie said.

Not to be outdone by the neighboring farm's singing hayride, Josie and Dan were in the process of transforming their potato farm into more of an "attraction." They added giant trampolines and jungle gyms in the shape of tractors. There was a *Ninja Warrior*–style obstacle course and a full-time walking, talking potato mascot that played the role of an overzealous announcer. Even the pigs and goats were put to work greeting visitors. Sometimes, if business was really bad, they were forced to race around a hay bale track.

Josie was entirely uninterested in the Erin Brockovich lifestyle I was living. I tried to tell her about my crusade against town hall. I told her that I was going to meetings and filing petitions. To this she said, "Are you okay?" This is when you know you've started to lose your mind. People start to regularly ask you if you're okay. They start to squint and look concerned when you talk to them. Maybe your emails and letters were coherent once, but now they read like the ramblings of a madman. People, often friends, are happy to let you know this. They encourage you to check with them before clicking Send.

The first sunny warm day, I decided to treat myself to a beach day. I settled into a beach chair and got myself comfortable with a light blanket wrapped around my shoulders and a novel about a woman who actually likes her beach house. I was so happy. I looked out at the sparkling blue water and squished my toes in the white sugary sand and I thought, *Who's better than me?* Then, what looked like a mother/daughter pair walked along the shore past me. The daughter looked at me and said to her mother, "She's bundled."

"You know what?" the mother said to the daughter. "Good for her. She got herself out of the house." This just about killed me. This is something you say about two kinds of people: the extremely elderly and the extremely insane. I don't know which this woman mistook me for and I don't know which I found more offensive.

After that, Josie decided to give me a job to prevent me from becoming the sort of person she could no longer, in good conscience, associate with. "Do some greeting cards," she said. "I'll sell them in the store. Or notecards, or postcards. Postcards are coming back, you know," she said.

"They are?" I asked.

"It doesn't matter," she said. "You're doing it." So, I did it and I found that painting watercolor seagulls with funny hats and cardigans was most likely something I could do for the rest of my life. I started making money from the cards I was designing. Josie said she couldn't keep up with the demand. They weren't a hit with the locals, just the tourists and the Manhattanites who popped out to their country homes for the weekends. I remember thinking that my home would make a wonderful second home. It made a god-awful first and only home. But, I imagined that everything that bothered me about my new neighborhood would bother me a lot less if I knew I could leave.

Everyone thinks these small rural towns are sleepy and charming and simple. They say life is slower. They say the people have time to enjoy one another. But, if you move to one of these towns, and I'm not saying you should because you shouldn't, but if you do, you'll find that the people who live in these towns are the busiest people you'll ever meet.

The meetings! I guarantee there are more meetings in my beach town than there are meetings in all of Congress. If Capitol Hill were beside a boardwalk overlooking the water, we would have universal health care. We'd have gun laws. We'd have sensible immigration reform. We could start manufacturing again. The minimum wage would go up. Our roads and bridges would be fixed. There are no Republicans or Democrats in a beach town. The right-wing conservatives want clean water protocols. The Democrats push big business. Nothing makes sense here. There are no friends. There are no enemies. There are just people. And each one of those people has at least one good idea and one stupid idea about everything.

I still don't know whether I love it or hate it here. All I know is, I'm in it. Once you've gone round for round at a civic association meeting about the height of a swing set, you know you're in it. I tried to ignore the fact that Tom was right in it with me. We lived fairly separate lives. I lived in the house. He lived in the Airstream. I thought perhaps this was the secret to a good marriage, or at least a good divorce. Someone needs to live in the driveway. Tom fit in in a way that I could not. He made friends with the town clerk and was able to woo Virginia Bittner in the Water Conservation Committee office into revealing that the owners of the Sugar Cube were planning a roof deck expansion. He had Roger certified as a therapy dog and made visits to the nursing home twice a week. Tom was just better. I don't know whether it was the salt air or some voodoo he had encountered on his trip around the world. But, he was better.

When I heard a knock on the door, I was hoping it was Rosemary. She was still out of sorts from the lifting of the stop work order. Her lack of interest in the roof deck expansion was unnerving. But, the knock at the door wasn't Rosemary. It was two police officers. One was holding Tom's bicycle.

"Hi," one of the young officers said. I looked at the bike and saw the front wheel twisted in a knot and a long branch sticking between the spokes.

"Your husband's had an accident," the other officer

said. "He's all right," he was quick to say. "Bump on the head. They took him to the hospital."

"Wasn't he wearing a helmet?" I said. "He always wears a helmet."

"I don't think so," the officer said. "He was talking and everything, though. He told us your name and where you lived. So, I bet he's okay. You can meet him at the hospital. He's probably already there."

"Thank you," I said and the young officer leaned the bicycle on the Airstream.

The local hospital looks like a yacht club. The parking lot is beside a marina and while stretchers are pushed through the emergency room doors on one end of the lot, fishermen are loading up coolers on the other end. Tom was accident-prone. He always had been. He had appendicitis on our honeymoon and the day Hattie was born he sliced his finger open while fixing the shed door and needed stitches. So, I wasn't nervous. Not really. The policeman said a bump on the head. They take people in ambulances for everything now. The week before I moved to Whitbey, I fainted in the supermarket in Kansas City. Just a little. Just for a second. I told everyone I was fine. I faint all the time. My doctor told me to start carrying cashews in my purse, which I usually do, but I didn't that day. I had to take a $1,200 ambulance ride to the hospital for them to tell me it was nothing.

So, I was expecting nothing or next to nothing. I was expecting Tom to be sitting in the lobby with a Band-Aid on his head waiting for me to pick him up. "Ridiculous," he would say. "I'm absolutely fine. I *was* wearing my helmet." But, he wasn't in the lobby. He wasn't absolutely fine. And he wasn't wearing a helmet. A nurse escorted me to the trauma bay where Tom was laid out on a stretcher, covered in blood. "CT," he said as his bloody hand grabbed mine. We were alone in the room. A woman had come into the emergency room just as I did. She was in labor, screaming, crying, wailing labor, and all attention had moved to her.

"Hello?" I yelled to the nurse's station outside the room. "We need a CT!" A few moments later, a doctor came into the room. She had long curly blond hair that was not tied back and I remember that bothering me.

"What seems to be the problem?" she said in a chipper voice. She clicked her pen open and looked at Tom's chart.

"Look at him!" I yelled. "How long has he been here? You're just asking now what seems to be the problem?"

Tom closed his eyes. His monitors beeped and flashed and whistled. He was rushed to CT. I chased after the speeding gurney while I rummaged in my purse.

"Ma'am," a nurse said while running beside me. "You'll have to wait outside."

"Okay," I said and continued on.

"Ma'am," the nurse said again.

"There!" I said as I splashed some holy water on Tom, most of which landed in his face. He winced as he disappeared behind a double door. "Sorry!" I called out. And then, I waited. I waited in the empty room. Blood stained the floor where the stretcher had been. The room began to spin as I searched for my cashews. I ate them furiously in the doorway and prayed that Tom would live. A woman was playing the piano in the lobby.

I leaned my head on the doorframe and watched as she swayed with the music. She was wearing a yellow dress and her hair was neatly pinned in a bun. Why couldn't the doctor pin her hair up like that, I thought.

I managed to avoid a fainting spell and Tom returned, eyes open and alert. "His CT looks clear," the doctor said. "No sign of blood on the brain."

"Good," I said. "Thank you. I'm sorry for yelling before." She nodded her head, clicked her pen once more, and left.

"They're going to admit him and move him to the third floor," a nurse said. "You're lucky, the plastic surgeon is here today."

"That's good," Tom said.

"It'll be a few minutes," the nurse said.

"Why did you throw water in my face?" Tom asked me.

"It was holy water," I said. "I grabbed it on the way out the door. You know, just in case."

"From Lourdes," Tom said.

"Right," I said. "From Lourdes. I've been using it. I use it every day."

"I knew you'd like it," Tom said.

"And that'll help," I said. "It's very healing. It's supposed to be very healing."

Tom nodded as he reached for my hand.

"It's fresh from the grotto," Tom said as he struggled to lift his head.

"Right," I said. "I know."

"My sternum's broken," Tom said as he gently put his hand on his chest.

"Is that what the doctor said?"

"No. But, it's a classic presentation," he said and closed his eyes once again. I took a wet towel and started wiping the blood from his arms. But, there weren't any scrapes or cuts. I soon realized that the blood was not coming from his hand or his arm or chest. It was coming from his head, which upon closer inspection, was split right down the middle. There was about a six-inch chasm that ran from the top of his forehead, straight back to the top of his head.

"Why weren't you wearing a helmet?" was the thing I shouldn't have said, but did.

"The strap broke," he said and pointed to the perfectly intact green helmet lying in a plastic bag by the door.

"You're going to be just fine," I said. He nodded. "You can come in the house," I said.

"Well, that's something," he said and the nurse came to wheel him upstairs. She said he'd need more scans and that I could see him in about an hour. She suggested I leave and go have dinner. But, I stayed. I sat in the lobby and ate cashews and listened to the woman in the yellow dress play the piano.

About twenty minutes later, the woman stopped playing. She closed the lid to cover the keys and collected her purse from inside the piano stool. "Is he going to be all right?" the woman asked as she passed me.

"Yeah, I think so," I said.

"Good," she said and smiled a sweet smile. "They're pretty good here," she said. "Doesn't look like it. But, they're okay. Does he have a brain injury?"

"No. They said there was no blood on his brain," I said and tucked my cashews back into my purse.

"Then you probably don't need to move him," she said.

"Is it common for people to get moved?" I asked.

"Yeah, well, they can't handle that much here. Nothing too serious. But, broken bones, fishhooks in fingers—they're pretty good at that stuff."

"My husband, actually he's my soon to be ex-husband . . . He thinks he broke his sternum."

"Well, there's nothing anyone can do for that. That needs to heal on its own. Can't put a cast on a sternum," she said and took a seat next to me. "I'm Nancy," she said.

"Kathleen," I said.

"Did a car hit him?"

"No," I said. "A stick went through his wheel."

"Must have been some stick," she said and I laughed.

"It's nice that you play the piano here," I said. "You wouldn't think it would help. But, it does."

"Yeah, I started doing it when I retired—something to keep me busy. Gets me out of the house."

That made me feel better.

"You can go up now," the nurse yelled to me from her station.

"I'll send up a prayer for him if you like," the woman said. "Just to be safe."

"Thanks," I said and went to the third floor to see Tom.

10

TO: Supervisor White (white@whitbey.gov)
FROM: Kathleen Deane (KDeane@gmail.com)
SUBJECT: Traffic committee

Dear Supervisor White,

Last week, the town's traffic committee joined the civic association in presenting a plan to address beach overcrowding and the ongoing parking woes in the hamlet. There are rumors flying that I attempted to blackmail the vice president of the traffic committee at this meeting. I don't know what you've heard, but I wanted to write to you and assure you of the fact that I did no such thing. If anyone was behaving unethically it was Mr. Jones, who led the meeting and proposed that a public street be gifted to a private business for its exclusive use. He said this not on his own behalf, but as the primary representative of the town. Mr. Jones neglected to tell the audience that his stepdaughter recently married the man who is soon to inherit the business in question.

I merely pointed out this fact and mildly suggested that perhaps Mr. Jones should not be the liaison to this committee due to what is obviously a blatant conflict of interest. Half of the room agreed with me. The other half did not and considered the relationship an inevitability of small-town life. Fine. No problem. I stated my opinion and that's all I could do. I didn't think anything else about it.

A few days later, I heard from multiple neighbors that Mr. Jones was under the impression that I had some sort of vendetta against him and that my words were akin to a threat. He told Maryellen on Plum Street that I called him at two in the morning trying to blackmail him. Owen heard the same story. This morning I received a handwritten letter in my mailbox from Mr. Jones. In it, he pleads with me to stop "infecting" the community with my "negative aura." He closed the letter with this sentence: "This community will not be intimidated. You will not succeed."

Let me be very clear, I don't know this man. I have nothing to blackmail him with. Even if I did, what kind of person would blackmail someone over hypothetical parking restrictions? I have never spoken with Mr. Jones. I do not know where he lives and I certainly have never called his house. But, I am starting to become very concerned. I would suggest that he be referred to the town's ethics committee, but I fear that will potentially make matters worse.

I saw that the new parking code will be discussed at Tuesday's work session. Do you think it is safe for me to attend? On the one hand, I would like to avoid any more interaction with Mr. Jones. But, on the other hand, I believe I am correct in questioning his motives for this legislation. Somehow, Mr. Jones has very skillfully painted himself as a victim, when in fact he is the one spreading lies and rumors. What do you think is the best course of action? Please advise. Thank you.

Sincerely,
Kathleen Deane

P.S. The metal cages have been filled with rocks.

My house was formerly an oyster shack, which was essentially a shed to store oysters. If I were to show you my house and tell you this used to be a shed to store oysters, you would say, "That makes sense." This is not a spacious modern home with an interesting history. This is a shed and it looks like a shed. I bought the house for the deck. That's what I tell myself. The deck has twice the footprint of the house. You can't beat the view. And, anyway, I was going for minimalism. How much space does one person need? A guest room implies that I want guests, and lucky for me, I don't want them. Hence, no guest room. I asked myself, *Does anyone truly require anything more than a galley kitchen? When did we all decide that bathrooms needed two sinks?* It was all so unnecessary, I thought—so frivolous.

What I didn't anticipate was my soon to be ex-husband requiring bed rest for three months in my oyster shack. If I had known that Tom was going to show up in an Airstream six months into my independent adventure and get into a terrible bicycle accident that left him with a broken sternum and vertebra and a Frankenstein-ish wound on his head, I might have sprung for a house with a guest bedroom. I might have rethought my opinion on two sinks. I would have said, "Screw the deck, I need four thousand square feet minimum." At the very least, I would have bought a pullout couch.

I threw out the $4,000, chic, white couch. I tried to give it away, but no one wanted it. No one wanted the ketchup-stained, slightly beige, formerly white couch. So, Steve took it to the dump for me. It was replaced with the mother of all couches, an ugly blue corduroy sectional that Tom ordered online while he was still in the hospital. "It's got hydraulics," Tom told me, as if that were a terrific selling point. "It can lift you with just a push of a button. It's like having your own hospital bed right there tucked away in your couch!"

It arrived the day before Tom was discharged from the hospital and it was as advertised. The men who delivered it took about an hour to explain all the features to me. There were remotes and temperature settings and firmness dials. It moved up and down and side to side. It tilted and turned. There was a massage feature and a collapsible tray table hidden in the armrest. It came with an app to track your sleep quality and a mini fridge to, presumably, keep your medications fresh. The main thing though, was its size. This couch took up every inch of the house. It was just couch as far as the eye could see.

"Do you like the blue?" Tom said as he hobbled with his walker into the house. His head was bandaged Civil War–style and he wore a plastic brace on his back.

"Yes," I said and held his arm. "I like the blue."

"I can tell you don't," he said.

"Can we get you in the door?" I said. "Can you focus on getting through the door and into bed?"

"The physical therapist is going to come to the house," Tom said as he carefully inched forward. "Did I tell you that already?"

"I don't think so, no. How often is she going to come?" I asked. The physical therapist told Tom he looked like Robert Redford, which inspired him to do the required laps around the hospital hallway, but also made him more insufferable than usual.

"Three times a week they said is best," Tom said. "She said she'll be here tomorrow at two. You know she thinks I look like Robert Redford?"

"I heard," I said and helped him into the blue corduroy cocoon where he would remain until summer.

People stopped by to see Tom every day. They brought books and soup and gossip from the neighborhood. They'd sit on the edge of Tom's enormous bed and look at me suspiciously as if to say, "Why are you always here?" Eleanor, who is nearly eighty and carries around a portable oxygen tank at all times, asked if Tom needed help walking Roger. "The poor thing never gets out," she said.

"That's all right, Eleanor," I said from the kitchen where I was preparing Norwegian steel-cut organic oatmeal for Tom that needed to be cooked and carefully watched for forty-five minutes. "I've been walking Roger."

"Well," Eleanor said and looked at Tom. "He's certainly not getting the same exercise he got with Tom, is he?" She grabbed Tom's foot over the blanket and gave it a little rub. So, I started taking Roger for more walks and longer walks. I made sure to pass Eleanor's house as many times as possible. When we weren't walking,

Roger slept with his head in the street and I hid in the Airstream.

Antoinette Wallace was another frequent visitor. Tom had many admirers in the neighborhood, but Antoinette was absolutely, without question, head over heels in love with him. She took one look at his salmon shorts and tattered Birkenstocks and decided, *This is the man for me.* A part of me sort of hoped they would run away together to Birch Street. Before Tom's accident, Antoinette stopped by the house all the time looking for him, asking if he could help her launch her kayak or if he would like her to bring over some tomatoes she had grown in the community garden. She touched his arm more than was necessary and would say things to me like, "How do you put up with this guy?" Antoinette thought everything Tom said was just hilarious. Unlike me, she could sit and listen to Tom talk about aortic aneurisms for days. She baked Roger homemade dog biscuits and knitted Tom a hat. Not me. I didn't get a hat.

Perplexingly, the gaping hole in Tom's head only fanned the flames of Antoinette's desire. She did daily "check-ins" and graciously volunteered to "take a shift" when I needed to do a grocery run. She made soup and baked bread. She brought over a stack of books and magazines and crossword puzzles. One afternoon, I was off at the drugstore fetching another vat of Vaseline to slather on Tom's crusting head, when Antoinette made an unannounced visit. What I found when I arrived home horrified me. There they were, Antoinette and Tom on the pullout couch.

"Tom!" I said when I walked in the door.

"Nothing happened," Tom said. "It's fine."

"What were you thinking?" I said.

"All the other plates were dirty," Tom said. "Antoinette made cookies. She just grabbed it. She didn't know."

"Give it to me," I said and held out my hand. I inspected the melted chocolate smeared on the porcelain.

"It's just a plate," Tom said. "I was very careful with it."

"I'll just let myself out," Antoinette said and tiptoed toward the front door. "I'm sorry, Kathleen. I didn't know they were special plates. I swear I have the same ones from the Christmas Tree Shop. I can pick you up some next time I'm there. You know what? I think they're on sale this week. I'll bring the circular tomorrow."

I have tried and failed to suppress the memories of the many years I wasted hunting for old radios at estate sales in Kansas. As a general rule, riffling through moldy basements and dusty attics for unusable relics is not the most fulfilling or worthwhile hobby. To be honest, I don't know why anyone would ever bother to collect old radios. Even if by some miracle you can get one of them to turn on, the chance of being electrocuted in the process is almost a guarantee. The only worthwhile radio in Tom's collection is the one that led me to my Limoges dishes.

About five years ago, Tom dragged me to a sale in Overland Park at seven o'clock in the morning because he had received a "hot tip" the night before via a radio collector's blog. Good news—the widow of a 1950s studio sound technician was going into assisted living. At the house, Tom tinkered with the radio and marveled at the vast record collection while I admired a service for twelve in the dining room. "It was my wedding set," the woman said to me.

"It's beautiful," I said.

"The man running the sale is going to buy it," she said. "Unless you want it."

"Oh, I can't afford it. We're here for the radio," I said and pointed to Tom, who had the radio proudly tucked under his arm. "Well, how much is it?" I asked as I carefully lifted a teacup.

"He said he'll give me two hundred," she said.

"You can't sell it for that," I said. "This is worth much more. You need to get someone else in here to appraise it."

"I have to get rid of it," she said. "I can't be bothered. I'm moving into my new place in two days. If you want it, match the price, and it's yours."

"Okay," I said. "If you're sure?"

"I'm sure," she said. "But, can I ask you for a favor?"

"Of course," I said.

"Can I keep six of the dishes?" She took a long pause. "I'll get them back to you. I just never ate off these dishes. No one was ever important enough. They've never been used. And now, you know, my days are sort of numbered and I'd like to enjoy them."

"Yes," I said. "You can hold on to as many as you want."

"No," she said. "Six will be plenty. And I'll return them to you."

So, I have these hand-painted Limoges dishes and even though I swore that I would enjoy them and find occasions to use them, I never did. I stored them away.

I protected them. I did exactly what the original owner did. It was true, these dishes were far too beautiful. No one was important enough to use them—that is, until Antoinette came along and plopped a Nestlé Toll House cookie on one. But, I'm over it. I swear.

Construction on the Sugar Cube finished in May and that was good. I almost thought it was worth celebrating. It was a monstrosity, there was no denying that. During the day, it cast a long shadow that draped my little shack in darkness and at night, the light that shone through the unobstructed glass walls provided a maximum-security prison atmosphere. Floodlights lining the perimeter of the illegal roof deck poured pools of light onto Harbor Road. In what I guess was a parting gift from the construction crew, one particularly bright spotlight was aimed directly at my house. Possibly, the most irritating development, though, was the sound of the three exhaust fans that rumbled at all hours and were only offset by the drip drip drip of a waterfall feature that cascaded from the roof all the way down four stories into the infinity pool. But, it was finished. At least it was finished. There weren't any jackhammers or cement trucks or flying debris. No one was there to say, "Good morning, Dorothy," and I could pull out of my driveway without fighting with twenty-five different people.

Just before Memorial Day, Tom found a listing on Airbnb for the Sugar Cube. Tom spent a lot of his time in bed researching real estate. "Maybe I'll move to Seattle when I recover. I'll be closer to Hattie," he'd say. The next day, it'd be Vermont. "The Thompsons had a place in Vermont. It was nice. I don't think they even paid a lot for it. Kathleen? What do you think about Vermont?" he'd call out as if I were in a different wing of a grand estate instead of three feet away from him whipping up yet another bowl of oatmeal.

"Good," I said. "Go to Vermont."

"I do like it here, though," he said and leaned back into his pillow and stared out at the water through the glass doors. I wasn't sure if I would live out the rest of my days in Whitbey, but I was sure Tom would.

The Sugar Cube was listed under the name "Seaside Retreat. Modern Wonder." The same day I saw the listing, I received a letter in the mail informing me that my drinking well had been contaminated and that I should seek medical attention if I had consumed large amounts of water in the last two weeks. Rosemary got the same letter. The Sugar Cube had a brand-new state-of-the-art septic system. It had three leaching fields and concrete barriers around each pool. Rosemary and I had heard a lot about this septic system. Every time our neighbors broke a law, a consultant or lawyer would show up at a hearing or meeting and make a big presentation about the marvelous upgraded, eco-friendly, nitrogen-reducing septic system. They'd dodge questions about how the house was fifteen feet higher than it was supposed to be or how the nonporous stone deck was now an infinity pool and they'd talk about the septic system.

I hate to keep writing the words *septic system*. But, seeing how it was the thing that almost killed me, I feel I have to bring it up. I wish I didn't live in a place that was so comfortable talking about human waste. But, I do.

In fact, this is probably the most disgusting part about living in a beach town. This is the thing they really don't tell you. Forget everything I said before. The real reason not to buy a beach house is all the poop talk. But, of course we don't come out and say *poop* or *feces* or *shit.* We never say that. We disguise it. We say things like *nitrogen levels* and *sanitary flow.* One of the biggest employers in town is Mr. Flush. Go for a drive in the spring just after the ground thaws and you'll see big trucks with giant green hoses plugged into people's backyards. We have pump-out boats that require pump-out operators. Every summer, the pump-out boat breaks from overuse. So, the town employs a pump-out boat mechanic for the season.

I don't know if this is true for all beach towns. I hope it's not just mine. That would feel terribly unlucky. I'd be happier knowing that the Clintons and Obamas and even Carly Simon are on Martha's Vineyard discussing sanitary flow credits. Here's a tip—don't go swimming next to a mansion that's close to the water. You know what mansions have? A lot of bathrooms. We know, thanks to my next-door neighbors, that the best septic system you can buy stops 50 percent of nitrogen. We also know it contaminates drinking wells that are within a fifty-foot radius. So, you do the math.

My favorite thing about this town is how everyone prefaces their complaints with some comment about the beauty of the area. We're miserable. We hate each other. Everyone is fighting nonstop. There are no sewers. We don't have public transportation. There's no mail delivery or garbage pickup. You can't leave your house on the weekends during pumpkin season. Everything's a rip-off. Homes are destroyed every year during hurricane season. But, boy that view is pretty. Children can ride their bicycles into town to get an ice cream cone. No one locks their front doors. Thank God we don't live in the city.

So, my well was contaminated. This was what I wanted—something big, something important, something that would make me more Erin Brockovich and less get-off-my-lawn guy. And now I had it. Someone was being poisoned! Finally! Unfortunately, it was me. It was me and Tom and Rosemary and Steve. But, it was mostly me. A few weeks before I received the contamination letter in the mail, I went to the doctor. I told her that my head was sweating. It was sweating all the time—day and night. When I was nervous, the sweat was rocketing from my head and dripping down my face and neck. She told me to drink more water. "Drop a little lemon in the glass," she said. So, that's what I did. I drank glass after glass of lemon water in an attempt to calm down and stop sweating and as a result I was poisoned.

I don't know how to make this business about the Sugar Cube interesting. I've yet to find anyone who can stand to hear me talk about it for more than a few minutes. Still, it doesn't stop me. You see, I have all this information in my head. I know all these things! So many laws were broken, not just by my neighbors, but by the town—by elected officials. They forged documents. They lied. They covered things up. God knows they took bribes. I have evidence! But, no one cares.

They still don't care. I'm sure you're reading this and saying, "I don't care." Because, at the end of the day, it's still just a house. It's height requirements and wetland permits and town code and there's just nothing sexy about it. There's nothing to really draw you in. Even the poisoning–you'd think that'd be something. You'd think a few people might be interested in that. And trust me, everyone enjoyed the story. They liked the part about me vomiting for days and requiring IV fluids and the rash on my butt and all of that. But, when I told them that the reason I was poisoned was because of a missing health department certificate, they quickly lost interest.

Hattie came out to visit the week I was hospitalized. She came to tell us she was pregnant, but delayed the announcement when she found Tom bedridden and bandaged on the couch, Roger lying with his head in the street, and me in the hospital being treated for God knows what. "What the hell, Mom?" I believe were the first words she said to me when she found me in the hospital. Hattie hates to be kept out of the loop and yet, we often leave her out of the loop. It's sort of one thing to burden your children with bad news when you have a whole slew of them. They can spread out the misery. But, when you only have the one, it seems unfair. So, we didn't tell Hattie everything. We told her bits and pieces. We left the bad stuff out. In our defense, she made a surprise visit and that was bad manners on her end.

Rosemary came to visit me in the hospital. She called me an idiot for drinking tap water and told me that Hattie had carved a dent in her lawn with her rented convertible. I told her that Hattie failed her driver's test four times. "The husband apologized, at least," Rosemary said about Andrew, whom Hattie had dragged with her across the country. "Not the brightest," she said, casually. "But, what can you do?"

"He was a Rhodes Scholar," I said.

"Fact remains," Rosemary said as she inspected the wilting flowers left over from my recovered roommate. "I told them you had tossed your cookies one too many times, so they took you to the hospital," Rosemary said as she settled onto the edge of my bed. "He thought I was actually talking about cookies! He asked me what kind."

"What'd you say?" I asked.

"Oatmeal raisin," she said.

"Andrew doesn't understand idioms," I said.

"Aren't there any more smart people?" Rosemary asked.

"No," I said. "We're the last ones."

"Well, at least he's nice," Rosemary said. "He is nice, isn't he?"

"Yeah," I said. "He's nice."

"Then she'll just be bored or small." She sighed. "Probably both. But, I guess there's worse things."

"Hattie will never be small," I said.

"Don't you be small either," Rosemary said. "This place will do that to you. Don't let it."

"It didn't make you small," I said.

"Yes, it did. I just got bigger with age," Rosemary said and started flipping through one of my beach-read romances that was lying on the bed. "I'd better get home," she said and tossed the book up toward me. "Steve's waiting outside," she said and grabbed her bag from the chair. "I'm catching the bus to the city in about an hour." She looked down at her watch.

"What are you doing in the city?" I asked.

"We're going to see the new Stoppard play," she said.

"Who?" I said.

"Tom Stoppard," Rosemary said. "He's a playwright."

"No, I know. I mean, who's going?" I said.

"Oh," Rosemary said. "Just a few friends. We meet up every month in the city. We go to a play, have dinner. Sometimes, we get drinks at the Roosevelt Hotel. Have you been to the Roosevelt Hotel? It's good to know about. They have a very nice bathroom if you're ever in Midtown and need one. The bar is nice too, but it's not as good as the bathroom."

"Wait," I said. "You're going to see plays every month in the city? How did I not know this?"

"I don't know," Rosemary said. "We've been doing it for years."

"You never said anything," I said.

"I didn't think you'd be interested," she said. "You're from Kansas."

"I can't believe this," I said as I searched for the remote to adjust my hospital bed. "You're going to Broadway plays and out to dinner. That's great. What am I doing?"

"You're recovering," Rosemary said and grabbed the remote that was dangling off the edge of the bed. She handed it to me. "And next month, you'll come to the city with us." She moved closer to the door and held onto the frame. "For now, rest."

"Okay," I said, trying to calm myself down. "Are you all right getting out? Do you know the way?"

"I was born in this hospital," Rosemary said and left.

For a long time, I took solace and real comfort in knowing that Rosemary was crazier than I was. Yes, I was tracking down ZBA agendas and snapping photos of license plates and crying in Building Department offices and calling in bad contractors and peeking out my windows, but so was Rosemary. I wasn't the only one with visions of dry wells dancing in her head. And, then, in an instant, blammo, I was the crazy one. Rosemary apparently had friends. She went out. She took the bus. She saw plays. She had dinner. She had drinks. And all I could think was, *Shit.*

In college, I took an advanced math course—Abstract Algebra with Professor Campbell. Up until that moment, I was good at math. I was practically a prodigy compared to everyone else in the Art Department. On the first exam of the semester, I got a 57 percent. The girl sitting next to me got a 53. For the midterm, I managed a 66. She bested me with a 67. She wasn't worried and so, neither was I. We laughed when we both scored lower than 50 on a pop quiz. Two weeks before the final, I joked that the course was going to sink our GPAs. The girl sitting next to me smiled and said, "Oh, I'm auditing this class." I almost passed out. Who in their right mind would audit Abstract Algebra? Italian Baroque Art—fine. Introduction to Classical Music—sure. Studio Pottery—okay. Abstract Algebra? No, sir.

Rosemary telling me that she was a theater buff felt remarkably like the day I learned you could audit Abstract Algebra. You think you're in something together and then suddenly, you're alone. And for whatever reason, it feels much worse. It's one thing to fail together. It's another to fail alone.

I will say, it was sort of a relief to be in the hospital. Everyone was very nice to me there. They brought me meals and asked how I was feeling. I watched a lot of TV and read my book. I kind of liked it. Hattie and Andrew were busy at the house taking care of Tom, even though Tom called to tell me that the two of them were very demanding guests. "They just sit around," he said. "I feel like I have to entertain them. Last night, we played three hours of Monopoly. When are you being discharged?"

Tom FaceTimed me every day while I was in the hospital. I was only in for a few days but each day he called about four times. In our mutual quest to be free and seek independent adventures, we had landed five miles away from each other, sick and immobile. The irony was not lost on us. Tom would call and complain about his aches and pains. I'd listen and nod my head and then I'd tell him about my aches and pains. After day two, I didn't really have any aches and pains, so I just made some up. We had conversations—long conversations. We told old stories, the ones we used to tell at parties—the ones we'd each heard a thousand times.

I started looking forward to Tom's phone calls. I don't know if it was the drugs or some strange side effect of the nautical-themed hospital room, but he seemed perfectly wonderful for those four days. He was considerate and charming. He was funny and silly and even slightly better-looking beaming into spotty hospital Wi-Fi. But, Tom, as always, knew just how to break the spell.

"Your sister called. She wants to know where you want to go," he said in between reminiscing.

"What does that mean?" I asked.

"Well, she doesn't want to be cremated," he said. "So . . ."

"So, when I'm dead? She called to ask where I want to go when I'm dead?" I said.

"No, Kathleen. God. She called to see how you were doing. She said you didn't answer your phone this morning."

"I was in the hyperbaric chamber," I said.

"I told her that," he said.

"And then she asked where I want to go?" I said.

"Only because she's getting her own affairs in order," he said. "Nothing to do with you. Absolutely nothing to do with you. Apparently, you both can't fit in the family plot. There's not enough room. One of you has to be cremated. And she doesn't want it to be her so she wants to know if it can be you." There was a pause. "So, do you want to be cremated?"

"Not really . . . ," I said, pondering it for a moment.

"Well, you can come with me," he said. "You'd be very welcome in Woodside. We have plenty of room."

"Where's Louise going?" I asked.

"I don't know," he said. "I think she and Jack might have gotten their own plot in Jersey."

"Because I don't want to spend eternity next to your sister."

"Well, I don't mind spending eternity next to your sister. Lilly said there's room for me if all three of us get cremated. What about that?" he asked.

"Do we have to discuss this now?" I said.

"No," he said and there was silence.

"Tell Lilly it doesn't matter to me, but I want to go with you. So, wherever we fit, that's where we'll go."

"Yeah?" he said.

"Yeah," I said.

My third day in the hospital, I got a roommate.

"Here's a nice lady you can talk to," the nurse said as she wheeled a bed through the door.

Upon first inspection, it was unclear what was wrong with the woman in the bed. But, then again, it would have been unclear what was wrong with me as well.

"Hi," I said as the nurse parked the woman's bed next to mine.

"There we go," the nurse said as she plunged her foot on the edge of the bed to lock the wheels, jolting the woman. "That's Kathleen," the nurse said as she wandered over to the whiteboard that was hanging below the television. "She's from Kansas!"

"I've never met anyone from Kansas," the woman said.

"Mary, I'm just going to write your name here next to Kathleen's," the nurse said from the front of the room.

"While you're there," I said, "do you think we can change my goal?" I asked the nurse. Underneath my name, one of the other nurses had written, *Goal: Smile!* She had written it after I explained to her that I had made a terrible mistake buying a beach house and that as soon as I got out of the hospital, I was going to put it on the market and cut my losses.

"Sure!" the nurse chirped. She erased *Smile!* and drew a big smiley face in its place. "Better?" she asked.

"I guess," I said.

"Mary, would you like a smiley face too?" the nurse asked.

"Why not?" Mary said and the nurse drew a smiley face with eyelashes under the name *Mary Williams.*

"I'll be back soon with your lunch orders, ladies!"

"I can't stand her," Mary said to me after the nurse had left.

"She seems nice enough," I said.

"Well, she's not," Mary said.

"How do you know?" I asked.

"She's my sister," Mary said.

The next day, I was discharged. I hadn't washed in four days and I had lost about ten pounds. "Do I look awful?" I asked Mary as I tugged at the lavender sweat suit Hattie had brought me.

"No," she said.

"How long before they let you out of here?" I asked.

"God knows," she said and clutched her side. "They don't know what's wrong with me. . . . I'm in here about once a month with something else. My sister says I'm making it up. She tells everyone here I'm making it up. It's a big joke. No one believes me."

"I'm sorry," I said.

"Yeah, well. Hope springs eternal, right?"

"Right," I said and collected my things. "Well, good luck," I said, not knowing what else to say.

"Hey, erase those smiley faces before you go."

"Sure," I said and wiped the board clean.

11

TO: Supervisor White (white@whitbey.gov)
FROM: Kathleen Deane (KDeane@gmail.com)
SUBJECT: Health department permit

Dear Supervisor White,

I don't know if you're even getting these emails, because I have yet to receive a response from you or anyone in your office. But, on the off chance that you do read this, I just wanted to let you know that I have recently been poisoned by some sort of unidentified waterborne bacteria stemming from my neighbor's new and improved septic system. On Wednesday, I received a call from the health department alerting me of the potential for minor illness and on Thursday, I was taken by ambulance to the hospital where I was immediately placed in the ICU. On my third day in the hospital, I developed a suspicious rash, which landed me in a hyperbaric chamber for the remainder of the day. I am not happy.

Do you remember when I spoke at the December ZBA hearing and asked as to whether or not my neighbors had been granted a health department certificate? Do you remember what you told me? "I'm sure that is all in order." That's what you said. Well, Supervisor White, it was not all in order. There is not and never was a health department certificate! There was an application for a health department certificate, but it was denied—eight times!

So, the good news is, my neighbors now have a septic system that accommodates four outdoor showers, five bathrooms, two washing machines, two full kitchens, and a waterfall. The bad news is, anyone who drinks the tap water on Harbor Road is likely to wind up hospitalized, if not dead. Yesterday, I received a letter from the town attorney offering to split the bill for a brand-new state-of-the-art $137 water filtration system for my kitchen sink. Simply put, I have had enough. I don't think it is too much to ask that a town government not actively participate in the poisoning of its citizens.

On a less dire front, I returned home from the hospital to find that six traffic signs have been erected in front of my house. Three read, SLOW CHILDREN. *One says,* DEAD END. *And the other two have pictures of bicycles on them. None of these, of course, are appropriate. There are no children currently living in my house or even on my street. Even if someone in the highway department suspected that there were children in the area, are three signs inches apart really necessary? And while my house certainly feels like a personal dead end, it is not located on a dead-end street. I don't know whether or not my street has been designated a bike route, but I will say that these two signs are especially triggering for my soon-to-be ex-husband, who is still recovering from a ter-*

rible bicycle accident. I would ask that all six signs please be removed.

Thank you very much.

Sincerely,
Kathleen Deane

Beach towns have rules because beach towns attract rule-breakers. People see sand and water and they just forget how to exist in a society. These are the three most said words in any beach town: *I didn't know.* I didn't know that I had to pay for the peaches at that farm stand. I didn't know that this driveway belonged to anybody. I didn't know this was your pool. You're not supposed to drive twenty bags of garbage to the nearest public beach and dump them in the parking lot? I didn't know that. I didn't know that you needed a sticker. What's a permit?

You would think that all the rules and restrictions and signs and threats would deter the rule-breakers. But, it only entices them. It's like their Olympics. In Whitbey, you can be in violation of fifteen laws just by sitting on the beach for an hour. But, nothing's going to happen to you. The sign says you'll spend fifteen days in jail, but you won't. Technically, you could be slapped with a $1,000 fine, but you'd be the first. So, go ahead and be barefoot in the deli. Take off your shirt and show off that dad bod to everyone in the artisanal cheese shop. Park wherever you like. Smoke whatever you've got. In a beach town, or at least in my beach town, there is only one rule that counts: don't fuck with the piping plovers.

You really have to hand it to the piping plovers. They did the impossible. These tiny sand-loving birds somehow managed to secure miles of prime waterfront property and get results from town hall all at the same time. The piping plovers don't so much as lift a feather to protect their slice of paradise. They don't spend their summers calling code enforcement or beating back the hordes of intruders like the rest of us. They don't have to lodge anonymous online complaints when people trample all over their beach. You won't see a piping plover arguing with a police officer about public access or high tide markers. No. These clever little birds bamboozled the highway department into serving as their own private security team. No charge. The roads in Whitbey are terrible, the sidewalks are a hazard, traffic lights never work—the highway department is never anywhere to be seen. But each spring, miraculously, a fleet of highway department employees emerges to install a grandiose gated community on the beach beside my house. It takes about a week to install and God help you if you put a toe inside that fence. In my next life, I want to be a piping plover. I want to sit on my own private beach inside a fence with a fat man named Mike in an orange vest telling people to get the hell off my property.

Tom loves the piping plovers, by the way. While I was in the hospital, he took it upon himself to tell someone from the highway department—Mike, presumably—to go ahead and extend the habitat. "Bring it right to the deck," he told them. Tom was a nuisance when he was bedridden, but at least he didn't talk to people.

"Stop talking to people," I said after he told me that he had also greenlighted a seagrass installation on the beach to protect the plovers from predators.

"Who do I talk to?" he said. "I don't talk to anyone." But, of course, he did. Tom talked to everyone and he talked about the only things you could talk about in Whitbey—the traffic, the parking, the construction, the Bay Mission. The problem was, Tom never had his facts straight. He downplayed things. He was always just to the left of the point and I wish I could say it was because he landed headfirst on the asphalt, but it was just the way he was. If you tell Tom that you had a fever of 105, he will tell people it was 102. If you say the Sugar Cube had twelve variances, he'll go around town and tell everyone it was seven. I don't know how many times I told Tom that I was poisoned because the septic system next door didn't have a health department certificate and it contaminated our well water. I must have said it three hundred times. But, I also said, once, that I thought the two-month-old questionable package of frozen baked clams didn't help matters. Well, of course, when neighbors inquired about my hospitalization, Tom said that I had a bad clam. To this, half of my neighbors said, "Well, what is she doing buying frozen clams?" The other half assumed I had some sort of very serious STD and, according to Rosemary, discussed my possible diagnosis at length while milling around the community garden.

Tom and I developed a morning routine around this

time. I got up first. I made the coffee. I cleaned Roger's bowls. I went outside and got the paper from the driveway. I gave Roger breakfast. Just as Roger gobbled his last nugget, Tom got up. He stumbled out of the Airstream and across the driveway and knocked on the door. I answered the door. He put the leash on Roger. I handed him his coffee. He said, "Thank you."

I said, "Don't talk to anybody."

He nodded and he left.

About twenty minutes later, Tom and Roger would return. Tom would start reading the paper. I'd say, "Did you see anybody?"

He'd say, "Nobody." Two weeks would pass and I'd bring up some juicy town-related news that I had just discovered and Tom would say, "Yeah, I know about that."

And I'd say, "How? How do you know about that?"

"George told me," Tom would say.

"When did you talk to George?" I'd say.

"A couple of weeks ago at the post office," Tom would say and so would begin the fight that we will apparently never stop having. I honestly can't tell you why I am so bothered by this and I don't want you to think that Sebastian the life coach and I haven't spent several sessions discussing it, because we have. Only someone you pay would listen to something like this. The first time I told Sebastian about this recurring fight, I was really confident about it. I knew he would see my side of things. Then, I heard myself say the words, "I don't know why he can't just tell me that he runs into people *when* he runs into people?" Sebastian didn't dignify that question with a response. So, I continued. "I just think it's weird," I said. "Does he forget or is he purposefully withholding information?" Still, Sebastian said nothing. "What?" I said.

"I just don't get it," Sebastian said finally.

"Get what?" I asked.

"How is he bothering you?" he said.

"Let's talk about something else," I said after a long sigh.

"Okay," Sebastian said and we sat in silence.

"Drink?" Sebastian asked as he always did around the half-hour mark. I nodded. "Back in a jiff," he said and headed down the long corridor toward the kitchen. I sat and waited and spiraled.

"I'm out of paprika," Sebastian said when he returned with two martini glasses and a platter of deviled eggs.

"I think I may have ruined my life," I said.

"I've only been gone five minutes," Sebastian said as he plated eggs and rearranged napkins on the coffee table. "French martini today," he said proudly and handed me a glass.

"I have a lonely feeling," I said.

"You're lonely?" Sebastian asked.

"No. I'm not lonely. I have a lonely feeling. That's what I used to call it. When I was a little girl, I would get this feeling and I would tell my mother that it was a lonely feeling and she would make me pancakes. And now I can't have pancakes because Tom ruined pancakes. And my mother is dead. And I have a lonely feeling."

"Should we talk about your mother?" Sebastian asked.

"Isn't that a little cliché?" I said and bit into an egg. "This is delicious," I said.

"Let's go back to the lonely feeling," Sebastian said. "What is that feeling?"

"I don't know," I said. "It's this bad, sinking, dark-cloud feeling." I held my stomach. "What is that? It's depression, right? I know it's depression." I paused while Sebastian closed his eyes and nodded sympathetically. "Tom's back in the Airstream," I said after a sip of martini. "Did I tell you that?"

"Do you think that's related?" Sebastian asked.

"To what?" I said.

"To the lonely feeling," he said.

"Well, he's only about ten feet farther than he was last week," I said.

"Here's what I want you to do," Sebastian said. "Close your eyes and imagine yourself happy."

"Okay," I said.

"Can you see yourself?" he asked.

"Yes," I said.

"Good," he said. "Where are you?"

"I want to say Illinois," I said.

"Why Illinois?" Sebastian asked.

"I don't know. I just feel like there's a Great Lake around," I said, my eyes still closed. "Maybe it's Ohio, like Cleveland area." I opened my eyes. "Did you see that article about climate change? They said we're all going to end up living by the Great Lakes. I bet Detroit comes back."

"Okay," Sebastian said. "Let's try something else."

"Okay," I said.

"Who are you with?" he asked.

"Tom," I said without hesitation. "Oh God," I said. "That came awfully fast."

"That's good," Sebastian said.

"Is it a breakthrough?" I asked.

"Sure," Sebastian said.

For as long as Tom and I have been together, I have been the social one. I was the one with friends. I threw dinner parties. I made chitchat with the neighbors. I coached Little League. I was the one who danced at weddings—the one who could make conversation. And then we moved to Whitbey. And for whatever reason, Tom got along with everyone and I got along with the one woman who no one could stand. Suddenly, I was the one who needed to be reminded to socialize. I was the one who needed checking in on.

Before Hattie left to go back to Seattle with Andrew, she sat me down and told me that she was worried about me in this soft-spoken "I'm speaking to a crazy person" sort of way. I assured her that everything was fine and that the doctors said I would make a full recovery. Her father was almost entirely healed and I planned on kicking him to the curb any day now. Someday soon I was going to defeat the Sugar Cube and all would be right in the world. I told her to have a good flight home and not to worry about a thing.

"Are you depressed?" Hattie said.

"Of course I'm not depressed," I said.

"Really?" Hattie said, almost too earnestly to believe.

"Yes, really," I said. "I'm very happy here. It's taking some time to settle in, but in a few weeks when I feel better and the weather gets warmer I'm going to call the painters and maybe a plumber and I'm going to really spruce this place up."

"So, you're not depressed?" Hattie asked again.

"No," I said, a little annoyed now.

"So, you just have fifteen brand-new unopened three-pair packages of classic white brief underwear in your top drawer for no reason?"

"I don't know why you're going through my drawers," I said. "But, if you must know, there was a sale," I said.

"It's a cry for help," Hattie said. "That's what it is. When Andrew and I found them, we were very concerned. I mean, it's forty-five pairs of underwear, Mom. What are we supposed to think?"

"Well, I'm glad you showed them to Andrew," I said.

"You need to make friends," Hattie said. "And not that crazy Rosemary. She probably has a stockpile of underwear too. That's the type, Mom. You know what she said to Andrew? She called him a dope, right to his face. He was very upset about it."

"I will try to make new friends," I said.

"I mean, I'm sure Dad can introduce you to people," Hattie said. "I was walking around the neighborhood with Roger the other day and a few people asked me who I was. I said I was Kathleen's daughter. Mom, they didn't know who you were. They just asked if I knew Tom. You have to get involved in the community. You have to find something to do."

So, I promised Hattie I would find something to do. I would join a group or take a class or teach a class or do something to avoid becoming the kind of person who hoards giant cotton underwear, whatever kind of person that is. Here's a question: Do people ever stop asking you what you do or is that a question that just crops up your entire life? Are there people who poke around nursing homes asking Alzheimer's patients what they're working on these days? Is there an age when it becomes socially acceptable to say, "Nothing"? Because that's the age that I'd like to be.

I spent most of my career avoiding the question "What do you do?" I worked in the arts and sometimes, it's great to work in the arts. There are perks. You get to be creative. There are flexible hours. Sometimes, you get free stuff. But, there's a downside too. Everyone is curious about the arts. You can't just say, "I'm a greeting card designer," and not expect a follow-up question. People want to know more. I don't know for sure, but I assume from the excited expressions on people's faces that they envision my rather ordinary corporate existence as some sort of Willy Wonka–esque world where cartoon characters crack jokes at the watercooler and people skip down the rainbow hallways with paintbrushes in their hair. There is nothing I can say to these people that won't disappoint them. Nobody says, "Oh, wow!" when you tell them you're a teacher or a doctor or a lawyer. They don't pitch you ideas or suggest ways to "save your industry." Teachers and doctors and lawyers take that for granted.

I thought things would be different when I retired. I could just say, "I'm retired," and that would be that. No further explanation required. But, I'm here to tell you that it doesn't stop. Even if you put in your thirty years, and collect your pension, and move far away from home, everyone is still very worried about what exactly it is that you are doing. Strangers will say things like, "You're retired? That's a lot of free time. How are you keeping busy? I hope you're volunteering." Well, I'm not. I'm sitting on my couch watching dark-money documentaries, scouting underwear sales online, and drafting angry emails to the town. I don't see why that's not enough.

As it happens, retirees in Whitbey are remarkably busy. There's so much that needs to be done! And apparently, the members of the geriatric jamboree are the only ones willing and able to do it! There are committees to join and commissions to form. Soup kitchens need to be manned. Nature trails need to be maintained. Beaches have to be cleaned. Osprey nests have to be monitored and repaired and improved. There are lectures to attend. Shelter dogs need to be walked. They need to be read poems every night before bed, preferably Irish ones. If you're not fostering a dog, then what the hell are you doing? Volunteering is good, but it's not enough. You really should take a class. If you don't want to take a class, then you absolutely must teach one.

In a beach town, people don't just do things. They don't wake up one morning and decide to take a crack at gardening or painting or paddleboarding. You won't find anyone blindly taking up woodworking or needlepoint. No one here is attempting to self-learn the guitar or the piano. They're not self-learning anything. They take a class. In Whitbey, there is a class for everything. Everyone here is a lifelong learner. The idea that you would sit down and start journaling without a six-week course about how to do it is absurd. And don't think you need any sort of qualifications to teach a class. Have you heard of the thing that you are teaching a class about? That's enough. You'll learn along the way with everyone else. In this case, believing is achieving. Confidence is everything. And if a course in watercolors or pickleball or handbag design or beekeeping doesn't strike your fancy, you can feel free to partake in a wide selection of twelve-step programs. Even if you don't have any kind of addiction or disorder, you'll have done something with your day and really that's the only goal. Either way, whatever you choose, you'll most likely get a stale doughnut out of the deal and that's something. It's definitely not nothing.

It's not like I didn't know that it was a bad idea to join the Bay Mission. I did. First of all, the whole enterprise was so sloppy and disorganized and misguided that it almost made you wish some psychopath billionaire with no moral compass would take over the operation. He would build some energy-sucking warehouse on the vacant lot and he'd fill it with low-paid workers and there would be horrible working conditions and everything would be contaminated with toxic sludge and he wouldn't pay a dime in federal taxes. But, at least it would be organized. He'd get it done. He'd have a goddamn plan.

The most appealing part of this scenario would be that we could all stop meeting every other week at the school cafegymatorium to discuss what to do with the property. There would be no need to go back and forth about how much it costs to renovate an antique carousel or what exactly is the definition of a snack bar. We could stop wondering about what the unintended consequences would be if we put up a few more picnic tables. The phrase *witch hunt* might not appear in every conversation. Talk of an amphitheater wouldn't necessarily warrant a call to police dispatch. Perhaps we could walk around the neighborhood without wanting to murder several of our neighbors along the way. Maybe a yard sign with the words *Save What's Left* wouldn't have to ruin a thirty-year friendship. But, then again, what would we do with all the spare time? What would we do every other Tuesday if not scream at each other about traffic studies and environmental impact reviews?

I, for one, sort of like the mental and physical challenge presented by navigating the neighborhood based on the ever-changing list of whom I am avoiding on any given day for any number of reasons. So many people just walk their dogs aimlessly from one street to the next without a thought in the world. Not me. I have to be sharp as a tack. I can walk down Plum Street, but I'll have to make a left on Queen because Sandy lives on Queen and at the last Bay Mission meeting Sandy called Rosemary a "nosy Rosy." I can't go down Birch Street for obvious reasons, and yet, to get over to Main Street, I'll have to pass by the harmonica player's house, which will no doubt ignite an hour-long conversation about his fear of a boat storage facility going up on the lot. If I cut through the park, I can make it back to Harbor Road without running into Owen on Maple, who, because of a small disagreement about the ownership of a door knocker, only speaks to me through Roger. "Hello, Roger," he'll say. "Did you see that the ladies installed a snow fence at the beach to keep all the non-Mainstays out? Do we think that's legal, Roger? No, it's not. Uh-uh. It's not. It's a public easement, Roger. Yes, it is."

"Hi, Owen," I'll say and he'll give Roger another pat on the head.

"See you later, Roger!" Owen will say and scurry back into his shop.

The second reason why I knew it was a mistake to join the Bay Mission was simply the fact that I hated everything about it and practically all the people involved with it. I had made such a habit of ridiculing the women of the Bay Mission that I developed almost uncanny impressions of the three head honchos. And let's just say they weren't exactly flattering impressions. I also know that there's allegedly a special place in hell for women who don't help each other, and if that's the case, Rosemary and I are certainly going.

The third and final reason against joining the Bay Mission was that it was Tom's idea. That's important to remember. This was all Tom's idea. "Join the Bay Mission," he said. "It'll be something to do." So, at the risk of having nothing to do, and in an effort to avoid that special place in hell, I joined the Bay Mission. Josie took me under her wing. She walked me through the ins and outs and ups and downs of running a nonprofit. I sat in on board meetings. I was reinstated as a "Mainstay," and this time I kept my mouth shut like I was told. I was almost immediately promoted to director of fundraising. Responsibilities included mowing the grass, cooking twenty gallons of clam chowder in my galley kitchen, weeding the community garden, cleaning bathrooms, and other menial tasks entirely unrelated to fundraising.

This was not the first time I have fallen for this trick. In 1967, I was elected president of the Tea Club. The Tea Club was a club that met in my living room after school. The members were my sister, Lilly, her best friend, Louise, and our neighbor Helen. Activities of the club included drinking tea, eating snacks, and talking. I was not in the Tea Club. I was not allowed. For about two months, I waged a campaign to get in. I begged. I pleaded. It was all I wanted. Finally, one afternoon, Lilly informed me that not only would she let me in the Tea Club, but I could be the president. Being the president of the Tea Club was a very important job. Duties included making the tea, serving the tea, making the snacks, serving the snacks, and cleaning up after the tea and snacks. It wasn't great. But, being the director of fundraising for the Bay Mission was even worse.

Let's be honest, I deserved what I got. I knew better. It's not like I wasn't warned. Rosemary told me exactly who the Bay Mission ladies were the first day I met her. But, when you turn your life upside down and spend all your money on an impromptu decision inspired by a thirty-year-old VHS tape, you want that decision to work out. You need it to work out. I didn't just want to be happy. I had to be. Otherwise, what was I doing? What had I done? I could leave. I could pack up everything and say it was a terrible mistake. But, where would

I go? This was my second chance—my fresh start—and I was spoiling it.

"I'm going to take the water," I said to Rosemary during one of our regular driveway rendezvous. "Jack and Sarah offered to pay for it and I'm going to accept."

"It's hush money," Rosemary said.

"It's a public water hookup," I said.

"Good," Rosemary said. "Fine." And she began to walk away.

"That's it?" I said. "Good? Fine?"

"Well, what do you want me to say?" she asked, stopping in the street.

"Well, that you think I'm doing the right thing," I said.

"You're not," Rosemary said.

"They're the ones who contaminated my well," I said.

"Right," Rosemary said.

"So, why should I have to lay out a thousand dollars?" I said. "Let them pay."

"Okay," Rosemary said and continued toward her house.

"Hold on," I said, following her into her yard. "You're seriously mad about this?"

"I'm not mad," Rosemary said as she started rearranging Steve's fishing poles that were propped beside the front door. "Why does he leave these here like this?"

"This is a win," I said. "They're finally paying a consequence."

"It's not a win," Rosemary said. "It's a bribe and you're an idiot. Let's talk about something else."

"Well, I have to go to Mitsy's house in a few minutes

to pick up her ride-on lawn mower," I said. Rosemary smiled. "I'm going to have to drive it all the way to the community garden."

"Serves you right," Rosemary said.

"All right," I said. "Better go. I have to stop at the gas station. Mitsy said she's on empty."

"Enjoy," Rosemary said.

"Will you forgive me if I take the water?" I asked as I reached the front gate.

"Yep," Rosemary said.

12

TO: Supervisor White (white@whitbey.gov)
FROM: Kathleen Deane (KDeane@gmail.com)
SUBJECT: Yesterday's meeting / Bay Mission special event

Dear Supervisor White,

As you know, I attended last night's town board meeting. I also popped into the tail end of the work session in the hopes that the subject of "big houses" would be revisited. But, I guess that subject has been delayed another month. Instead, I caught your discussion regarding the town's renewed efforts to bolster community involvement and improve attendance at town board meetings and public hearings. There was talk of social media campaigns and newspaper ads and I believe it was Councilwoman Lyons who suggested that a private public relations consultant be hired to help "get out the word" using professional marketing strategies. Councilman Fisher spoke at length about the need for a new and improved audiovisual sys-

tem and proposed gutting the meeting hall to make way for the installation of professional-grade microphones. This is a laugh. First of all, does Councilman Fisher think the public cannot connect the dots between his pitch for a new sound system in town hall and his son's new electronics store opening this weekend on West Bay Avenue? Second of all, I think Councilman Fisher, of all people, is well aware that it is not a lack of audio quality that is keeping citizens away from the public meetings.

Two weeks ago, during the town board's leaf blower discussion, Councilman Fisher, whom we all know owns the largest landscaping business in Whitbey, announced his opposition to any regulations on the use of gas blowers, citing the dangerous environmental impacts of batteries and electricity. This, of course, was an asinine comment that went unchallenged by the other members of the board. My soon-to-be ex-husband and I were the only two citizens in attendance at that meeting. I may or may not have rolled my eyes at Councilman Fisher's statement. I can't say whether or not Tom made any inappropriate facial expression, but nonetheless, Councilman Fisher thought it necessary to tell Tom at the close of the meeting that he would "kick his ass." It should be noted that this was picked up loud and clear on the meeting hall's current aging and outdated microphones. The video has now been posted on the town website for all to see. So, if the board's goal is to encourage community involvement and public attendance at meetings, I think a good place to start would be to dissuade town employees from telling citizens that they are going to have their asses kicked if they so much as roll their eyes.

On another note, I wanted to get your advice on the Bay Mission's latest charitable venture that is tentatively set for June 1. In an unexpected turn of events, I am now serving as the Bay Mission's director of fundraising, and despite my best efforts to pump the brakes on this latest proposed event, it is fast approaching. I raised my concerns to the directors of the Bay Mission and they do not share those concerns. They advised me to seek your guidance on the subject. My good friend Josie Friedman, treasurer of the Bay Mission, assured me that you would assuage my fears and perhaps offer some helpful ideas to improve what I foresee to be the unintended optics of the event.

If you are not aware of the event, this is the email that was sent out yesterday to the Mainstays:

> Help give the homeless a taste of paradise. Volunteer next weekend for our first-annual Bay Mission Day in the Sun! We need folks to man the grills, pass out beverages, and donate picnic blankets and tables if you have them. Thanks to the support of our generous patrons, the Bay Mission has decided to give back. Lucy Williams, vice president of outreach for the Bay Mission, has connected our team with a nonprofit organization in New York City specializing in services for the homeless population. With the help of our partners, we have selected one hundred lucky "un-housed" people to spend a day in our beautiful village. They will be boarded on luxury coach buses in the morning and transported to Whitbey, where we plan to treat them to a day of relaxation, sunshine, good food, and scenic vistas. Transport for our guests back to the city will take place at 4:00 p.m. Hope to see you all there!

I just worry that this may be doing more harm than good. Of course, the intention is sincere and kindhearted and all of us should be doing everything we can to help ease the homeless crisis. But, I'm just not sure that scooping up people from the streets of New York City, busing them three hours to a small seaside town with million-dollar homes, giving them a hot dog, and then dumping them back on the streets of Manhattan later that night is the best way to help. Am I overreacting? Please advise.

Thank you.

Sincerely,
Kathleen Deane

I always wanted to live in an interesting place with interesting people. The words *artist community* always appealed to me. I thought it would be wonderful to live in a neighborhood where people had creative ambitions and unique life stories. Wouldn't it be something to live down the road from someone who was, I don't know, a professional harmonica player? What if there were a town where half the residents had self-published novels in their spare time? Was there a place where everyone fancied themselves an amateur painter and where faux finishers outnumbered lawyers?

Well, I found that place. It exists. And even with all the adorable craft sales and book signings and en plein air painting, there is an unsettling strangeness that runs straight through the heart of it. There is a retired faux finisher who lives around the corner from me. A few years ago, he suffered a botched spinal surgery that left him in terrible pain and addicted to morphine. Now, every night he screams at midnight. Sometimes, he is yelling at the dogs. Sometimes, it's his wife. But most times, he just lets out a terrific wail that echoes throughout the neighborhood. It's bloodcurdling, but we've all sort of gotten used to it, as bad as that sounds.

There is a wealthy man on Queen Street who married his hairdresser. He leaves for work at four o'clock in the morning. But, before he leaves, he sits in his car in the driveway, eats a frozen breakfast sandwich, and listens to Céline Dion on full blast. Before he arrives home at five o'clock, his wife goes around the yard and picks up stray leaves like a madwoman. In the winter, she frantically uses a broom to wipe away each and every snowflake from the stone path.

There is a hoarder who lives on Mill Street. She has the most beautiful piece of property—a rolling acre with a private sandy beach. The grounds are maintained by a landscaper. The house is regularly painted. But, she sleeps on a futon in the sunroom surrounded by Christmas decorations and antique dolls and old cereal boxes. Josie tells me she sees her at the tag sales every weekend. Sometimes, she'll leave with a pearl necklace, other times a half-empty bottle of Windex for a nickel. She volunteers at the soup kitchen every Tuesday and Thursday.

The group of ladies who walk in the mornings and play pickleball in the afternoons like to garden at night. Late in the spring, they wheel four ten-foot-tall flood lamps into the community garden. Why we have a community garden, I can't tell you. Everyone in the community has an ample yard where they could plant their own garden. But, they don't do that. Instead, they plant their vegetables and herbs on a contaminated plot of land near the restaurant parking lot. Just before dinnertime, you'll see the ladies head down to the garden with their wicker baskets to collect their harvest. They'll pick one tomato, perhaps a cucumber, and maybe one sprig of rosemary. And they'll make a tremendous show about it. They linger by the parking lot as long as they can, hoping someone will stop and say hello.

You won't see any of these things if you come for the day. The tree-lined streets are dotted with houses that are lovely and well-kept. The landscaping is neat and tidy and thriving. The beaches are pristine. The harbor is bustling. But, behind closed doors there is often a sort of sadness. I suppose that may be true of any place, but it's almost unnerving in such an idyllic setting, where you're constantly reminded of how lucky you are to be here. There are newspaper articles that come out every day about Whitbey's beauty and charm. They interview people who practically call it nirvana. Tourists sit in traffic for hours just to spend an afternoon here—just to get a ten-dollar blueberry muffin. So, how do you say, "I don't really like it"? How do you say, "I'm not happy"?

Nightly entertainment in Whitbey is limited. In the winters, it is nonexistent. And in the summers, what few activities do exist past 5:00 p.m. are almost exclusively on Wednesday nights. There are one-act plays at the gazebo on Elk and Main, dancing in Frederick Park with the steel drummers, pickleball tournaments at the West Creek field, weekly sailboat races around Gull Island,

and, my favorite, the town board meetings at town hall. Josie was the one to kindly point out to me that this scheduling inadvertently created a sort of pathetic high school cafeteria-style pecking order in which she was at the top and I was, regrettably, at the bottom. According to Josie, anyone in Whitbey could be easily summed up based on their Wednesday night location—jocks at the pickleball courts, theater kids at the gazebo, stoners at the park, the cool/popular types at the sailboat races, and the nerds at town hall.

"Come and watch the races with us," Josie said as I aimlessly milled around her store, something I did regularly to avoid the chaos on Harbor Road. Josie and a few of her girlfriends met every Wednesday night at the beach to watch the races, have dinner, drink wine, and gossip.

"I can't," I said. "There's a public hearing about the rental code tonight."

"So, you miss a public hearing," Josie said as she organized baby quilts neatly stacked in the front window.

"Those are nice," I said.

"They're beautiful," Josie said. "Handmade. You should get one for Hattie." She tucked one under her arm and hopped down from the windowsill. "When's the baby due again?"

"October," I said.

"Coming up," Josie said and handed me the quilt. I looked at the tag.

"Three hundred dollars?" I said.

"Well, it's an heirloom piece, Kathleen," Josie said. "It's all hand done."

"Right," I said and ran my finger along the carefully

stitched white squares and safari shapes. "Okay," I said and fished for my wallet.

"Hold on," Josie said and dashed off to the back of the store. "I just got these in," she said and held up a silk scarf. "Isn't this so Hattie?" she asked.

"She might like that," I said.

"She'll love it," Josie said. "One hundred percent silk."

"Throw it in," I said. "What the hell."

"Good," Josie said as she swiped my credit card with gusto and carefully folded the quilt and scarf into a paper bag.

"What's going on here?" I said and flicked a small patch of white hair that seemed to be deliberately framing Josie's face. "You ran out of things to paint white? We've moved on to the hair?"

"I'm going to ignore that comment," she said and carefully swept her hair to the side. "I'm doing an open mic at Ray's on Saturday. Bonnie Raitt. Get it?"

"Got it," I said.

"I thought it might be a fun touch," she said and fluffed her bangs once more.

"It is fun," I said. "What song? 'I Can't Make You Love Me'?"

"'Something to Talk About,'" she said, as if it were obvious. Josie loved open mics and karaoke and really any excuse to hop on a stage. For about eight months in 1987, she seriously pursued a country-and-western music career. She bought a steel guitar and cowboy boots and headed down to Nashville with a notebook full of songs about growing up in the mountains of Appalachia. "It's better odds in country," I remember her telling me. "I can always pivot to pop," she said.

Sadly, Josie's thick Long Island accent proved to be her kryptonite in this endeavor and she was back on Sixty-Fourth Street before ever getting the opportunity to hit it big at the Grand Ole Opry.

"I do like the hair, though," I said. "It suits you."

"That's what Dan said," Josie said. "I might keep it. You'll come to the open mic, right?"

"Sure," I said.

"And bring Tom," she said. "He's fun. He'll enjoy it."

"I'm fun," I said.

"You know who always goes to these things? Supervisor White. You can talk to him about the rental permit then."

"That's true," I said.

"So, you'll come to the races tonight?"

"Can I bring Rosemary?" I asked.

"If you must," Josie said and handed me the bag. I was halfway out the door when Josie asked me to bring a dish. "Tell Rosemary to bring one too!" she called out.

I spent the rest of the afternoon preparing spareribs, being sure to douse them with barbecue sauce every hour on the hour until race time at six o'clock. Rosemary, after a great deal of convincing, reluctantly threw some local sweet corn in a pot. She soaked them in butter before haphazardly wrapping them in aluminum foil for transport.

"Do you think they'll pass the rental law tonight?" Rosemary asked as we lugged our beach chairs and mini coolers down the length of Harbor Road.

"Don't know," I said as I watched the tourists vying for position on the crowded pier.

"You believe this?" Rosemary said as we passed Owen, who was sitting on his stoop, head resting in his hands. He shook his head.

"Planning board meeting on Friday," he said.

"About what?" Rosemary asked.

"Picnic tables," he said and pointed across the street to the Bay Mission lot. "You want the agenda?"

"I've got my hands full at the moment," Rosemary said and lifted the cooler.

"I'll leave it in your car," he said.

"Thanks," she said and we proceeded in step with the towering sails making their way to the starting line.

"No stickers," Rosemary said when we reached the beach's sand-covered parking lot. She shimmied next to a wooden barrier and inspected a row of bumpers. "Not a one," she confirmed.

We kicked our sandals off near a pile of similarly discarded footwear. An excited wave of a Lilly Pulitzer arm flagged us over to the eastern edge of the shore where just beyond the rock jetty, sailboats twisted and turned. Beyond a *No Public Access Beyond This Point* sign, we found Mary, Sue, Margaret, and Patty seated in a semicircle, divvying up shrimp and uncorking wine. "Don't take too many of those," Patty said as Rosemary and I joined the coven. "They're from Whistlers. I paid a fortune. Two each," she instructed. "Hi, Kathleen," she added. "Rosemary," she said with a dismissive nod. Patty was Patty Tilley, feared leader of the Bay Mission. I could see Rosemary dreaming up an exit strategy as she plopped our coolers into the sand.

"Here," Mary said. "Don't put it in the sand. I have

something in my bag." She pulled out an intricate, multicolor quilt from a tote bag and spread it in front of us.

"I'm not putting the food on here," Rosemary said. "This is too nice. We brought ribs, for God's sake."

"Oh, no," Mary said. "I have a million of them. I make them for fun."

"I can run back to the house and get an old blanket," I said.

"No, no, no," Mary said and took the cooler from Rosemary's hand. "It goes right in the washing machine."

"I just bought a quilt today," I said.

"At Josie's?" Mary asked.

"Yeah," I said.

"That's mine," Mary said. "I made that."

"Oh my God," I said. "It's beautiful. I got it for my granddaughter. My daughter's due in the fall."

"Oh, how exciting!" Mary said. "Can you believe Josie pays me fifty dollars for them?" She raised her eyebrows. "I'd make them for free. Did you pick up some of the knitted hats and mittens that she has for newborns?"

"No," I said. "I didn't see them."

"Those are mine," Sue said. "I knit them."

"Huh," Rosemary said. "Sue does the hats and mittens. Mary does the quilts. Kathleen does the greeting cards. Patty, what do you do?" Patty rolled her eyes and peeled back some tinfoil to inspect Rosemary's contribution.

"You know," Patty said. "The grass is getting a little long over at the community garden, Kathleen."

"Yeah, I know," I said. "I'm going to get that done tomorrow."

"Well, good," she said. "Because we want it done before the Flower Festival on Saturday."

"Right," I said just as the air horn blared to start the race.

"Oh, look!" Margaret said with a laugh and pointed to the water. "She is too much!"

"Hi, girls!" Josie yelled from the bow of one of the sailboats. She waved excitedly as she rounded the first buoy.

"What boat is she on?" Patty asked, cupping her hands over her eyes.

"*Three Ring Circus,*" Sue said and the others nodded. I looked at Rosemary, confused.

"Supervisor White's boat," she said. "Guess they're not passing the rental law tonight after all."

I used to need a white noise machine to fall asleep. I had the same one for fifteen years. It was big and ugly and beige and took up the entire nightstand, but I loved it. It had only a few settings—jungle, rain, and ocean, each of which had a very obvious two-minute loop that apparently drove everyone who bought it insane. It was quickly pulled from the shelves and replaced with a better, slimmer, less annoying version. But, if people had just stuck with the machine long enough, they would have realized that after about six months the whole thing breaks just enough to incorporate a moaning fan noise that practically drowns out the loop altogether. This combination is what really creates the ideal sleeping conditions. I took this thing everywhere. I absolutely could not sleep without it.

On Memorial Day, my beloved sound machine broke. It died a slow death—a painful one. I watched for weeks as the humming turned to clanking and gargling and whistling. I knew the end was near when it started running a fever. Hot air started to pour out of the vents and left a circular scar on my nightstand. Finally, I woke up one morning and it was gone. The room was silent. After that, I had nothing to help me sleep except the sound of the actual waves crashing outside my bedroom window and the real live seagulls fighting over clams on the beach. They kept me up all night. Each wave crashing against the bulkhead felt like an assault.

During my bout of insomnia, I thought mostly about Supervisor White. "Call me anytime," he said when he scribbled his cell number on the back of a town board agenda. "If anything comes up," he said, "you just call me." I hung the piece of paper proudly on the refrigerator door using a magnet shaped like a seahorse that I had bought in Josie's store. I felt very important—very seen. Getting that number stopped me from officially reporting the outdoor shower that was illegally installed and the impervious pavers that lined the driveway. It stopped me from calling the police when my electricity was cut and when my tap water turned brown the second time. I had someone on my side—the top guy—the supervisor. Sure, he didn't answer my emails. But, he didn't have to. He understood. He got it. I stopped bothering with code enforcement complaints and the police. I didn't need them. If something really came up, I could call the supervisor. I could call him anytime, anytime I wanted. I was above the anonymous online complaint form. That wasn't for me.

The problem was, nothing ever seemed big or bad enough to warrant calling the supervisor's cell phone. I'd run over the imaginary phone calls while I lay awake at night. "Oh, hello? My neighbors have planted ten-foot-tall trees in the street." "Hi there, it's me. I just wanted to let you know that a thirty-foot ladder has been leaning on my house for three days." "Me again! What would you say if I told you that the contractor screamed good morning at me today several times and in a very threatening way? Is there something in the code about that?" So, I never called. I let things go. I focused on Tom and my greeting cards and the chowder fest that was fast approaching.

I was never one of those girls who cried over a school dance. I didn't do much waiting by the phone for someone to call or pining over someone else's boyfriend. If someone I was seeing wanted to see someone else, I said, "By all means, good riddance." But, I'm sorry to say that I was absolutely devastated when Rosemary informed me that Supervisor White had handed out his cell phone number to everyone in town. "It's on his Facebook page, for God's sake," she said. My heart absolutely sank. He had given his number to all the women with bad neighbors.

"He said I could call him anytime," I said to Rosemary when she ripped the paper from my fridge.

"And did you?" she asked, waving it in the air.

"No," I said.

"It's a tactic!" Rosemary shouted. "They're all tactics—schemes! When will you wake up?"

I was always disappointing Rosemary. I was a bad judge of character. My emails weren't strong enough—

weren't mean enough. I was gullible. I took the money for the public water. So, I was susceptible to bribes. I said the wrong things. I couldn't keep a secret. I forecasted my next moves. I picked rotten friends. I believed people. I didn't notice things. I couldn't remember names. I forgot dates and times. I was late to meetings. Sometimes, I knew we were mad about something, but I couldn't remember why. I misquoted the town code. I involved Tom in things I shouldn't have. I took things personally. I cried. I cried a lot. Too much.

But, Rosemary forgave me. She forgave me for everything—for joining the Bay Mission, for taking the money for the public water hookup, for hanging around with Josie and the Birch Street Bitches at the community garden. She stood up for me when I didn't deserve it. Still, it all weighed on her. That was obvious. We were losing. There was no other way to look at it. We were losing the battles. We were losing the war. We were losing all of it. I was fighting what I perceived to be a great annoyance. Rosemary was fighting for her hometown. It was different. It chipped away at her in a way that I couldn't fully understand.

As the losses started to pile up, Rosemary abandoned what little politeness and political correctness she had left. I went with her to a historic preservation meeting where she stood up and accused the president of being a fascist. She told the ladies in the garden to get a life when they asked for a donation for the new picnic tables. Part of me loved Rosemary. She said all the things I wanted to say—all the things I was too chicken or polite or nonconfrontational to say. In a way, she was my hero. She did exactly what she wanted and said exactly what she thought. She was the only person I'd ever met who wasn't instantly taken with Tom. But, she understood me taking him back when no one else did. "He's just decent," she said about him and she was right. Decency was really all Rosemary expected from people, and yet on Harbor Road it was hard to come by. She could forgive mistakes and foibles and bad judgment. But, a lack of decency was unforgivable. It was more than unforgivable. It needed to be confronted. And that's what Rosemary did.

Rosemary had a long-running dispute with a restaurant down the street. The dispute was less with the restaurant and more with the woman who owned it. This had been going on for years, could have been decades. When you speak your mind and you make it your personal business to call out injustices, you're bound to make a few enemies and Rosemary did. But, Cassandra Pennelli topped the list.

The restaurant is popular. It's the designated hangout for police officers and firefighters and town employees. So, no one really minds when they go over capacity or overserve or, in this case in particular, store garbage in a dumpster near the public beach. I've never been to this restaurant, so I can't comment on the quality of the food or the ambiance or any of that. I once thought about getting a lobster roll to go and Rosemary nearly smacked me. Rosemary did what she could. She complained about the dumpster. She spoke at the town board meeting. She wrote a letter to the editor. Nothing happened and probably that should have been the end of it.

But, at some point the lid to this offending dumpster broke and that's when things really escalated. One morning, Rosemary was walking on the beach and she saw that a flock of seagulls and crows had taken most of the contents of the dumpster and scattered them all over the beach and into the water. So, she picked up every last piece of garbage, walked it over to the restaurant, and scattered it on the doormat.

The next day, there was a pickup truck parked in front of Rosemary's house. By midafternoon, it was filled with twenty open bags of garbage. The first day, Rosemary called the police. The second day, she called the supervisor. The third day, she took Steve's putter and smashed it through the truck's windshield. Then, she was arrested. I don't know who called the police, but they were fast to arrive on the scene. It was just the one officer, a young man with a slender frame and a soft voice. "I'll need to take you to the station," he said sort of indifferently as he acknowledged Roger, who had moseyed across the street amid the commotion. "Nice dog," he said to Tom and patted the top of Roger's head.

"I'm not going to the damn station," Rosemary said and loaded the golf club back into the trunk of Steve's car. "If you want to arrest someone, you can head right across the street to the criminals next door. Or better yet, go have a talk with Cassandra. I'm sure she'll give you a free drink while you're there."

"Okay," the policeman said and took out his notepad. "I just need to take a statement first."

"About what?" Rosemary said and folded her arms.

"About you smashing this window with a golf club," the officer said.

"I don't know what you're talking about," Rosemary said.

"Listen," the officer said. "It's not a big deal. You tell me what happened. I write it down. I'll drive you to the station. You fill out some paperwork. Half hour later, your husband can pick you up. Okay?"

Rosemary considered this for a moment. She looked at the young officer, then at the broken window, then at me, and then did a thing that I never imagined she'd do: she ran. She took off down Harbor Road like a bat out of hell. Rosemary is many things. She is smart. She is wise. She is funny. She is not, however, fast. Officer Davis decided to forgo a vehicular chase and opted rather to apprehend Rosemary on foot. "Rosemary!" he called out as he briskly walked behind her. "You're not helping, Rosemary!"

Tom, Roger, and I stood at the end of the street and watched this slow-motion scene unfold. Neither Tom nor I knew what to do. We just stood there, watching in disbelief. What was she thinking? Did she think she could outrun him? Where was she going? Finally, about half a block later, Rosemary made the ultimate runner's mistake. She looked back. She checked to see the progress of her competition and that was it. She lost her footing. She tripped on absolutely nothing and went tumbling down onto the pavement. One loud yelp followed. Tom and I ran to her. We passed Officer Davis, who radioed for an ambulance.

"Are you all right?" I said.

"These damn cops," Rosemary said as she clutched her leg.

"Rosemary, you had a fall," Officer Davis said as he knelt beside her.

"You think?" she said.

"Did you hit your head?" he asked.

"Yes," she said. "I hit my head very hard because you were chasing me. Police brutality," she said.

"You did not hit your head," Officer Davis said.

"Then, why'd you ask me if I did?" she said.

"Because I have to," he said.

Rosemary looked up at Tom.

"Well, are you going to take a look at this thing or just stand there?" she said.

"Your hip's most likely broken," Tom said after a twenty-second evaluation.

"Oh, for God's sake," Rosemary said. "I hope you're happy," she said to Officer Davis, who was now visibly shaken by the whole ordeal. "While we wait," Rosemary said, "write up a ticket for that fence." She pointed to the Sugar Cube. "You people keep telling us you're going to write a ticket for a code violation. But you never do. Now's your chance. You have the time. It'll be another fifteen minutes before the ambulance comes."

A few weeks and one hip replacement later, Rosemary moved into the rehab facility at the Cliffs. If you're looking to die in Whitbey, you have three options. One—die young. Two—go to Shady Shores Nursing Facility against your will. Three—sell everything you own, borrow money, liquidate funds, cut people out of your will, and buy a spot at the Cliffs. If on the off chance you're not dying and just want a glamourous monthlong staycation, break a hip and rehab at the Cliffs. The Cliffs is the Beverly Hills of retirement communities. The first day I visited Rosemary, they were setting up for a celebrity wedding that was taking place in one of the old stone mansions on the property. You know your nursing home is posh when there's a two-year waiting list to have a wedding there.

"They don't know what the hell is wrong with me," Rosemary said as we walked along the winding path that overlooked the bay. We passed a few ladies in wheelchairs being wheeled by nurses and two old men with walkers discussing flag etiquette. There were benches everywhere filled with people taking a rest. "Doctors here are idiots," Rosemary said as a golf cart with an emergency light zipped past us. "One says anxiety, another says dementia. The latest is post-traumatic stress disorder. Oh, and bipolar. A student nurse told me yesterday that she thought I was bipolar. She read about some celebrity having it and she thinks I have it too."

"What about your hip?" I asked, confused.

"Yeah, they're less interested in that," Rosemary said. "You know, you yell at one cafeteria worker and suddenly you're bipolar."

"You're not bipolar," I said.

"Well, just to be on the safe side, I told Steve to shove me off the cliff if I start to really lose it," she said with a laugh.

I told her that Tom had already stopped in at the main office to inquire about pricing. He loved it. Everything he saw, he loved. He loved the swimming pool and the tennis courts and the library with the leather armchairs. He thought the cafeteria deserved a Michelin star. He absolutely did not stop talking about it.

Meanwhile, while Rosemary was away, we got a new

neighbor. The small blue house on the corner was sold to a nice couple from Brooklyn. They had two little girls and twins on the way. It was a matter of weeks before a Zoning Board of Appeals certified letter came in the mail. They wanted to build an extension. They wanted cathedral ceilings, walk-in closets, a mudroom, a den, a few extra bedrooms, and an attic playroom for the children.

Every weekend, they came to marvel at their new home. They never officially moved in. The only thing I saw them bring into the house was one roll of toilet paper and half a roll of paper towels. On Saturday mornings, a red Mercedes would pull into the oyster-shell driveway. The girls would sprint out of the car and head for the beach and their parents would conference with architects and builders and contractors and landscapers. By week two, there were signs surrounding the property that said, *No Trespassers. Twenty-Four-Hour Video Surveillance.*

At first, I hesitated to tell Rosemary about our new neighbors. I thought for sure, it would send her into a tailspin. The nurses told me that Rosemary was becoming more and more agitated. She fought with the other residents and insulted the staff. But, that was hardly out of character. I tried to talk about happy things when I visited. I told her about the Fourth of July parade and that Hattie was entering her third trimester.

"How's she feeling?" Rosemary asked.

"Good," I said. "She called yesterday to tell me to apologize to Andrew. So, I have that to look forward to."

"Apologize for what?" Rosemary asked.

"For sending the package with the quilt for the baby and the silk scarf for Hattie and nothing for Andrew. She said it sent a terrible message."

"No good deed," Rosemary said, shaking her head.

"And I guess I have to get him something now," I said. "What do you think, like a sweatshirt? A hat? I have no idea."

"I don't give a damn," Rosemary said. That conversation took about three minutes. Then, I was out of things to say. So, I told her about the blue house. I only brought it up once.

"They have all these plans for a big extension," I said. "You can't believe what's in their application."

"Don't worry about it," she said.

"I am worried about it," I said. "I can't go through all that again. I'll have to move. I'll have to sell the house."

"You won't have to move," she said.

"I'll have to get a lawyer, then," I said.

"We'll figure something out," she said. "Anything else?"

"Well, you'll like this," I said and Rosemary widened her eyes.

"I went to the Bay Mission meeting last night," I said.

"Oh, right. I forgot yesterday was Tuesday. Any fireworks?"

"A few," I said. "At the end of the meeting, the harmonica player asked about the finances again. You know, he did what he always does. He said, 'Let's see the finances, let's see the books, what are you hiding?' on and on."

"Mm-hmm," Rosemary said and sipped her coffee.

"So, the ladies of course dodged the question. They said everything is in good order," I said.

"Like they know," Rosemary said.

"Right," I said. "I mean, everyone in the audience basically told them they were idiots and liars."

"Sure," Rosemary said. "And that was it?"

"No," I said. "So, the harmonica player listened to all of this and then he got up out of his seat and said he wanted his money back."

"Oh," Rosemary said and took a bite of her scone. "That's new."

"And Bunny told him he should sit down and show some common courtesy or she would have to ask him to leave."

"Nice," Rosemary said.

"So, the harmonica player said he was going to call the IRS," I said, "and everyone started clapping."

"How much did he donate?" Rosemary asked.

"I had Tom look it up," I said. "Two hundred dollars."

"You know he's loaded," Rosemary said.

"Is he?" I said.

"Yep," she said. "Well, good. I hope he really does call the IRS."

"I think he will. I mean, he was mad. He left before the meeting was over."

"Good," Rosemary said. "You're right. That did cheer me up a little."

Rosemary and I never talked about nice things or good news. We complained. We whinged. That's what we did. That's all we did. Without a fight, without the Sugar Cube, without trips to town hall, what was my life here? What was my friendship with Rosemary without a common enemy? On my drive over, I would rack my brain to think of positive conversation topics. I couldn't talk about the news or politics. I tried that once and Rosemary called me a communist. Anything about the neighborhood was suddenly out of the question. Even the weather had been miserable. I honest to God could not think of one nice thing to say about anything.

In the early days, we'd meet in the cafeteria and drink coffee and talk. We'd do our best not to be negative. I'd say the food was delicious. She'd say it was edible. We'd settle on it could be worse. I remember questioning her treatment a lot, mostly because I wanted her back on Harbor Road. "I don't see why they've still got you in here," I said to her. "You're walking fine."

Most days, Rosemary didn't want to talk. I couldn't bear to sit in silence in the cafeteria. So, we stopped having coffee and talking. We started going on walks. Every day at exactly one o'clock we went for a walk. The grounds were beautiful with giant oak trees and ballerina sculptures. We followed a path that ran along the cliffs and always stopped to rest on the same bench beside the blossoming cherry tree.

Every day, we passed the same woman on our walk. She always walked alone and always wore pink. She'd smile sweetly and say, "Hello again," or "Lovely day," as she approached. This went on for weeks. She never missed a day and neither did we. It took one very blustery day for us to finally meet. "Do you mind if I join you?" she asked as Rosemary and I sat on our bench and stared out at the whitecaps on the water. The wind whipped the cherry blossom petals into tiny tornadoes at our feet.

"Of course," I said to the woman and slid closer to Rosemary.

The woman readjusted her dusty rose cardigan and ran her fingers through her wild, windswept hair.

"Phew," she said as she sat down to recover. "I thought about not coming out today. But, I figured you'd worry where I was!"

"We would worry," I said with a laugh.

"It's some day," she said. "I heard they canceled the ferries."

For a long time, we sat on that bench and talked about the weather. We talked about Rosemary's hip. The woman told us about her late husband. She explained that she had one very successful son and another less successful son. There was talk of grandchildren and stories about Whitbey in decades past. I gave a brief summary of my recent melodrama with Tom. We discussed the new art installation in the sculpture garden and the upcoming performance of *A Doll's House* in the amphitheater. We were having a very nice time.

Then, it started to rain. "My cottage is just there," the woman said and pointed to the gingerbread-like house with the turquoise shutters. "I'll make a pot of coffee," she said and we trudged like three old witches up the hill in the rain. Here's what I found out about the woman on the bench that afternoon. Her name was Grace. She loved the color pink. She was a nurse. She trained Seeing Eye dogs for twenty-five years. She had bad taste in art. She liked her coffee weak with a lot of milk. She didn't care for the meatloaf from the cafeteria. She collected all things frogs. And her son, the more successful one, owned the Sugar Cube.

"Wow," I said when I walked inside Grace's cottage.

"I know," Grace said. "Isn't it something?"

"It really is," Rosemary said. Hanging in Grace's living room was the ugliest painting that I have ever seen. I don't have the words to describe exactly what this painting looked like. It was almost otherworldly. All I can say is that it featured a somewhat demonic-looking woman, lounging in a corpse-like state on a textured lumpy yellow surface that I assume was meant to represent a sandy beach. It took up one entire wall in Grace's living room.

"You won't believe what my son paid for it," Grace said as she looked at it admiringly.

"I've seen this before," Rosemary said as she studied the curdled surface and gazed into the portrait subject's lifeless black eyes. "It was featured at one of the Bay Mission events."

"The first Bay Mission event," Grace said. "My Jack outbid everyone," she boasted. "He's very generous."

"It's lovely," I said and Rosemary gave me a look.

"Thank you," she said. "But, it's too big for this space. Jack will hang it in his house once the construction's done. He's building a beautiful house right on the water. It was supposed to be finished by now. But, he's having a little trouble getting it done."

"Oh?" I said.

"Neighbors," Grace said. "You know, they don't want their view blocked. So, they make up things, call in complaints, write nasty letters. Guess they have nothing better to do."

"Huh," Rosemary said.

"What are you going to do? There will always be jealous people, right?" Grace said with a shrug.

"Right," I said.

"Right," Rosemary said and we drank our weak coffee and looked at the ugly painting and waited for the storm to pass.

13

TO: Supervisor White (white@whitbey.gov)
FROM: Kathleen Deane (KDeane@gmail.com)
SUBJECT: Airbnb / ongoing issues

Dear Supervisor White,

I am forwarding you the Airbnb listing for 900 Harbor Road. The "House Description" was updated last night. It reads:

> Modern Retreat. This spectacular architectural wonder boasts panoramic water views from every room of the house. Guests will feel as if they have been transported to a remote island paradise. Located in the desirable hamlet of West Creek—a pristine beachside artist community. Escape the city noise and enjoy the peaceful sounds of nature at this secluded seaside retreat. Services include

> massage treatments, farm-fresh fruit / vegetable delivery, in-home private chef, wine club membership, and chauffeur. Perfect for corporate retreats, wedding parties, and bachelorette weekends. This house was designed to be on par with a five-star hotel. We offer every amenity to make our guests' experience truly special. The property is divided into two spacious, fully equipped apartments, which may be rented separately if desired. Features: infinity pool, roof deck with professional sound system (DJ available upon request), five bedrooms, five bathrooms, two chef's kitchens with Wi-Fi-enabled stainless steel appliances, two W/D units, outdoor showers, smart home technology, Tempur-Pedic mattresses, 800-thread-count sheets, kayaks, paddleboards, bicycles, and more!

As you know, my neighbor, Rosemary Preston, and I have mentioned at several meetings, over the course of many months, that we suspected that this property was nothing more than a business venture. I specifically said, "This house will be on Airbnb before June." We were dismissed by the Planning Board, the ZBA, and the Water Conservation Committee. Instead of heeding our advice, the town instead decided to believe that the owners of this home were "astronomy buffs," who needed the roof deck for "stargazing purposes." Mr. Walker claimed that he illegally divided his home into two separate apartments merely to accommodate his extremely sick and elderly mother.

He wanted her to live out her last days comfortably. Last weekend, I discovered that his mother is alive and well and living in a cottage at the Cliffs. I don't know why the pool was approved. But, the town attorney told me over the phone that he suspects it was the result of a "basic bribe."

Two months ago, the Water Conservation Committee ordered the immediate removal of several violations on this property. They included

1. *Trees in street*
2. *Floodlights*
3. *Metal cages*
4. *Waterfall*
5. *Hot tub*

As of today, these things are still in place. When can we expect them to be removed?

In other news, another home on Harbor Road was recently purchased by a couple from Brooklyn. I understand that they have grand plans for its renovation. I would hope that the mistakes of the past will not be repeated. But, I fear we are headed down a very familiar road. Two weeks ago, I requested the new owners' building permit application and was told by the secretary that I did not have permission to see it. A few days later, after a conversation with the town attorney, the secretary called to say that she would email it to me. Yesterday, I was told it was lost. Perhaps you will have better luck.

Thank you very much.

Sincerely,
Kathleen Deane

By summer, the Sugar Cube became a popular destination for bachelorette parties. The listing name was changed from "Modern Retreat" to "Girls Just Wanna Have Fun" and each weekend, a stretch limousine, sometimes two, would dump about twenty thirtysomethings onto Harbor Road. There's no way I can describe these women without sounding like an old hag. I know this, because when I tried to describe them to Tom, he told me that I sounded like an old hag. And he was right.

Sometimes, I worry that I'm a sorry excuse for a feminist. I used to be a proper feminist. I read all the right books and marched in the marches and burned my bra. I did it all. But, now I find myself saying things like, "Does a thirty-four-year-old woman wearing a tiara and a sash really advance the cause?" It just seems to me that twenty fully grown women need not risk death to capture the perfect selfie on a rotting dock. But, they do. They do it every weekend. They pop on their floral maxi dresses and their wedge sandals and their wide-brimmed straw sun hats and dangle clumsily on a narrow piece of rotted wood over a collection of jagged rocks. After the photo is taken and taken again and laughs are shared after Sally or Sandra or Sarah narrowly avoids falling to her death, the liquor store delivery truck swings by. From there, it's a lot of vomiting and screaming and music and unicorn pool floats and "Oh my God" and "Tag me in that" and so forth. And you think to yourself, *Well, they're young and it's nice to be young.* But you know what? We wouldn't do that in my day. There, I said it. You can't stop me and I said it and there it is. I'm an old hag and girls just wanna have fun. Let's just leave it at that.

The police and code enforcement were suddenly very accommodating when it came to responding to bachelorette-related code violations. They were not only willing but eager to respond quickly to noise complaints and calls about illegal fireworks. I don't particularly want to tell you that the town's chief code enforcement officer called me Kitty. But, he did. The only other person who ever called me Kitty was my aunt Ethel, who used to berate me at the dinner table about my posture and my crooked teeth.

Stanley was not the best code enforcement officer. He was always just missing a crime. He'd arrive on the scene moments after the perpetrators drove away. He misplaced evidence. He was gullible. He got locked out of his car. He'd forget the machine that measures decibels when he'd come to assess a noise complaint and when he remembered it, he didn't know how to work it. But, he always wanted to help. Truly. He was always in hot pursuit of justice. And one good thing about him was that he never hesitated to call. He always followed up. He never had good news to deliver, but he was very prompt in calling with the bad news.

For months, Stanley had been on the case, investigating an alleged second apartment in the Sugar Cube. He became aware of the illegality after some careful sleuth work revealed that 1) the owner admitted he installed the apartment, and 2) it was advertised in the real estate listing. But, according to the town, that wasn't enough proof to issue a summons. "Now, I just need a way into the house," Stanley said to me over the phone. "We'll have to wait until they let their guard down." I suggested a search warrant, but Stanley said that he'd prefer to avoid the paperwork. "It's best if we don't go the search warrant route," he said. He told me to call him when the house was rented. "Here's what we'll do," he said. "They don't have a rental permit. So, you call me when you suspect the house is rented. I'll go knock on the door and ask if it is indeed being rented. They say yes . . . bam! That's one summons. Then, I'll say something to the effect of, 'Do you mind if I inspect the property?' "

"Who would say yes to that, Stanley?" I asked.

"Oh, you'd be surprised," he said. "People see an authority figure, someone with a uniform, at the door . . . nine times out of ten they let that person in."

Each time Stanley and I tried this stunt, it failed. Every Saturday afternoon, he was rejected by a dozen women in rhinestone tiaras. One particularly cheeky group told Stanley that they weren't renting, they were sisters of the owner, Jack. They said they had flown in from Finland to celebrate his fortieth birthday with him. "False alarm," Stanley came over to tell me. "It's just his sisters."

One thing I've learned about these bachelorette parties, and I feel confident in saying I am nearly an expert, is that there is always at least one girl who doesn't want to be there. She doesn't pose for the mandatory selfie and she's usually the one emptying the liquor bottles into the appropriate recycling bins in the morning. In my case, she's the one walking on the beach beside my bedroom window at one o'clock in the morning telling her mom or boyfriend or sister or whoever what a miserable time she's having. This girl exists in every group and she's the one who will open the door. She respects authority. If anyone is keen to set off a weekend sabotage, she is.

Rebecca was sulking in a lounge chair while her group practiced making a human pyramid by the pool. "Be my guest," she said to Stanley when he asked if he could inspect the house for a possible violation. There it was—the second kitchen, the locked entrances, the washer-dryer combo on every floor. Stanley asked Rebecca to sign an affidavit confirming his observations, which she did, happily. A lawsuit was filed by the town the next week. About a week after that, Tom checked on the real estate listing. "Two spacious, fully equipped apartments . . . two chef's kitchens" was removed. He read the rest of the Sugar Cube's primary features, searching for other modifications. "Stainless steel appliances, infinity pool, Tempur-Pedic mattresses, smart home technology . . ." Tom read the list aloud as I painted seagulls with striped turtlenecks nearby. The seagull notecards had become the most popular item in Josie's shop. Tourists couldn't get enough of this dopey seagull character I had created. He always wore cardigans and turtlenecks and eyeglasses. Tom rattled off about ten more items included on the listing, before pausing.

"Oh my God," he said. "Kathleen, listen to this."

"I am listening," I said as I dabbed my paintbrush

into the crystal goblet I always used as my designated water glass.

"WBFP—Tom and Kathleen—Kiss Kiss Bye Bye," Tom said and looked over at me. "What the hell does that mean? What's WBFP?"

"Wood-burning fireplace," I said. "God, Tom, you know what *WBFP* means."

"Well, that's great!" Tom said. "That's just great! Wood-burning fireplace, Tom and Kathleen. Kiss Kiss. Bye Bye. So, what? They want to put us in the fireplace?"

"It seems that way," I said.

"Would you please get over here and look at this with me!" Tom said and carried his laptop over to the table.

"Better screenshot it," I said as I leaned over his shoulder.

"Screenshot it?" Tom said. "I'm calling the police. I'm shaking. Look at my hands," he said and held them out. "They're shaking."

"Would you stop it," I said. "They just want a reaction."

"Well, they're going to get one," Tom said. "And why the hell am I included? What did I do? You're the one who's always calling in complaints! I told you to stop talking to that Stanley, that idiot! Why does it say, 'Tom and Kathleen'? Why am I going in the fireplace? Call the supervisor," Tom said. "You have his number."

"Okay," I said a little too quickly, thrilled to finally have a worthy reason to make the call.

Supervisor White spoke very slowly and calmly. I apologized for calling and he said I was right to call. We had him on speakerphone. He told us that if we perceived the listing to be a threat, which he believed it absolutely was, then we should go straight to the police station and file a report. "Might as well forward the whole thing to the town attorney in an email as well," he said. "It's good to have these things on the record." Before we said goodbye, he told Tom that his Airstream being parked in a residential driveway was a violation of town code. "We received a complaint about it this morning," he said.

At the police station, we met with Sergeant Johnson. We told him that we'd like to file a report. We showed him the listing that we had printed up. He studied it for a few moments. "They put an awful lot of money into this house, huh?" he asked.

"Yes," I said. "They broke every town law. I mean you wouldn't believe what they've done."

"Fifteen hundred dollars a night. Wowzah," Sergeant Johnson said, still studying the listing.

"It's the bit about the wood-burning fireplace that concerns us," Tom said.

"I don't see anything about a wood-burning fireplace," he said.

"WBFP," I said.

"Are you sure that's what that means?" he asked.

"Yes," I said. "I'm sure. *WBFP* means 'wood-burning fireplace.'"

"Do they have a wood-burning fireplace?" he asked.

"I don't know," I said. "There's a chimney."

"Well, that doesn't necessarily mean that there's a fireplace."

"It doesn't matter," Tom said. "It doesn't matter if there's a fireplace or not. It's a threat."

"All right," the officer said with a sigh and scribbled

down the information on a sheet of paper. "Anything else?" he asked when he'd finished writing.

"So, that's officially filed, then?" Tom asked. "That's the report?"

"Yep," the officer said. "That's on the record," he said and folded the paper in half.

Tom started getting more involved after that. He came with me to the ZBA hearing for the blue house on the corner. We spent an entire weekend drafting a letter of opposition to the renovation proposal. It took seven drafts and three timed rehearsals. We worked on it while simultaneously collaborating on a mandatory wedding craft sent to us via expedited priority mail from Tom's sister in New Jersey. "I'm not doing this," I said when I opened the box filled with scrapbook supplies and heart confetti.

"We have to do it," Tom said. "I'll never hear the end of it. It's for our niece."

I moaned and peeled back the pastel tissue paper as if it were radioactive.

"'Celebrate Emily and Stephen,'" Tom read aloud from a glitter-covered card. "'Help us make their day special!'"

"This is because I didn't surrender the figurine," I said. "This is what I get."

"No," Tom said. "I'm sure everyone got it."

"What are the pom-poms for?" I said, lifting the bag of rainbow fluff. Tom read on.

"Here we go," he said. "Here it is at the end. We have choices. . . ."

"Oh, great," I said.

"We can write a family history," he said.

"No," I said.

"Share a personal recipe and/or a recipe for a happy marriage," he said. I laughed.

"Create a scrapbook page with the enclosed supplies," Tom went on. "Use it to share a sweet message to the happy couple. Feel free to enclose photos."

"Oy," I said.

"Or make a video tribute. Please keep to less than two minutes."

"Done," I said. "Video tribute." And I went to the deck and propped my phone against the egret statue. It was late afternoon and the sky was filled with swirls of pinks and oranges. I pulled two chairs together and positioned them carefully near the bulkhead, making sure to showcase the sun setting behind the whale- and donkey-shaped dunes in the distance. An air horn blared across the water, summoning a gaggle of miniature sailboats back to the ramshackle yacht club a few doors down. "Ready?" I called out to Tom, who was still riffling through an assortment of rose-gold stickers.

"Yep," he said and moseyed over to the edge of the deck, casually tucking in his shirt and fixing his hair as he walked.

"Quick," I said, already seated and in position. "I want to get the shot with the sailboat passing behind us."

"What are we saying?" Tom asked as he sat down, glancing over his shoulder to see the boat's progress.

"Missed it," I said.

"There'll be another one," Tom said reassuringly. "Is it all right that we're both wearing navy? Does that look odd?"

After about an hour, two outfit changes, and fifty-five takes, we gave up.

"Forget it," I said. "We'll do the scrapbook."

"You can paint something," Tom suggested as he untucked his shirt and headed back through the sliding glass doors.

"Thank you," I said and dumped the craft supplies onto the kitchen counter.

So, we hot glued and we stuck stickers and we painted and we tied tiny ribbons and bows as we drafted our ZBA letter. We wrote the letter. We rewrote the letter. Whatever they said, whatever insane argument they made, we were ready for it. I briefed Tom on the ZBA members while we cut hearts out of construction paper like we were unwitting participants in a corporate team-building exercise. We pored over the blueprints. We studied environmental assessment reviews. Who needs crossword puzzles? I introduced Tom to what had become the source of all my wisdom and arguably my most prized possession. Let's just say that if the house caught on fire, it wouldn't be the diamond engagement ring or the Limoges dishes or even Louise's damn figurine that I would save. I'd save the cardboard Christmas box with the snowman on the lid—no question. This box, which later got me out of a terrible jam, was overflowing with letters and emails and proposals and blueprints. There were copies of agendas and minutes and tax maps. There were newspaper articles and hundreds of bits of paper and blank envelopes and Post-its and business cards where I had scribbled random pieces of information. Every time I made any contact with the town, I made a note of it and threw it in the box. I secured the whole thing with a red grosgrain ribbon.

But, it just so happened that we didn't need the box. We didn't need the five-page, triple-spaced, size-sixteen-font speech or the photos or anything. All our arguments and counterarguments and debate prep was for naught. The application was denied on the spot. The hearing only lasted a few minutes. No discussion, no comments, no nothing. Tom and I couldn't believe it. We were robbed. All that preparation and time wasted. Tom was going to quote Oscar Wilde and everything. "It was a good speech," I said to him as the ZBA members moved on to the next agenda item.

"Yeah," he said and folded the paper in half.

"I don't get it," I whispered to Tom as the lawyer for the blue house, seeing our obvious disappointment, came over to commiserate with us.

"Do they usually do this?" the lawyer asked us, leaning over one of the folding chairs.

"Never," I said, finding myself suddenly on the same team with the enemy.

"Well, it's not like we were in favor of the application," Tom was quick to tell the lawyer.

"Right," I said. "But, still . . ."

"Exactly," the lawyer said. "You want to make your case."

"We had a whole thing prepared. You know you lied in the application about the square footage of the lot. It's fifty-four hundred, not seven thousand, six hundred fifty."

"It's based on a tie line," the lawyer said.

"Oh, please," I said. "You think I haven't seen that trick before? You draw a line out in the middle of the water and say it's yours. Come on."

"All right," Tom whispered. "We got what we wanted, right, Kathleen? Let's go."

"They've got twins," the lawyer said.

"Oh, they have twins. Why didn't you say so? Tom, you hear that? They have twins. Never mind, then. Build whatever you want."

At that point, the ZBA chairman scolded us and asked us to leave.

"Please respect the board and the other applicants," he said. "This is not a public forum."

"Yes, it is!" the lawyer and I both said in unison.

In the lobby, Tom, the lawyer, and I continued our discussion. Tom unfolded his speech and started to read excerpts from it and I did everything in my power not to be a stereotypical local and say the words that, regretfully, immediately came to mind: "Go back to Brooklyn."

In the end, we won. The lawyer went home and the next day, a lady in a silver sedan pulled into the blue house's driveway and placed a For Sale sign in the front yard. *The Twenty-Four-Hour Surveillance* signs were removed and the landscapers stopped coming.

"Well?" I said to Tom about a week later. "What do you think about that?"

"About what?" he said.

"About the house, Tom," I said. "About the ZBA denying the application for the blue house."

"I did hear that Mitsy wrote a letter about it to Supervisor White. That might have done it," he said.

"Mitsy?" I said. "You think one email from Mitsy did it?"

"Could be," Tom said.

"Not me or Rosemary?"

"No, you too," he said. "You both did a lot. But Mitsy, she's really upset about all this stuff. You know? She's fired up about it."

"Mitsy doesn't know what planet she's on," I said.

"Oh, I'm sure she does," Tom said. "She's a hell of a pickleball player."

The point is, I was at the finish line. Nothing was resolved with Tom. He was still somehow both the best and worst person I knew. But, the town was officially suing the owners of the Sugar Cube. All plans for the blue house had been stopped in their tracks. I should have been happy or at least relieved. Tom was. He sold the Airstream and bought a sailboat. He anchored it directly in front of the house and used a rowboat to reach it.

"What is your plan?" I asked him one day while he was musing about his sailboat.

"What do you mean?" he said, as if nothing had happened between us. As if he hadn't left me for the *Queen Mary*. As if we weren't in the throes of a divorce and basically coexisting in a seven-hundred-square-foot house.

"I'd just like to know what your plan is, so that I can know what it is," I said.

"Okay," he said.

"So, what is it?" I said.

"I don't know," he said.

"Okay," I said.

"Okay," he said and that's all we said about that.

The next week, I turned sixty. I spent the day serving cheese balls and washing dishes at a Bay Mission fundraiser. I was a rotten director of fundraising. Josie put me on cheese ball duty after she caught me refusing to accept a $10,000 check for a lousy painting of a tulip. After that, Josie took over. She successfully tricked seven very gullible people into buying truly terrible paintings for outrageous prices. And she did it all while wearing a floor-length peasant skirt. The best was, they were happy to do it. Some paid more than she asked. A few put their names on waiting lists and provided generous down payments. And by the way, when I say the paintings were lousy and terrible, I don't mean they weren't my taste. I mean they were lousy and terrible. I should know. I was the artists' teacher.

Every Monday and Thursday, I taught beginning watercolors to a group of retirees on the pier. It was a "senior arts outreach program," run by the Bay Mission. Josie, of course, was the brainchild behind it. "It'll be a bit of art therapy," Josie said. "Just show them the basics." So, I did. We started slow. We mixed colors. We tried gradients. In the third class, we tried a basic landscape. By the end of the second week, each and every one of my students was selling their paintings for five-figure sums. All money was donated to the Bay Mission.

"People just want to contribute to the cause," Josie assured me. "It's not about the paintings. They'd give money anyway."

"I guess," I said as we sat together at the end of the night and shared a piece of leftover strawberry shortcake. The tent had cleared out and only a few stragglers remained.

"It's like when you adopt an elephant or something," Josie said. "You're not really doing it for the stuffed animal and the certificate that comes in the mail."

"Right," I said as Josie gathered up the checks and neatly tucked them in an envelope. "It's just a lot of money," I said.

"Well, depending on what we decide to do with the property, it's going to cost a lot of money," she said. "The bulkhead repair alone is going to run us half a million." This made sense to me. "Sign this," Josie said and slid the event report across the table. I looked over the paper and signed on the dotted line.

"Forty-five thousand dollars tonight?" I said.

"Yep," Josie said. "I think next time we'll do a theme night. Spice things up," she said. "Maybe we can get a local band to play. Do you think these events are feeling stale?"

"A little," I said.

"God, I can't believe you're sixty," Josie said and took a sip of champagne.

"You're fifty-nine," I said.

"Exactly," she said. "Happy birthday." She reached in her bag, pulled out a small box, and plopped it on the table in front of me. "Seeing how you're a beach girl now," she said.

"I'm going to be so disappointed if this isn't what I think it is," I said as I peeled back the lid.

"Well, you've only been asking for it for fifty years," she said.

"Oh my God," I said as I pulled the dashboard hula girl from the box. "I love her," I said as I set her down and gently gave her little grass skirt a push.

"It was hell trying to find her," Josie said. "I searched every box in the attic. And then, I had to call Johnny, which you know I love to do."

"How is he?" I asked, still admiring the hula girl on the table.

"Still rotten," she said. "Mom spoiled him."

"And he had the hula girl?" I asked.

"Well, he denied it at first," she said. "But, last week she arrived in the mail. She's still a little dusty. God knows where she's been."

"She's perfect," I said and dusted her off. "This shouldn't make me this happy. But, it does," I said.

"I'm glad you're here," Josie said as she dove her fork onto my plate and finished off the last bite of cake.

"Me too," I said.

I found out rather quickly that I didn't particularly like being sixty. No one does. For one thing, your knees hurt. That's probably the biggest thing. Knees don't last. No one tells you that. They have a shelf life. They stop working. I don't care who you are. I don't care how much yoga you did or how many kale salads you ate. You can get steroid injections. You can have surgery. You can take pills. But, the best and most popular remedy is commiserating with other people whose knees hurt and you can find them just about anywhere.

I've stopped going to the doctor altogether. As you get older, they start finding stuff. They start ordering tests. Last year, I broke a rib while cleaning the bathtub. I went to the emergency room and found out that, beside the broken rib, I had twelve other abnormalities that showed up on my CT scan. Now, I have a list of bumps and lumps on various organs that my doctor and I have to "keep an eye on" until the end of time. Last week, Tom tried to get new reading glasses and he came out with an appointment for cataract surgery. Speaking of eyes, don't be alarmed when you suddenly see wiggling tentacles appearing in your peripheral vision. That, apparently, is merely a side effect of the sixty-year-old jelly in your eye gradually liquifying.

And, by the way, don't expect any special treatment or sympathy when you get these diagnoses. Post sixty, doctors become very cavalier about non-life-threatening things. You are meant to just take it. Unless the hideous mole on your back is malignant, it is staying right where it is. And if it is malignant, fear not, it will be scooped out and replaced with a tremendous crater. You'll get used to the tentacles and flashes of light in your eyes. Try not to think about them. Don't worry about that clicking in your shoulder. Be happy that only one of your fingers locks in a bent position. Lose weight.

So, suddenly I was sixty and almost overnight I realized that I had bad knees and eye floaters and a trigger finger and moles on my back and cysts on my liver. I accepted these things. I made peace with them. They were a nuisance to no one but me. And it isn't really your own aches and pains and medical curiosities that you have to worry about when you get older. It's everyone else's. Tell me this: Do all men over sixty have a perpetual cough, or is it just the ones I know?

Here's a piece of marriage advice you won't hear

anywhere else. It involves one word and if you happen to be marrying a man, it will be a word that will rear its ugly head throughout your marriage. The word is *phlegm.* Now, you may say to yourself, *The man I intend on marrying has never and would never talk about phlegm.* You are wrong. He will. That handsome thirty-year-old in the tux at the other end of the aisle will one day start coughing and, believe it or not, he just won't stop. You'll think it's walking pneumonia or allergies or tonsilitis. But, it is not. It never is. You will spend the rest of your life or his listening to your former dreamboat painting you a vivid picture of the phlegm that will be caught in his throat from now until eternity. So, do yourself a favor and ask yourself a question before the wedding day: *Would constant coughing and throat clearing and talk of phlegm make me love this man any less than I do today?* That's the barometer.

Tom, I'm happy to say, has a mild case of this condition. He has a permanent dignified lump in his throat that he delicately jostles with a polite "ahem" every few minutes. Rosemary's husband, Steve, on the other hand, has a sort of blitzkrieg-style cough. It is an infrequent, but impressive attack that occurs when you least expect it. It just about stops your heart every time it happens.

The night Rosemary was checked into rehab, Steve came over for dinner. Tom invited him. "He can't cook," Tom said. We had salmon and roasted potatoes and asparagus. Tom even made a batch of vegan oatmeal-raisin cookies for dessert. We mostly talked about bicycles. After dinner, Tom and Steve got their fishing poles and "threw a few casts" off the deck for an hour while I scowled at them from the medical-grade couch inside. The next night, Steve was back. We had roast chicken. I asked Steve how long Rosemary was expected to stay in rehab.

"A month," he said. "Maybe two."

"Huh," I said.

He was right. Rosemary spent over a month in rehab. She wined and dined at the Cliffs while I listened to a cacophony of coughs in the oyster shack. The good news was, it did inspire me to get out of the house more. I went to restaurants by myself. I went to a concert alone. I even took Josie up on her offer to do hot yoga, an experience I cannot recommend. If there was a reason why I started gravitating more toward Josie and the Bay Mission and the Birch Street Bitches, it was Steve's cough.

14

TO: Supervisor White (white@whitbey.gov)
FROM: Kathleen Deane (KDeane@gmail.com)
SUBJECT: Renters

Dear Supervisor White,

Could you please give me an update on the status of the pending litigation for 900 Harbor Road? As I understand it, there have been at least six appeals filed by the owners and there appears to be no end in sight. This has been going on for months. Every time a construction crew arrives at the property, I expect one of the many outstanding violations to be removed as per court orders. But, that never happens. Instead, more illegal structures are added and/or improved. Our town code requires an engineer-certified rental permit and states that no property shall be rented for less than thirty days. So, how are my neighbors, who do not have a rental permit, allowed to rent their house with a million violations to a new group of people every weekend?

I have tried to be patient. After being threatened with a wood-burning fireplace execution, I have opted not to report the last ten groups of renters to code enforcement. I have looked the other way. But, I cannot be silent anymore. As I've explained to you before, this property was exclusively being used as a bachelorette weekend destination. Every Friday afternoon, like clockwork, limos full of bachelorettes would arrive on the scene. This was not my favorite thing in the world, but I could live with it.

This latest group of renters, however, are not bachelorettes. On the evening of Friday, June 25, approximately fifteen people were dropped off by six black SUVs with tinted windows. The next morning, a truck came and unloaded very large professional lighting equipment, a refrigerator, tripods, and what looked like antique steamer trunks. I have not seen one person leave the house. It's been two weeks! Every day, more people are dropped off. But, no one leaves. There is no noise. No lights. The only thing that is delivered to the house is more people. Most don't have luggage. There are fourteen unopened copies of The New York Times *piled in the driveway and every morning there are at least fifteen bags of garbage neatly stacked outside the house. Who are these people?*

At least, with the bachelorettes, they would say good morning and hello and I knew I was living next to basically normal people. Now, I don't know what to think. At first, I was horrified at the idea of this property possibly being used as some sort of underground drug den. But, then, my husband, who, by the way, has gotten rid of his Airstream per your request, told me that he suspected that this new group of renters are in the pornographic film industry. And now I find myself hoping that it is a drug den and praying for the day that the bachelorettes return.

I know there is nothing you can do about this. But, I thought I'd let you know. I also wanted to say that I was very surprised with the recent determination of the ZBA regarding my newest neighbor's construction plans. Of course, I wish the ZBA had come to its senses sooner. But, either way, good for the town for finally erring on the side of preservation and common sense.

Sincerely,
Kathleen Deane

P.S. Every night between 11:30 p.m. and midnight, someone drives by my house in a white pickup truck and blasts their horn. I have tried and failed to catch a glimpse of the license plate. Do you know, by chance, if Mr. Jones of the traffic committee drives a white pickup? If yes, then, I think now is the time to make a formal complaint to the ethics committee.

I had anxiety before it was trendy to have anxiety—before the entire world needed weighted blankets and soothing essential oils and adult coloring books just to get through the day. I was deep breathing and meditating twenty years before there was an app to help you do it. I'm pretty sure I invented the fidget spinner in 1994, but who can remember? When *The Secret* came out in 2006, I started journaling. I wrote, "I will own a beach house," on the top of every page. And it worked. It really worked. I manifested my very own beach house. Of course, along the way I also lost my husband, my very nice Kansas house, all my friends, my mother's art deco furniture, and worst of all, my mind. Here is a list of all the brand-new never-before-seen anxiety symptoms that I have developed since moving to so-called paradise:

1. Sweating—intermittently, profusely, and only from the top of my head.
2. Severe headache in the middle of my left eyebrow—don't know why, hurts like hell.
3. Heart palpitations—only when shopping.
4. TMJ—jaw pain—caused by clenching of teeth when sleeping and writing emails to Supervisor White.
5. Skin crawling—previously thought to be bedbugs—casualties include one mattress, one mattress topper, two sheet sets, all pajamas.
6. Numb right foot—especially helpful when driving.
7. Pityriasis rosea—splotchy red skin rash all over back and stomach—very attractive, no cure.
8. Teeth grinding—$800 custom-made mouth guard now required.
9. Feeling like throat is closing—sometimes when eating apples at home—always when eating apples in car.
10. Appendicitis—not yet, but I'm waiting for it, and I always feel like I have it.

I'm sure there are more. . . . I wouldn't even bring this up, because honestly, when I look at this list now (which, by the way, I compiled as part of a therapy exercise) it makes me look insane, which I guess was the point of the exercise. But if you happen to be suffering from anxiety, which, of course you are, take comfort in the fact that you are not alone, and whatever you have, I've probably had something weirder.

The truth is, anxiety is the least of my troubles. In the last year or so, I have aged. I look about ten years older than I did in Kansas City. I found out the hard way that scowling over a stockade fence for over a year causes deep frown lines and crow's feet that no amount of creams or lotions or jade rollers will eliminate. Let's face it, if your computer screen is covered with Post-it Note references to wetland permits from the '70s, chances are things are not going great for you and you are in all likelihood suffering mental deficits as a result.

Around this time, when the summer tourist merriment was truly in full swing, I closed the windows and the shades in my little oyster shack. I blasted the air-conditioning, not to relieve the heat, but to block out the noise from the revelers. I stopped showering every day. I cursed my neighbors daily. I dreamed up ways to ruin everyone's fun. I could poke holes in their pool floats and throw sand in their ice cream cones. I could gather up their beach balls and pails and fishing poles and pickleball rackets and put them in a big sack and throw them over a cliff. If you think about it, there are very few things that separated me from the Grinch. I had a lair. I was smelly. I lived alone. I hated a particular season. I couldn't stand my neighbors and I wanted desperately to steal their toys. Sadly, the only difference is that, at the end of the day, it wasn't my heart that grew three sizes. It was my ass.

Sebastian, the life coach, told me that I needed to find purpose. I was feeling very good about myself for a minute. After all, I was doing things. I was volunteering and teaching classes and walking Rosemary around the Cliffs every day. "But are those things purposeful?" Sebastian asked me.

"I don't know what else they'd be," I said.

"I mean are they necessary?" Sebastian asked.

"No," I said. "None of this is necessary. And yet, here we are," I said.

"It's a very common problem for retirees," Sebastian said. "They feel like they're not needed."

"I am needed," I said.

"For what?" Sebastian said and raised his eyebrows in anticipation.

"Well, for one thing, I'm the only one keeping this town government in check. Me and Rosemary," I said.

"And is that your job?" Sebastian said.

"Apparently," I said. "No one else will do it."

"Does it make you happy?" he asked. "Does it fulfill you?"

"No," I said. "I hate it."

"So, why do you keep doing it?" Sebastian asked.

"Well, maybe I should just open a store and sell overpriced tchotchkes like Josie. Would that be purposeful?" I said.

"Yes," he said. "Josie is purposeful."

"And I'm not?" I said.

"That's right," he said. "Josie is doing things that benefit Josie. You are doing things that benefit who?"

"Society," I said.

"Nobody," Sebastian said and took a sip of his mimosa. "And frankly, I'm tired of hearing about it," he said. "When was the last time you had fun?"

"Well, now I don't want to tell you," I said.

"Go on," he said.

"You'll say it's not purposeful," I said.

"Having fun is always purposeful," Sebastian said. "As long as no one gets hurt, it's purposeful."

"Fine," I said and proceeded to tell Sebastian about the time I caught a quorum of the traffic committee clandestinely meeting at a coffee shop in town.

"Kathleen," he said, exasperated.

"No, listen," I said. "They haven't met in nine months; you know, after Rosemary and I called them all crooks at the December meeting. Remember that?" I said.

"I remember," Sebastian said and drooped ever so slightly in his seat.

"Right, so they're supposed to be meeting and everyone said, 'Oh, they're not meeting anymore, you know, because of what you did in December.' But, it turns out they are meeting. At the coffee shop. Six of them. Twice a month. Mondays. There's only ten of them on the committee. Six is a quorum. They're not allowed to do that."

"And this is fun for you?" Sebastian said.

"Yeah, well, I caught them red-handed," I said. "They were just sitting there with their coffees and Danish and I walked right up to them and I told them, I said, 'This is a quorum, right here, fellas.'"

"Fellas?" Sebastian said.

"Yeah, well, if you saw them it'd make sense. They're sort of fella-type guys."

"Okay," Sebastian said. "And then what?"

"And then nothing," I said. "I got them. I caught them. That's it."

"And that was the last time you had fun?"

"Yes," I said.

At my age, I shouldn't have needed a life coach. But, the thought of it was so appealing–someone to coach you on life. What could be better than that? It was exactly what I wanted. I wanted instructions–a handbook–someone to tell me exactly what to do and when to do it. Go here, see this, do that, and voilà, happiness. I didn't want to talk about my "issues" or my childhood or the neuroses I have honed and perfected over the course of a lifetime. I didn't want someone to understand or empathize or hear me out. I wanted a coach. I wanted someone with a clipboard and a playbook–someone who would blow a whistle in my face when I said things like "Why me?"

Sebastian tried to do this for me. He gave it his best shot. He told me to be purposeful, to meet new people, to learn to let things go. We talked about goals and dreams and vision boards and the power of positive thinking. Sebastian told me that in his professional opinion, having been certified through a now unaccredited three-week intensive life-coaching crash course, it was the town that was the root of my unhappiness and overall anxiety-related issues. It wasn't Tom or Kansas or being a retired empty nester. It was the town and the Sugar Cube and the Bay Mission and all the rest of it. "Lose it," he said. "If you do nothing else, disassociate from the town government. Stop emailing the supervisor. Stop going to the meetings and weighing in on the parking situation. It's a crutch," he said. "It's holding you back."

Sebastian was very wise when he wanted to be. He made an excellent case. It was good advice. It made sense. And the best part was, it was simple. It didn't require medication or workbooks or digging up old traumas. This didn't have to be something I worked on for years. I could solve it overnight. It was a behavior. It was a bad habit. Just stop doing it. Change one little thing. How hard is that?

In 1971, my mother hired a man to install a fence in our backyard. My father thought it was a bad idea. Our neighbor Mr. Beneventi thought it was an outrage. Mr. Beneventi loved our backyard. He used it all the time. In the winters, his children would sled down our hill and in the summers, the whole Beneventi clan would have cookouts and picnics. Every morning, Mr. Beneventi cut through our yard for his morning walk and when he came home, he did his daily stretching in front of our kitchen window. So, the fence went up. My mother said it was for the best. After all, good fences make good neighbors. For a while, Mr. Beneventi was able to squeeze through a skinny slot where the new fence met the old oak tree on the corner of the property. Mr. Beneventi was not a small man. So, it was only with great difficulty that he was able to shimmy through. My mother chose to let this go and look the other way.

Then, one morning, Mr. Beneventi got tired of shimmying. He took a saw and carved out a nice big chunk of our hundred-year-old tree to widen the gap. The next day, my mother had the fence man install another slat. The day after that, Mr. Beneventi parked his station wagon at the foot of our shared driveway and left it there for a year. And, so, it became the year of the fence. My father complained every morning about parking on the street. My mother spent a lot of time peering out the kitchen window diligently surveilling the slats in the fence and keeping watch over the old oak tree. Mr. Beneventi stopped speaking to us. We stopped speaking to Mr. Beneventi. The day the fence came down my father turned to my mother and said, "I knew that shared driveway was going to be a problem." And that was it. We were all friends again. A few years before my mother died, she asked me if I remembered the Beneventis. I said I remembered the fence. "What fence?" she said.

I don't know whether or not people are capable of change. But, I know they don't like to change. I know that if you give a dog fresh chicken when he's sick, he's not going to eat dry nuggets when he feels better. I know that once you have a dishwasher, you can't go back to washing dishes by hand. And I knew that even though it was bad for me and even though it was against professional advice, I was going to keep emailing the supervisor. I was going to continue to wake up each morning and check the town website for news bulletins. I wasn't going to stop writing down the dates of the renters' arrivals and departures in my marble composition notebook. And you can be sure that when I got a call from the newly appointed citizen concern coordinator for a sit-down meeting with the supervisor, I accepted.

Arthur Quigley was the citizen concern coordinator for the town of Whitbey. He was a central vacuum salesman, turned youth minister, turned retiree, turned president of the shellfish committee. He was also arguably the nicest guy in town. Just before Memorial Day, Arthur was promoted from unpaid volunteer shellfish committee president to official citizen concern coordinator, a two-hundred-thousand-dollar-per-year, full-benefits, totally made-up position that I, for one, thought was an entirely worthy investment. Rosemary thought so too. He was her prom date in 1968.

A month or two after Rosemary was sprung from the Cliffs with a clean bill of health and a still undiagnosed source of irritability, we went to town hall to meet with Arthur Quigley and Supervisor White about parking restrictions. Rosemary and I had drafted a proposal. It started as a way to pass the time during rehab and sort of evolved into a formal traffic study, complete with graphs and maps and photos and interviews and data. When we were done, I emailed the draft proposal to the supervisor, who emailed it to the clerk, who forwarded it to Arthur, who called to tell me that he was very impressed. He even thanked me for all my hard work. Then, he invited me in for a "chat." He said he'd love to hear more of my ideas. It just about took my breath away.

For better or for worse, it didn't take long for Arthur to become the go-to guy in town hall. All complaints, concerns, and questions landed on his desk. No matter who you called, no matter what number you dialed, if there was even a hint of a complaint in your voice, your call was going to be transferred to Arthur. I don't know whose idea it was to hire Arthur, but whoever it was, they knew what the hell they were doing. They knew that at the end of the day, people in Whitbey didn't care if things got done or fixed or resolved. They just wanted to be heard. "A willingness to listen" was what the supervisor called it. People just wanted someone to say, "You're exactly right," or "That does sound terrible," or "I can't believe that happened to you." Arthur couldn't do anything. He didn't have any power. All he could do was commiserate and amazingly, he was the only person employed by the Town of Whitbey who was capable of accomplishing that task.

Suddenly, Arthur handled everything. He was in charge of all the things no one else wanted to do. You were overcharged for your dump sticker? Call Arthur. Someone needs to fill out a long, complicated legal form to receive a crucial grant to keep the town running? Arthur can do that. Did the board create another unenforceable law? Did it illegally destroy incriminating documents? That's Arthur's fault. What can we say? He's new.

"Now, you know what you're going to say, right?" Rosemary said as we walked up the steps of the familiar old brick building on Main Street. "I don't want you embarrassing me." I grabbed her arm to help her up the steps and she slapped it away.

"So, what did you wear?" I said.

"When?" Rosemary said.

"To the prom?" I said.

"I swear to God if you say anything about my hip while we're in there," Rosemary said. "Pink tulle," she added as we entered the lobby.

"I can't picture that," I said.

"Yeah, well, it's still in my closet," she said. "And don't say anything about that either."

Supervisor White's office was on the second floor of the building across the hall from the Planning Department. It was not what I expected it to be. For one thing, I expected him to be in it. "Bad news," Arthur said when we arrived at the supervisor's door. "Supervisor White won't be able to make it."

"Shocker," Rosemary said and Arthur cracked a smile.

"How are you, Rosy?" Arthur said and gave her a kiss on the cheek. With that, all was forgiven.

"Where is he?" I said, still disappointed at the news.

"Budget meeting," Arthur said and shrugged. "But, I'll fill him in on everything. Don't worry. Come on in," he said and waved us to the two leather captain's chairs beside the desk. Rosemary started in with our presentation straightaway. She pulled a stack of papers out of her bag and jumped into statistics and beach capacity and parking violations. "You know how it is down there," she said and Arthur closed his eyes and nodded sympathetically. Soon after that, Arthur and Rosemary took a stroll down memory lane. They reminisced about old classmates and bonfires. They asked about each other's spouses and children.

I wasn't listening. I was too busy surveying Supervisor White's office. There was something odd about it—something strange, and yet very familiar. At first, I didn't think anything of the white mason jar holding pens on his desk. I didn't give the photo of his family in the whitewashed driftwood frame a second look. But, then there were the decorative white seashells in the white ceramic bowls. There were the white thimbles and the antique glass doorknobs sitting on the bookshelves. Like a real-life Hansel and Gretel, Josie had left a trail of bread crumbs in her wake. Only in her case, the bread crumbs were freshly painted knickknacks and tchotchkes.

"What do you think about that, Kathleen?" I heard Arthur ask, jolting me back to reality.

"I'm sorry, about what?" I said.

"For God's sake, Kathleen. Are you even listening? The committee. Arthur is asking if we'd like to run a new oversight committee."

"Oh," I said and Rosemary started widening her eyes and nodded her head in my direction. "I guess, yes," I said.

"Fantastic," Arthur said. "You two will be cochairs and we'll leave it up to you on how you organize the committee . . . how many members . . . mission statement . . . and so on. . . ."

"And Supervisor White is okay with this?" I asked.

"It was his idea," Arthur said. "He's thrilled. You know, just the other day he said to me, 'We need more people like Rosemary and Kathleen in this town.'"

"He didn't," Rosemary said.

"He did!" Arthur said. "He said exactly those words and then he brought up the committee idea."

"Huh," I said.

"That's wonderful," Rosemary said.

"Well, we want you to hold our feet to the fire. That's democracy, right? If there's something that's not right, we want to hear about it and we want to fix it. It's as simple as that. Listen," Arthur said and leaned over the desk. "We know what happened with the Sugar Cube wasn't right. Supervisor White knows it. We all know it. Everyone who drives by the damn thing knows it. But, it happened. And our job is to make sure it doesn't happen again. Right?"

"Right," Rosemary said.

"But, why did it happen?" I asked.

"I don't know," Arthur said. "I mean, I wasn't here."

"Right," I said.

"But, that's the kind of thing this committee will address, you know? It's a new day here in Whitbey thanks to you two."

We walked out of that office on cloud nine. We had won. This was it. This was what victory felt like. There was an admission of wrongdoing and the slightest hint of an apology. All the emails and the meetings and the phone calls, they had paid off. It turns out, you can fight city hall. Persistence. Tenacity. That's what it takes to really make a difference. I felt a wave of relief wash over me as I exited the building. Everything seemed possible, doable. *Now,* I thought, *I can live. I can fix up the house. I can deal with Tom. I can go visit Hattie. I can be better. I will be better. Life will be wonderful.*

"Hey," I said to Rosemary as we crossed the parking lot to our cars. "Did you notice . . ."

"Yeah, I'm sure he's sleeping with her," Rosemary said.

"I knew you were going to say that," I said.

"So, why'd you ask me?" she said and opened her car door. "Anyway, I told you that Josie was no good."

"No, you didn't," I said.

"Well, it was implied," she said.

"It's probably just something with his name, you know? Supervisor White . . . it's all white stuff—the thimbles, the mason jars, the picture frame. Josie probably just saw it as a business opportunity."

"I bet she did," Rosemary said and lifted her eyebrows in a way I'm sure she thought was cute, but wasn't. "Who cares? Didn't you hear? It's a new day in Whitbey. There's an oversight committee now," she said. "We're in charge. We'll have the whole affair investigated if we want to! We have the power!" she said, shaking her fist in the air.

"It's already gone to your head," I said.

"You bet," she said as she carefully guided herself into the driver's seat, making sure not to let on to any residual hip pain. "And, hey," she said, rolling down her window. "Good work."

On my way home, I swung by the Cultured Pearl to do some snooping. The hand-lettered sign on the door read, *Meet us at the beach,* a common expression used by the businesses in Whitbey to say, "Closed," while also implying a whimsical taste of small-town charm and carefreeness. I peeked in the windows to see if Josie was busy in the back spray-painting antique lamps or rearranging baby's breath or, perhaps, entertaining a certain visitor. But, there was no sign of her. So, I stopped in at the farm stand up the road and got a celebratory cochair of the oversight committee cider doughnut to eat on the drive back to Harbor Road.

As I made my way down the causeway, I took in the

sights with fresh eyes. It was a hot summer day with just enough of a breeze to whip up a few whitecaps on the water. I ate my doughnut, rolled down the windows of my station wagon, and pretended I was in a convertible. I turned up the radio. I sang. My dusty 1950s hula girl danced on the dashboard. I tapped one hand on the side of the car along to the beat and the other hand I casually drooped over the top of the steering wheel like I was a man with a Porsche and a delayed midlife crisis. I regretted the fact that I didn't have a silk scarf handy to wrap around my windblown hair. Still, I made do with Tom's old Kansas City Chiefs baseball cap that I found crumpled in the cupholder. I may not have looked it, but I felt terrific.

I arrived home to discover a shiny black sedan parked in my driveway. *Probably a renter from next door,* I thought. I blocked him in. *Let him wait,* I said to myself. Then I saw a man nervously poke his head out the car window and I thought better of that idea. I was going to rise above it and be the better person. After all, it was a new day in Whitbey.

The man introduced himself as Agent Hart. "We're canvassing the area," he said as he stepped out of his car and into the driveway. "May I come in?" he asked and held up his badge.

"Okay," I said, reluctantly recalling Stanley's statistic and sort of wishing I were brave enough to be the one out of ten people who didn't let the authority figure in a uniform into the house. "Nice view," he said as he studied my little house and looked out the sliding glass doors that lined the back wall.

"Thank you," I said.

"So," he said and started fishing through his briefcase. "We're looking for a sexual predator in the area."

"Is it the harmonica player?" I asked.

"What?" the agent said.

"Nothing," I said.

"Here's a picture of him," he said and handed me a photo. The man in the photo looked like a stock image of a serial killer. This was not a person that you would see and forget. His face still flashes in my mind from time to time.

"No," I said immediately and handed him the photo back. I was sort of sorry to disappoint Agent Hart. So, I said, "Let me ask my husband."

"Okay," Agent Hart said. "Is he here?"

"He's over there," I said and pointed to the blue sailboat bobbing in the water. "It'll just take a minute." Tom mostly stayed on his boat at night and rowed in to shore to have breakfast in the mornings at the house. He picked up a pair of walkie-talkies for us. "There's no cell service on the boat," he said when he handed me the blue-and-green device. "You know, if you need me," he said. I said that I would never need it. I said I didn't want it. But, then again, I hadn't anticipated a federal agent showing up to the house.

"Tom?" I said over the walkie-talkie. "Can you come to the house? There's someone here who needs to speak to you."

"Who is it?" Tom asked.

"Just come over," I said.

"Ten-four!" he beamed back. Agent Hart and I watched

as Tom plopped into his rowboat and started rowing toward the beach.

"I tried to knock on your neighbor's door across the street but there was no answer," Agent Hart said.

"That's my friend Rosemary's house," I said. "I was just with her at town hall. I think she said she was stopping at the supermarket on her way home. She should be back . . ."

"No, not that house," Agent Hart said. "The one on the corner. The blue house," he said and pointed in that direction.

"Oh, sorry," I said. "They don't live here full-time. Actually, I haven't seen them since a ZBA hearing a few months ago. They wanted to do a big extension like this monstrosity next door. But it was denied. Thank God."

"I saw that driving up," Agent Hart said.

"Well, it's hard to miss," I said as Tom climbed the stairs to the deck. "Tom," I said. "This is Agent Hart. He wants to know if you've seen this sexual predator?"

"What?" Tom said.

"Show him the photo," I said to Agent Hart.

Tom looked at the photo carefully.

"He looks familiar," Tom said.

"What?" I said. "He looks familiar? Well, where have you seen him?"

"I don't know. I can't place him," Tom said.

"You can't place him? Well, that's great, Tom," I said.

"Hold on, now," Tom said. "Let me try to think of it."

"That's all right," Agent Hart said and put the photo away.

"How could you not remember?" I said to Tom.

"It's absolutely fine," Agent Hart said. "So, the blue house. You said you saw the owners at a ZBA hearing?"

"That's right," I said. "Tom was with me."

"What?" Tom said.

"The ZBA hearing," I said. "When we talked to the lawyer."

"For the Sugar Cube?" Tom asked, puzzled.

"Tom, I swear to God. The blue house. The application was denied. We were all asked to leave. They didn't let anyone talk. . . ."

"Oh, right. That's right. I was there. She's right. Too bad they changed their minds about that."

"What do you mean they changed their minds? About what?" I said as Agent Hart helped himself to a seat on the couch.

"I must have told you," Tom said.

"No, you didn't," I said. "This is what I mean. This is exactly what I was telling Sebastian." I turned to address Agent Hart. "This is what he does," I said. "I ask him every day, 'Did you see anyone? Did you hear anything? Is there any news?' and every day, he says no. And here we are, now there's news. Well, what is it?"

"Who's Sebastian?" Agent Hart asked.

"My life coach," I said and he nodded his head and made a note in his notepad. "Are you writing that down?"

"No," Agent Hart said.

"Good," I said. "So, what happened with the blue house?" I asked Tom.

"Nothing," he began, as he always did. "I was talking to Marjorie. . . ."

"Marjorie is on the Bay Mission with me," I interrupted to tell Agent Hart. "She lives on Fourth Street."

Agent Hart nodded.

"Right," Tom said. "I bumped into her on my walk with Roger the other day and we were talking about the parking and the traffic and whatnot. You know, she brought up Howard's hedges again, the ones that are planted on town property."

"Oh, she never misses a chance to bring that up," I said.

"Exactly," Tom said. "Actually, I know what it was. She said something about the new house that is going up on Plum Street, the giant one with the steel skeleton, and then the blue house on the corner came up. I said something like, 'We dodged a bullet with that one,' and then she told me that she heard that the ZBA had rescinded their earlier denial and now the application was approved and construction was going to start soon."

"She heard from where?" I said.

"Josie, I think," Tom said. "I don't know. I don't remember what she said. I think it might have been Josie. So, I guess there was a special hearing and we missed it."

"That can't be," I said. "There wasn't a hearing. We didn't get a notice or anything. Did you see a sign in the front of their house?" I asked Tom. He shook his head. "They have to put a sign in front of the house if they're holding a hearing," I said to Agent Hart.

"You mentioned the Bay Mission," Agent Hart said. "Is that what I drove by just down the street here? The lot with the little garden and the party tent?"

"Yes," I said. "That's it. The tent usually isn't there. We had an event two nights ago."

"It's a charity," Tom said.

"A nonprofit," I corrected him.

"You know what?" I said. "I did see the owners of the blue house after the ZBA hearing. They came to our Shellfish and Sunset Night a couple of weeks ago. I talked to the wife. Just for a minute, but she didn't say anything about the ZBA or construction on the house or anything. She bought a painting. I don't even know if she picked it up after the event. Sorry," I said to Agent Hart. "Here I am going on and on. I know you must be busy. We'll let you go."

"It's all right," Agent Hart said. "We're just gathering information at this stage."

I took this as an invitation to tell Agent Hart the entire story of my life. Tom and I told him about our pending divorce and our reunion. I talked about the Sugar Cube. I talked a lot about the Sugar Cube. We sat in the living room and I told him the whole Sugar Cube saga from start to finish. He asked about the Bay Mission and the paintings. He asked me about the town.

"Well, they're crooks," I said. "They're all crooks."

He was such a good listener. That's really what it was about him. He asked questions. He smiled. He asked me about my friendship with Rosemary. He extended his good wishes for a fast recovery from her hip operation. His mother had the same procedure done. He asked how she was feeling and her prognosis. He asked how I was feeling. I told him about Tom's bicycle accident. Tom showed him the scar that stretched from his forehead to the middle of his head. We talked about the neighborhood and the police and the Birch Street Bitches. By the end of the conversation, I was fairly certain that I could live a very happy life with Agent Hart.

"Hope you find the guy," Tom said as Agent Hart stepped out the door. "Sorry we couldn't help with that."

"What guy?" Agent Hart asked.

"The sexual predator," I said.

"Right," Agent Hart said. "Listen, I shouldn't say anything. But, I don't want you to worry. There isn't actually a sexual predator in the neighborhood."

"Phew," Tom said. "Well, that's good."

"It's just I needed to speak to you and well, sometimes it's easier this way," Agent Hart said.

"What's easier?" I asked.

"I can't say much more. I shouldn't have said anything," Agent Hart said. "All I can tell you is that there is a bribery, racketeering, and money-laundering investigation involving the town. I can't go into the details."

"Well, you know what? I'm not surprised," I said. "You could have said that in the first place. I already told you they're all crooks. I told you that I thought they were taking bribes. Who is it? The Building Department?"

"I can't say," Agent Hart said.

"I mean, how else could you explain what's going on here? With the variances? With the overbuilding? Haven't I said it was bribes, Tom?"

"You have," Tom said.

"Okay. Most likely we will need to speak more. If you wish to get a lawyer, that's up to you," Agent Hart said.

"Why would I need a lawyer?" I asked.

"Well, you don't. I can see that you don't. But, you are named in the investigation. So . . ."

"So, what, I'm an informant?" I asked.

"No," Agent Hart said. "You're not an informant."

"A person of interest?"

"I wouldn't say that exactly," Agent Hart said.

"You wouldn't say that exactly? But, you'd say it? I don't understand this. I'm the whistleblower. I'm the hero," I said.

"We're being framed," Tom said. "Or, rather, you're being framed," he was quick to add.

"That's right," I said. "Do you know what these lunatics next door did a few months ago? They said they were going to put me and Tom in a wood-burning fireplace. Now, they've got me mixed up in a racketeering scheme? I don't even know what racketeering is," I said. "Do you know what that is?" I asked Tom.

"No," Tom said. "Wire fraud, something like that," he said. "I don't know. It's not good. Is this going to be in the newspapers?"

"I don't want you to panic," Agent Hart said. "We're in the preliminary stages of the investigation. We got a tip and now we're following that lead. That's all. Right now, we're just getting information. You're not being charged with anything today."

"Oh, great," I said. "You hear that, Tom? I'm not being charged with racketeering or money laundering or bribery *today*? What a relief."

"I'm sorry," Agent Hart said. "You seem like nice people. We'll be in touch."

15

TO: Supervisor White (white@whitbey.gov)
FROM: Kathleen Deane (KDeane@gmail.com)
SUBJECT: Racketeering?

Dear Supervisor White,

Firstly, if it's not already obvious, I would like to formally resign from the position of cochair of the oversight committee to which I was appointed yesterday at the meeting that you neglected to attend. I cannot speak for Rosemary Preston, but I suspect in light of recent events that she will also want to resign.

I spent most of my morning interviewing lawyers and seeking legal advice from friends and family. I'm sure you've already heard that I was sobbing on the phone with the town attorney this morning. I was up all night last night researching racketeering, which I now know carries a twenty-year prison sentence. Needless to say, I am enraged.

I assume you have met Agent Hart. If you haven't, let me

fill you in. Agent Hart is a very nice federal agent who came to visit me at my home yesterday afternoon. I don't want to get into all the details, but I'm proud to say that I can now add becoming a person of interest in a racketeering, bribery, and money-laundering investigation to the ever-growing list of horrible things that have happened to me since moving to Whitbey. The good news is, you are also a person of interest. Finally, we have something in common. So, my question is What exactly is going on?

I haven't lived in Whitbey for long, but I know one thing to be true—all roads lead to the Sugar Cube. There is no doubt in my mind that the owners of the Sugar Cube are responsible for all of this. I don't know how or why or to what end, but they're involved. I can't begin to tell you how tired I am of being harassed, threatened, and generally tortured by these people. I am a law-abiding citizen trying my best to live a comfortable and quiet life. Apparently, in Whitbey, this is asking too much.

I have spent the better part of a year wondering why the town government has turned a blind eye to what was obviously blatant lawbreaking on Harbor Road. I suspected bribery or blackmail or quid pro quo. More often than not, I believed the selective enforcement was the result of laziness, incompetence, and maybe a touch of apathy. Ultimately, I wrote off the town's misdeeds as simply a symptom of a tried-and-true, good-old-boy network. But, I guess I was wrong. It appears this is something else entirely. I very much doubt federal agents would get involved if variances were being traded for chicken barbecue tickets as one zoning board member alluded to earlier this month.

I have been repeatedly belittled, patronized, and humiliated by members of this town at several public meetings. My hus-

band has been threatened with violence on camera by a town employee. Rosemary Preston and I have been painted at best as busybodies and at worst as conspiracy theorists. We have been laughed out of hearings and have been the subjects of more than one nasty rumor spread by board members. Well, enough is enough. I will not allow the town to continue to disrespect me or, for that matter, any other citizen. I certainly will not permit my name to be dragged through the mud or in any way associated with the criminal enterprise that is this town government.

I don't know how I got mixed up in this investigation and I don't know what the investigation will reveal. But, let me assure you, I will cooperate completely and share every detail of the events that have unfolded over the course of this nightmarish year. If necessary, I will spend the rest of my days fighting to bring justice to this town. Feel free to share this email with whomever you like.

Sincerely,
Kathleen Deane

In the first week of August, Hattie made a special trip all the way from Seattle to tell me that I was a horrible mother. At the time, she was unaware that I was also a possible felon facing twenty to life. But, looking back I doubt that would have made a difference. I'm sure she has a version of this story. In fact, I know she does. Here's my version. . . .

It had been two weeks since my initial meeting with Agent Hart. I was neck-deep in lawyers' fees and interviews and witness statements when I got a call from

Hattie. She wanted to visit. She was bringing Andrew. It was going to be their babymoon.

"I don't know if now is a good time to visit," I said as I sat on the floor of the oyster shack, crying, surrounded by the hundreds of documents I had tucked away in my snowman Christmas box on the off chance I would need them on a rainy day. There had been developments in the investigation—or rather, I was made privy to the information that had been known all along by many. Agent Hart, when he got tired of me asking questions and/or doubted my mental capacity to cook up even the simplest of schemes, described the whole thing as a web. The Sugar Cube was on the web. It was on there somewhere. But, it wasn't at the center, not even close. The ZBA was on the web. The Water Conservation Committee was too. But, at the center of the web was the Bay Mission, specifically fundraising at the Bay Mission. So, essentially me—the director of fundraising at the Bay Mission. I was at the center of the web.

"How about at the end of the month?" I asked Hattie. "Could you visit then?"

"No, Mom," she said. "The first week in August is the only week Andrew and I are both off from work before the baby comes," she said. "It has to be that week."

So, I agreed.

I started cleaning. I hired painters. I disposed of the industrial-size hospital-grade blue corduroy couch and bought a sleek leather mid-century modern couch and a matching coffee table. I bought new towels and linens. I hung paintings. I regrouted the bathtub. I bought two stand-up paddleboards and a kayak for good measure.

I hid all the packages of giant white cotton underwear along with the bankers' boxes full of legal documents and investigation-related evidence.

Tom and I had a long talk before Hattie arrived. It was the kind of talk all children accuse their parents of having—and the same one that all parents deny ever occurs. Children, adult children in particular, are time bombs. They all are. Even the happy, successful, well-adjusted ones are walking around the world carrying a lifetime's worth of injustices that they are ready to detonate at a moment's notice. And you can be sure that when that detonation is initiated, its sole target will certainly be Mom and Dad.

It's hard to accept. One minute you're a parent to a small child. You have all the power. You say what's for dinner. You say when bedtime is, when the homework gets done, whether or not so-and-so can sleep over. And then, suddenly that power is gone. Motherly advice is now an insult. Fatherly wisdom is offensive. Opinions are hurtful. Everything is a judgment. So, what do you do? You take a step back. You hold your tongue. You say to yourself, *It's their life.* You say it so many times it loses its meaning. You try to diffuse the bomb.

That's what Tom and I did. Well, it's what we aspired to do. We said we wouldn't mention the investigation around Hattie and Andrew. We wouldn't say anything about the town or the Sugar Cube or Agent Hart. We would try to be positive. We wouldn't complain. We would talk about the beautiful weather and how Tom's pickleball game was improving. We'd talk about the baby. When we went on walks around the neighborhood, we weren't going to say anyone was "nuts" or "insane." The "Birch Street Bitches" were not to be mentioned, at least not by name. In fact, there would be no name-calling at all. I wasn't going to talk about building violations or egregious variances or beach parking. If Hattie said something like, "That's a nice house," about any of the newly built monstrosities around town, I would simply nod my head and agree. I wasn't going to correct Andrew when he said things like, "I forgot to pack a bathing suit. It totally blew my mind." No one was going to roll their eyes at any of Andrew's comments. We weren't going to say a word when Hattie ate thirty pregnancy pops a day. She was an adult. She could eat pickles and Cheetos all day if she wanted to. We were going to be a nice, normal family. We would have manners and wait to talk about each other after everyone had returned to their respective time zones. We would have the good sense to be opinionless and judgment-free.

That lasted six hours. They came. We hugged. We had lunch. We laughed. Hattie took a nap. She woke up. Andrew went for a run. I made lemonade. Tom cut up a farm-fresh watermelon. We sat on the deck and watched the sailboats. And then, I made a mistake—a big mistake. I said something. I had an opinion. I did the thing I said I wouldn't do. Hattie was talking about baby supplies. She was overwhelmed. She said something about a mini crib. I said something like, "Hattie, that's ridiculous. You don't need a mini crib. You have a big apartment. Buy a regular-size crib. I'll buy you a regular-size crib," and that was it. Detonation initiated. Target secured. Ready. Aim. Fire. BOOM. The next words out of her mouth were "I'm ridiculous? You're ridiculous!" And then she left. She waddled out in a fury, holding her bump in a protective cradle.

She was back approximately three minutes later, this time with a very sweaty Andrew by her side. "All we wanted was to have a nice babymoon," Hattie said. "And you've ruined it."

"I don't know what I did," I said. "Dad and I have been cleaning all weekend. We bought a kayak. I'm sleeping on the couch. There are about three boxes' worth of onesies and swaddles and rattles and linens that I bought for you that are sitting in the closet."

"Please," Hattie said. "You've been totally absent this whole year."

"Hattie, stop it," I said. "You're embarrassing yourself."

"I'm embarrassing you!" she yelled and flung a newspaper that was sitting on the kitchen counter across the room. Tom, hero that he is, took this slight lull to announce that he was going to take Roger for a walk.

"Andrew, why don't you come with me?" he said and Andrew pried his hand away from Hattie.

"Well?" Hattie said.

"What, Hattie? What? I'm not allowed to have an opinion? This is all because I said something about a mini crib? Fine, get a mini crib. Knock yourself out. Buy an expensive mini crib and replace it with a bigger one in a month. I don't care. I don't need this, Hattie. I don't. I have a mountain of things on my plate here. . . ."

"You're right, Mom. I'm sorry my pregnancy is not as interesting as goddamn building permits and code violations. You know, a normal person would be excited about the birth of their first grandchild. A year ago, *you* would have been excited!"

"I am excited," I said.

"You didn't even consider coming to the gender-reveal party," Hattie said. "You dismissed it. You made a joke about it."

"I said don't start a forest fire."

"That's right. And how is that supposed to make us feel? Andrew's parents planned that party for weeks. And you know what you said when I told you the date of the party? You said you had a zoning board hearing to go to."

"Well, don't worry, zoning board hearing or not, I wasn't going to fly to Seattle for a gender-reveal party. You know how I feel about them."

"You think they're stupid!" Hattie said and threw her arms in the air.

"Yes. I think they're stupid," I said.

"So, now I'm stupid. I'm ridiculous and I'm stupid. . . . Great. That's great, Mom."

"I didn't say you were stupid or ridiculous. I said the mini crib was ridiculous and that gender-reveal parties are stupid and you know what? I'm allowed to think they're stupid. I didn't say don't have the party. I didn't say one word about it. I told you I'd come for a long stay when the baby is born. Have a little mercy, Hattie. Could you please?"

"It didn't cross your mind to move to Seattle when you sold the house in Kansas, did it? You just picked up and moved to the other side of the country without thinking about anyone but yourself."

By this point, we were both sobbing. The sweat from

my head was running down my face and neck and I felt as though the room were spinning. I was sure some sort of medical emergency was imminent. Hattie went into the kitchen and poured me a glass of water. She slammed it on the new mid-century coffee table before continuing her assault. She brought up third-grade traumas. The quilt and scarf fiasco was relitigated. I stopped fighting. I stopped yelling. I tried to imagine myself somewhere else. I thought about Agent Hart and the investigation. A jail cell might not be so bad, I thought. I sort of wished I could summon Rosemary over. She was a better yeller. She could really put Hattie in her place.

But, Tom was the one who ended the whole thing. "Enough," he said to Hattie in as stern a voice as he could muster. That was all it took. She had a brief conference with Andrew in the driveway before Andrew returned to pack up their suitcases.

"We're just going to get an Airbnb," Andrew said in a hushed and cautious voice. "Don't worry, we're not leaving."

"Maybe you should leave," I said.

"No," Tom said. "An Airbnb is good. I think that's a good idea, Andrew."

"Okay," Andrew whispered, sort of pleased with himself, as he hurriedly collected Hattie's things from my bedroom floor.

There was only one Airbnb available on such short notice at the height of the summer season—one that had unfortunately run into a few bureaucracy-related construction hiccups that regrettably delayed its rental permit application. The property was officially listed as unavailable, as per court requests. But, an option to "contact the owners" through a private email address to "discuss possible arrangements" was highlighted in yellow. If said owners deemed you to be a "good fit," a.k.a. "cool," a.k.a. "discreet," a.k.a. "okay with criminal activity," you were in. Upon booking, lessees were asked via email to kindly park in the garage and to keep the garage door closed at all times. If tenants wished to park in front of the house or on the street near the house, owners requested that they please remove their license plates—front and back. Due to the extremely minor, yet ongoing, legal matters with the Building Department, lessees were not to feel obligated or pressured to speak to any town official regarding their stay and/or any details about the property. The owners could not demand that you not speak to town officials, but then again, further booking opportunities would be at their discretion.

I think the part that really sold Hattie on the property was the email's mention of the nuisance next door. She was to be avoided completely. "She will try to engage you," the email read. "Ignore her." What followed was a rather lengthy description of a bitter, old, lonely woman who had nothing better to do than to call in code enforcement complaints and rain on everyone's parade. "Please accept our apologies for this inconvenience. We hope you understand that like family, we can't choose our neighbors." Before I was able to protest, or even threaten to call in a complaint to Stanley at code enforcement, Hattie booked the Sugar Cube. She did it with a swipe of a finger.

For the rest of the day, I sat and stewed. Rosemary came over and we stewed together.

"Ungrateful," Rosemary said.

"I shouldn't have said anything," I said.

"And to stay over there . . . ," Rosemary said.

"I know," I said.

"What are you going to do?" she asked.

"Tom's over there now," I said. "Presumably smoothing things over. I don't know what to do. I'm stuck. I can't leave here. I'm certainly not going over there."

"I know," Rosemary said. "Would be nice to see the house, though."

"Oh God, Rosemary. I'm not thinking about that right now," I said.

"Right," Rosemary said. "Right. Of course not."

"Have you ever heard of a babymoon?" I asked Rosemary.

"No," she said and shook her head. "Is that what this is?"

"Apparently," I said.

"It's terrible," Rosemary said. "They're all terrible. These damn millennials. They won too many awards as kids. Trophy for everything—now look at them."

"Don't say that. I hate when people say that," I said.

"Well, didn't they?"

"The fight wasn't even about any of this," I said. "The problem is Hattie has never had to deal with bad news. Never. Tom and I made sure of it. We protected her. She never had to worry about anything."

"And now there's bad news . . . ," Rosemary said.

"Right," I said. "Now there's bad news. Tom and I are, well, whatever we are. I bought this ridiculous house.

I'm fighting with everyone, you know, with the town. Tom and I have both been hospitalized in the last few months. I'm seeing a life coach. Tom's on antidepressants. And, for once, everything is not about Hattie. There are other things."

"And she doesn't like it," Rosemary said.

"And she doesn't like it," I said.

"Can't stay here forever, though," Rosemary said as she peeked through the window at the Sugar Cube. "Looks like they're on the third floor," she said as she pressed her nose to the glass. "God, I wish I could see if there was still a kitchen up there. Have you heard anything from Agent Hart?" she asked.

"Not for about a week," I said.

"Steve thinks they're all going to go down—like jail," Rosemary said. "I say all these lizards slither their way out of it."

"I'd like to slither my way out of it," I said.

"Oh, you're out of it," she said. "They're just using you for information. You didn't do anything. They know that," Rosemary said.

"You know I have never been in trouble. Not even a speeding ticket. Nothing," I said.

"Not wire fraud?" Rosemary said with her signature crooked grin.

"No," I said and looked out the window myself to see the progress of Tom's de-escalation tactics.

"Well, I for one am happy," Rosemary said. "I've been fighting these bums for about a decade with no success. You show up and bam, federal agents are knocking down Supervisor White's door!"

"The two are unrelated," I said.

"Either way," Rosemary said.

"All right," I said. "I'm going over."

"Can I come?" Rosemary said.

"Fine," I said and we walked cautiously together across the perfectly landscaped threshold.

I quickly lost Rosemary somewhere on the second floor. She pushed past me on the industrial metal staircase to see if the rumors were true about an alleged sauna room. I reluctantly hiked the rest of the way to the third floor alone, where I found Hattie, Andrew, and Tom having a deep, tearful discussion while seated around the famous wood-burning fireplace that happened to be located in the much-talked-about, but never confirmed, illegal second apartment. I recognized it immediately as a second apartment because there was a kitchen with an oven and according to the great philosopher Supervisor White, an apartment is an apartment if it has a kitchen and a kitchen is only a kitchen if it has an oven. If an oven falls in a forest, is it a kitchen? I noted the presence of the oven before turning my attention to Hattie.

"I'm not apologizing," she said.

"Me neither," I said and Hattie looked to Tom for guidance.

"But, I may have overreacted," she said. "Because you—"

"Okay," Tom interrupted. "I think we all need to just take a breath. There are a lot of hurt feelings and maybe some hormones are raging."

Hattie nodded her head at the mention of hormones. I sighed. I didn't even sigh. I breathed in deeply through my nose.

"You have no idea what I'm going through!" Hattie yelled and so it began again. In fact, we started taking shifts. We spread out. We made sure to point fingers and name-call in every inch of the Sugar Cube. For a while, I fought with Hattie in the third-floor living room while Andrew and Tom got into a heated discussion on the roof deck. Next, I had a long talk with Andrew in the second-floor kitchen, while Hattie and Tom conferenced in the first-floor den. Rosemary and I made a quick stop on the third-floor landing to say hello to our old friend, the curdled demon lady, whom we were glad to see had safely made the journey from the Cliffs and was looking larger and more dead-eyed than ever before. At some point, Rosemary and Hattie were screaming at each other in the wine cellar. Tom and I strategized in a bunk room that we discovered above the art studio while Andrew and Hattie did a fair bit of arguing in the master bath on the second floor. As we made the rounds, we all poured ourselves a drink from the fully stocked bar near the cabana by the pool. It was a marathon and we needed to hydrate.

I was on my way to rebut a three-hour-old comment from Hattie when Rosemary summoned me into one of the three laundry rooms—the one with the cathedral ceiling. "Isn't this one of yours?" she asked and pointed to the oil painting that was hanging above the toilet.

"Yes!" I said and tore the painting from the wall. I tucked it under my arm and continued in a fury to the roof for the sole purpose of informing Hattie that it was *her* not *me* who wanted her to leave her study-abroad program ten years ago. Eventually, everyone, including Rosemary, found themselves drooped across red leather couches in the media room on the second floor. It was almost midnight. We were exhausted. Everyone had said everything they could possibly think to say—every nasty word and accusation had been fired.

"All right," I said. "Good night."

"Good night," Hattie said as she rubbed her forehead. "Did you pack the Tylenol?" she whispered to Andrew.

"I don't know if you should be taking so much . . . ," I began to say.

"What?" Hattie said, her eyes half-open. I paused and reconsidered.

"We're going to get everything you need for the baby," I said. "I don't want you to worry."

"Okay," Hattie said.

"Tomorrow we'll make a list," I said.

"Okay," Hattie said.

"I'm sorry, Hattie," I said.

"Me too," she said.

Tom, Rosemary, and I, walking wounded that we were, exited the Sugar Cube with an almost collective limp.

"I can't believe you got rid of my couch for this," Tom said as he shuffled into the house and awkwardly positioned himself on the new leather couch. "Here's your phone," he said and pried it from between the cushions. There were two missed calls and two voice mails. The first was from Agent Hart. I was officially not, nor was I ever, a person of interest in Operation Seashell. My time, patience, documents, and cooperation were much appreciated. The second voice mail was from Josie, who for weeks had been unreachable. Her store was closed.

Her phone was off. Emails went unread. "Can I come over tomorrow night?" she asked in an uncharacteristically meek voice. "You can say no," she said.

I texted her, "Yes," ordered a mini crib, and went to bed.

16

TO: Supervisor White (white@whitbey.gov)
FROM: Kathleen Deane (KDeane@gmail.com)
SUBJECT: Sugar Cube update

Dear Supervisor White,

I apologize for the tone of my last email. I'm sure you can understand my distress and concern after being visited by a federal agent. However, now that things have calmed down and I have been cleared of any wrongdoing, I could see how my reaction might have been perceived as a slight overreaction.

I know you have a lot on your plate right now what with the investigation and the pending wire fraud charges. But, I wanted to drop you a quick line to let you know that yesterday, due to a series of unforeseen events, I was able to gain access to the Sugar Cube. I don't know where the town is with their lawsuit against the owners of this property and I suspect that with everything going on this will be of little interest to you, but

I just wanted to let you know that the illegal second apartment on the third floor of the Sugar Cube was never removed as previous court documents state. There is a six-burner stainless steel stove/oven. I can have Rosemary forward you a photo of the kitchen if that would be of use. There are also three laundry rooms, not two.

As always, thank you for your interest in this matter and best of luck with your upcoming court appearance.

Sincerely,
Kathleen Deane

P.S. Construction on the blue house on the corner (1873 Harbor Road) began last week. It has been brought to my attention that despite being dismissed at an earlier public hearing, this large-scale project was approved without any public notification or comment during a "special hearing" of the Zoning Board of Appeals. Two months ago, the ZBA denied this application outright, stating in its report that it was "not in the character of the neighborhood." Members of the public were not permitted to make comments because as the ZBA chairman put it, "That would be a waste of time. The application is going nowhere." The house has been listed for sale since the day after that hearing and I thought the matter had been resolved. Now, the owners are back, the house is off the market, the ZBA application denial has been rescinded, and a new identical application has been approved. Most importantly, all of Harbor Road is once again filled with cement trucks and bulldozers and cranes due to a construction project that is obviously out of scale with the lot size and in dangerous proximity to the wetlands. Can you explain this?

I assume, like always, this is yet another bell that cannot be unrung. Still, I believe the public is due an explanation. How could the ZBA deny an application in May and then approve it without any alterations or conditions in July? It doesn't make any sense. I know you're busy, but if you could look over this file (Application #4602 in the ZBA "Approval" folder), I would really appreciate it. Also, I heard that the owners of this property are toying with the idea of installing a new IA septic system. Can the town please make sure that a health department certificate is in place before such a structure is approved so that my neighbors and I do not end up hospitalized again? If my water is going to be contaminated, I would at least like a heads-up. Sorry for the length of this email. Again, best of luck with everything.

Let's just imagine for a moment that this were a story about a normal town with normal people. If that were the case, this would probably be the point when I would have no choice but to describe a long and arduous trial. People would be charged with crimes. They'd have to hire expensive lawyers and wear suits and appear in court. There would be a jury and a judge. Headlines about an all-too-familiar tale of small-town corruption would be splashed across every newspaper in the region. If I know anything from watching TV, it's that there would be evidence and opening statements and witnesses and examinations and cross-examinations. I'd assume at some stage in the process there'd be sentencing. Some people would be found not guilty. Some would be guilty. They'd go to jail. There would be consequences. You'd feel some sort of relief at the finality of the whole thing. One way or another, it would be resolved. Justice would be served.

But, sadly, this is not a story about a normal town with normal people. It is a story about a beach town with beach people. So no, there was not a trial. Of course there wasn't. There was no evidence or witnesses or opening statements. A jury was never selected. No one had to wear a suit or drive to court or hire a lawyer. But, I'm getting ahead of myself. I just thought it was important for me to tell you right now to lower your expectations and remember to never trust a woman over fifty wearing overalls.

Josie was not a punctual person, but she was on August 20. She arrived at my house at exactly seven o'clock as promised. She brought a bottle of "local" wine and a giant art deco antique armoire that was almost identical to the one I left behind in Kansas City. Josie hadn't had the opportunity to paint it white yet. "Isn't it gorgeous?" she said as she walked Tom and me out to the driveway to inspect the piece that was balancing in the bed of her pickup.

"It is gorgeous," I said. "You know it looks just like . . ."

"I know! Your mother's furniture! Can you believe it?" Josie said. "I found it last week at a tag sale in Connecticut. Here, grab that end, Tom."

"Grab the end?" Tom said. "Are you crazy? This thing's a ton. We can't lift this into the house. Even if we could, where would we put it? Forget it, Josie. It's a nice gesture. But, take it back to your shop. It's too big."

"No, I don't want it sitting around the shop," Josie said. "Especially not tonight. This is an expensive piece."

"What do you mean especially not tonight?" I asked.

"Oh, the two of you are impossible. It's light. Let's go. Take that end," Josie said and we did. With Josie at one end and Tom and me at the other, we hoisted the massive wooden armoire out of the truck and teetered it awkwardly across the driveway and onto the deck. "That's good enough," Tom said when we got it past the gate. "Let's leave it here for the meantime."

"Tom, we can't leave it outside," I said.

"There's no room for it!" Tom said as he began massaging his still healing sternum. "I'm going to have to start physical therapy again because of this."

"Here we go," Josie said. "Few more steps." And we heaved it through the sliding glass doors and into the middle of the living room.

"There," Josie said. "Perfect." And she took a step back to admire it.

"I'll put the clams in the oven," Tom said and grunted as he maneuvered around the armoire and into the kitchen.

"Tom made baked clams," I said to Josie.

"Did you catch them yourself, Tom?" Josie called out to the kitchen. Tom ignored her. So, she turned her attention to me. "My friend Amy takes me out clamming sometimes. She has a house right on the creek over by Goose Bridge. Do you know Goose Bridge?" she asked.

"The one the kids like to jump off of?" I said.

"That's it," she said and took a sip of her wine.

"So, are we going to talk about what's going on?" I asked.

"Let's wait for dinner," Josie said.

"Okay," I said. "But, you're going to tell me, right? Because, I'm still in the dark here, Josie. I mean, I have the CliffsNotes version of things. But, that's it."

"Don't worry," Josie said. "By the end of the night, you're going to know everything."

Tom, who had recently enrolled in a farm-to-table cooking class at the community center, didn't let the suspense of unraveling what was a very real crime rush his dinner preparations. Although, it should be noted that Tom had a lifetime aversion to rushing. He simply wouldn't do it—not for a late connecting flight, not when driving his laboring wife to the hospital, not for anything. Tom played Enya in his operating rooms when performing open heart surgeries. Let's leave it at that. So, for more than a half hour, I sat with Josie and talked about Dan and things on the farm while Tom carefully garnished plates and molded potato skins into roses.

Finally, dinner was served. And I have to say, Josie didn't disappoint. But, then again, she never did. Sometimes, it's good to have an interesting friend like Josie. She can't be your best friend. She's not going to show up when you need her or give you a lift to the airport or anything like that. But, every few years she will tell you a story so outrageous that you will suddenly deeply appreciate your own boring life. If you are able to keep this friend at an arm's length, you will be greatly entertained and more or less unharmed for years to come. I have been a captive audience for Josie's antics since we were eleven years old. But, despite my best judgment, I have broken the arm's-length rule and been swept up as collateral damage on more than one occasion. Still, this one took the cake.

It started with a Jumbo Jumper. There is this thing called a Jumbo Jumper and it is essentially a giant piece of rainbow-colored plastic that you stick in the ground and inflate with air. It is the object of many a toddler's desire and the crown jewel of any agritainment operation. And Josie really wanted one. But, it was expensive. So, she did without. She tried to drum up business at the farm in other ways. She declared every weekend a brand-new festival: Peach Festival, Garlic Festival, Blueberry Festival, Asparagus Festival, Corn Festival, and so on. When that didn't work, she started selling ice cream with funky farm-inspired flavors. But, it wasn't enough.

"Then, I ran into Charlie one day at the bank," Josie said as she polished off her pumpkin ravioli.

"Who?" Tom and I asked in unison.

"Supervisor White," Josie said and we both nodded and waited for her to continue.

"I was at the bank to deposit the money from one of the Bay Mission events. I don't remember which one. I think it was Country Night. Were you here for that one?" she asked.

"No," I said.

"Okay, it doesn't matter. Supervisor White was at the bank and he was at one teller and I was at the other. And at this point, I only knew him through Dan, you know because Dan is on the agriculture committee. I mean I knew he was the supervisor, but I had only met him once or twice. Anyway, I handed the teller the envelope with all the checks and cash in it and she said that I'd have to wait a moment because the account could not be accessed by two tellers at the same time. And that's when I knew," she said and slapped the edge of the table.

"Knew what?" I said.

"That he was taking money out of the account," Josie said. And with that, there was a knock on the door. "Shit," Josie said. "They're early. I'll finish the story later."

Josie sprang out of her seat and rushed to the door while Tom and I sat dumbfounded at the table. I was still chewing a ravioli when I saw Richard Hill, the town justice, standing in my doorway. "I'm early," he said. "I know."

"It's fine," Josie said and ushered him into the house as if it were her own. "Thanks for doing this," she said.

"Fire department's there now," Judge Hill said.

"Good," Josie said. "That's good."

"Got the armoire out, I see," Judge Hill said with a smile.

"Just in case," Josie said.

"They should be here any minute," the judge said and checked his watch. Josie looked nervously out the window and nodded. Tom and I were so enthralled and puzzled by this scene that we momentarily forgot to be participants in it. We just sat there and watched from the dinner table as Josie and the town justice paced across the floor. They checked the windows. They looked at their phones. They spoke in a tense, hushed tone. There just didn't seem to be a natural moment to jump into the action and frankly, I wasn't sure I could stand up from the table without passing out. So, I sat and watched and waited while Tom entered a sort of self-protection-inspired dreamlike semicomatose state.

"Hello," Judge Hill said when he noticed Tom and me sitting like wide-eyed gargoyles at the table. "I'm sorry we have to intrude like this. But, it shouldn't be long. We'll be out of your hair in just a few minutes," he said and looked at his watch again.

"Okay," I said, hesitantly. Tom didn't react.

"Here we go," Judge Hill said. "That's them." Flashing blue and red lights filled the room. I felt my heart sink to my stomach and as if on cue, the sweat began to drip down my forehead and into my eyes.

Tom, his frozen spell having been lifted by the suggestion of a police presence, handed me his napkin and approached Judge Hill confidently. "Excuse me," he said in a stern and scolding voice. Then, there was another knock on the door. Actually, there were seven knocks.

Judge Hill calmly opened the door to greet two uniformed police officers who were each holding an arm of a handcuffed Supervisor White. They took one step into the house before Josie barreled toward them and threw her arms around the supervisor's shoulders as if he were a soldier back from the war.

"Are you sure you want to do this?" she asked as she cupped his face in her hands. He nodded solemnly.

"It's going to be fine," he said. "Hi, Kathleen," he added when he saw me at the other end of the room. "I got your email about the second apartment. I let code enforcement know."

"Oh," I said. "Okay. I mean it's not dire or anything."

"They should be around sometime next week to take a look," he said.

"Okay," I said.

"Come in. Let's get this over with," the judge said and the officers escorted Supervisor White deeper into the house. "Here," the judge said and started clearing the plates from one end of the dinner table. "This will be fine." He handed a few dishes to Tom, who carried them into the kitchen in a mystified stupor.

"Okay," I said as one of the officers handed me three wineglasses. "Someone has to tell me what's going on here."

"Just let them do what they have to do," Josie said and took the glasses from me. "I'll explain later." She handed the glasses to Tom, who had decided to go ahead and run the dishwasher in the middle of all of this.

"All right, there we are," the judge said and took a seat at the table. He took a few papers out of his briefcase and began tapping his pen against them. "Now, you understand you're being charged with arson?" the judge asked.

"Yes," Supervisor White said, unfazed.

"Misdemeanor, most likely," Judge Hill said.

"Right," Supervisor White said.

"Okay, good," the judge said and made a note on one of the papers.

"Arson?" I said. "Now, hold on—"

"Please," the judge said and held up his hand in my direction.

Judge Hill asked the supervisor a few more questions

before bringing up the words *mental incapacity* and then just like that the whole thing was over. "You'll have to stay there for three months," the judge said. "Any less and it will look suspicious."

"That's okay," Supervisor White said. "Can I take the handcuffs off now?" he asked.

"Best keep them on," the judge said and packed up his briefcase.

"Will I be able to visit you?" Josie asked desperately from the corner of the room. A few tears streamed down her cheek.

"Probably shouldn't," Supervisor White said. "Don't worry. Three months will fly by." He smiled as the officers, once again flanking him on either side, guided him outside and into the back of the squad car. It was late now—about ten o'clock. A flash of light beamed from a pinched venetian blind next door and I gave Rosemary a small wave as Supervisor White, the officers, and the judge loaded into their cars.

Josie, Tom, and I spent the rest of the night talking. It took a few bottles of wine and a lot of tears, but eventually we got the whole story, or as much of the story as we could stand to find out. Listening to Josie try to not only remember, but explain this convoluted, half-baked yearlong crime was worse than the crime itself. Somehow, Josie had managed to cook up a racketeering and money-laundering scheme and then forgot entirely how she did it. Josie had good stories, but she stopped being able to tell a coherent one around the same time she lost half of her retirement fund in the financial crash of 2008. Don't ask me how the two are related. I can't tell you. All I know is that the same day Lehman Brothers went down, Josie forgot how to tell a story. Suddenly, she left out names. She mixed up time lines. She started in the middle and ended at the beginning. If she did mention someone's name, she said it at the end of the sentence like Yoda—"He said he'd pay the money back, Supervisor White." Josie's stories were filled with unrelated tangents. She'd spend a half hour telling you about a particularly ornery cashier at Costco in the middle of a story about a romantic affair. So, if there are holes in this story, I'm sorry. But, there's nothing I can do about it. I simply do not have the mental fortitude to hear this story told by Josie one more time. So, like me, and the rest of my aging comrades, you'll have to settle for the gist of it. Also, to make things even for everyone, I will be telling this story in the order in which it was told to me.

Supervisor White bought Josie a Jumbo Jumper. He bought her a $15,000 piece of plastic and it made her heart sing. It was an instant hit. Tourists flocked to the farm from far and wide for the rare opportunity to do a bit of bouncing while picking up a half-rotted pumpkin and maybe a bag of corn organically grown in Florida.

"But why?" I asked.

"What do you mean why?" Josie said.

"Why did he buy you a Jumbo Jumper?" I said.

"Oh," Josie said. "Well, I confronted him, you know, about the money and seeing him at the bank that day."

"Right," I said, confused.

"And he admitted it," Josie said. "He admitted that he was taking money from the Bay Mission account. Just like that. You know, he's an honest person. He did this bad thing. But, it didn't start big."

"Wait," I said. "How did he even have access to that account?"

"I don't get this," Tom said. And with that, Josie launched back in time to the birth of the Bay Mission.

Supervisor White, prior to his election, was a founding member of the Bay Mission. The ladies recruited him into the organization as a way of beefing up their credentials and at the same time cozying up to the all-too-powerful wine industry, of which Supervisor White's family reigned supreme. He was a member of the board only in name. It was a simple agreement—a small favor for a few well-meaning, conservation-loving, bored-out-of-their-minds retirees. Once things were off the ground, his name was pulled from the website. He stopped going to the meetings. He had fulfilled his duty. The ladies thanked him. They bought him a fruit basket. And they never looked back.

"So, he had access to the account," Josie said. "He always did."

"And no one knew?" Tom asked.

"Well, they knew. They just forgot," Josie said.

"Okay," I said. "So, he's taking money from the account and doing what with it? Buying Jumbo Jumpers?"

"No," Josie said. "Would you stop it?"

"What?" I said.

"You're being deliberately obtuse," Josie said.

"I wish it were deliberate," I said.

"Fine," Josie said with a sigh. "He had a fender bender, okay? He had one too many glasses of wine and he drove into a telephone pole. That's how it started. It was a town car and he didn't want to report the damage or have it in the police report in the paper, so he just paid to have it repaired."

"Using the Bay Mission's money?" Tom asked.

"Right," Josie said. "It was a few hundred dollars, that's it. It was mostly a paint job."

"Couldn't he have just paid for it himself?" I asked.

"Yes, Kathleen," Josie said, annoyed now. "Obviously, that would have been the better choice. But, we're not all perfect. The Bay Mission money was just sitting there. Charlie is the supervisor, but he's not made of money or anything. He doesn't see any of that money from his parents' winery. His salary is barely anything."

So, Supervisor White started taking money from the account–a little here, a little there. He bought a new watch and took a trip to Big Sur. He paid his cable bill and chipped away at student loans. And no one noticed. Until Josie.

"So, I told him. I said, 'You have to stop,'" Josie said.

"And what did he say?" I said.

"Well, he brought up the Jumbo Jumper," Josie said.

"Oh my God, Josie," I said.

"What?" Josie said. "Don't judge me. Dan and I were talking about shutting the farm down. I mean, we were drowning."

"What about the store?" I said.

"Oh, the store doesn't make the sort of money it used to. No one wants any of it anymore. They all just want T-shirts and key chains. They don't want to spend more than ten bucks on anything. No one appreciates crafts."

"So, what? You just looked the other way?" I asked.

"Well, I didn't just get the Jumbo Jumper," Josie said. "I'm not an idiot."

"What else did you get?" Tom said, intrigued.

"A variance," Josie said. "I couldn't install it without a variance from the ZBA and Charlie put in the word to get it approved."

"Did I tell you this would have something to do with that damn ZBA?" I turned and said to Tom.

"You called it," Tom said.

"Anyway, do you remember my friend Joan?" Josie said. "You met her at the chowder fest a couple of months ago."

"I think so," I said.

"Short hair, glasses, a little heavy? Well, she owns Cedar Wines," Josie said in a "there you have it" sort of way.

"Okay?" I said.

"Oh," Tom said. "I see."

"See what?" I said.

"They just did that big extension at Cedar Wines," Tom said. "They added a kitchen."

"Right," Josie said.

"I don't get it," I said.

"Wineries are not allowed to have kitchens," Josie said. "You know that, Kathleen."

"Right, I know. But, what does . . . oh," I said. "She needed a variance."

"She needed a variance," Josie repeated. "And one day we were out at lunch and she was complaining about her ZBA application being denied and she mentioned my Jumbo Jumper. She said, 'I don't know how you got approval for it.' So, I told her to go see Supervisor White and make her case. I told her that that's what I did."

"More or less," I said.

"We could live without comments like that, Kathleen," Josie said.

"Sorry," I said. "It's late."

"Well, this is no picnic for me either," Josie said. "I've lost everything tonight. What have you lost?"

"What do you mean you've lost everything?"

"I lost Charlie. I'll probably lose Dan. I'll have to get rid of my Jumbo Jumper and that'll be the end of the farm. Then, there's the store. . . ."

"What happened to the store?" I said.

"Burned," Tom said. "Is the whole thing gone?" he asked Josie.

"The whole thing?" Josie laughed. "God, no. The fire department was waiting around the corner."

"What?" I said. "How are you getting this and I'm not?" I said to Tom.

"Just finish the bit about Joan," Tom said and Josie continued.

"Right," Josie said. "So, Joan went to Supervisor White and she pitched him her in-house catering idea and he told her it was a tough sell. Wineries are supposed to be strictly agriculture. There's always a big pushback against the idea of making them commercial. Same thing for farms. And so, Joan asked if there was anything she could do to help her application and Charlie told her that a donation to a local cause was always an excellent way to show goodwill within the community and that the ZBA sometimes took things like that into consideration when making their final decisions."

"Oh, this is gross, Josie," I said. "So, she buys a painting from the Bay Mission, gets the variance, and White pockets the money. That's great. And all this time, a year, you're letting me go on and on about public hearings and meetings and emails to the supervisor and you don't say anything. I'm mowing the grass and weeding the community garden all summer like an idiot."

"Well, I couldn't say anything, could I?" Josie said. "You would have reported it."

"That's right, I would have reported it," I said. "And then you made me director of fundraising? Why? So, I could go down for the whole thing?"

"Oh, please," Josie said. "I told you to just focus on the painting classes. You're the one who said you wanted to get more involved. So, you went to Bunny. She made you director of fundraising. Not me."

"You didn't stop me," I said.

"Yeah, well, what kind of a director of fundraising never looks at a bank statement? You're not exactly innocent in all of this."

"Oh my God," I said. "Are you kidding me?"

"All right," Tom said. "Let's take a break." The sun was just starting to rise. We had been at it all night. "I'll make some breakfast," Tom said as he hoisted himself off the couch and creaked into the kitchen. "That couch is awful," he said and braced his hands behind his back.

"It really is a beautiful view," Josie said as she admired the sunrise glistening across the water. Tom made three omelets and put on a pot of coffee. We ate, we watched the sunrise, and then we jumped back in.

"When did you start sleeping with him?" I asked.

"About six months ago," she said.

"Does Dan know?" I asked.

"Does Henri know?" Tom asked.

"Dan knows," Josie said. "He found out three weeks ago when the investigation started."

"And?" I said.

"And he says he needs time," Josie said. "You know, to process." She took a long pause. "And I'm not sleeping with Henri, if that's what you think," she said.

"I didn't think that," I said.

"Do people think that?" she asked Tom.

"No," Tom said unconvincingly. "No," he said again.

"God," Josie said. "I'm going to have to move."

"You won't have to move," I said. "And if you do, take me with you."

"Did you hear they confiscated all the paintings?" Josie asked.

"No," I said.

"Hart told me they're just missing one," she said and pointed to the painting I had stolen from the Sugar Cube the previous night. It was sitting upside down on the floor, leaning against the wall.

"Oh, that's good," I said. "At least the painting prices make sense now. How many were there?"

"About a hundred," Josie said. "It was easy to find them all. They just went through the ZBA agendas."

Tom laughed.

"It's not funny, Tom," I said.

"It's a little funny," Tom said. "All these big fancy houses with these crappy little paintings. You're fighting the town and also supplying the source of the bribes. I mean, it's comical."

"Let's not forget you were the one who told me to

join the Bay Mission," I said to Tom. "That was your bright idea."

"Did I know it was a criminal enterprise?" Tom said.

"I'd still like to know where arson comes into all of this," I said and Josie explained it.

On the morning of August 19, Agent Hart called the town attorney to inform him that on the following morning at exactly 8:30 a.m., the supervisor of the town of Whitbey would be arrested for charges that included money laundering, racketeering, and wire fraud. He was facing a minimum prison sentence of fifteen years. So, naturally the town attorney called the town justice, who happened to be the brother-in-law of the president of UWMC Psychiatric Hospital. A few phone calls were made, a few favors were called in, and a sensible plan was hatched. At eight o'clock, Supervisor White would strip down to his boxer shorts. He would walk the two blocks down Main Street to the Cultured Pearl, light a match, throw it inside, and wait for a police escort to the oyster shack where Justice Hill would be waiting for him. And that's exactly what he did.

Back at my house, Supervisor White was formally arrested for arson. After a three-second mental assessment from a judge with no medical qualifications, the supervisor was declared mentally incompetent and committed to a psychiatric hospital for an evaluation and a short stay. The money was returned to the Bay Mission coffers from an anonymous donor and the ZBA chairman resigned and moved to La Jolla.

"It's just buying us some time," Josie said. "You know, until they work things out with Hart."

"And what about you?" Tom said. "Aren't you in any trouble?"

"Well, technically, I didn't take any money from the account," Josie said.

"What about the Jumbo Jumper?" I said.

"It was a gift," Josie said.

"Huh," I said.

"What?" Josie said.

"Nothing," I said. "Rosemary was right. You all slithered away like lizards."

"Oh, screw Rosemary," Josie said. "She's got something to say about everyone."

"And why the hell did all this have to happen at my house?" I asked.

"Well, it's not like we could do it at the judge's house. He has five kids. My house was out, of course, because of Dan. Breaking into town hall in the middle of the night seemed like an incredibly dumb idea. . . ."

"Oh, that would be the dumb part?" I said.

"Listen," she said. "It's not like I had a week to plan this thing. I got the call yesterday. I panicked. Judge Hill asked where we should do it and I said your house. It was the first thing that came to mind."

"Or you're trying to implicate us," Tom said.

I gasped at the thought.

"Oh, don't flatter yourselves," Josie said.

"And what happens to all the people who bought the paintings, who made the bribes?" I said. "What happens to the owners of the Sugar Cube?"

"Nothing, I guess," she said. "I mean, they're not getting their money back, if that's what you mean. But, what else could they do to them? Make them tear down the houses?"

"Yes," I said. "Or arrest them. Isn't it illegal to bribe a government official?"

"Well," Josie said and shrugged her shoulders. "How do you prove it?"

"Right," Tom said. "They all made contributions to a legitimate charity. They can just say they didn't know."

"Well, this sucks," I said.

"Yeah, well. Welcome to Whitbey," Josie said and peeled herself off the couch. "Listen," she said. "I know you didn't exactly volunteer to help us with this last night, but thanks."

"It's going to come back to bite us," I said.

"Nah," Josie said and collected her bag from the corner of the room. "It'll all work out."

17

I'll never be a native. I'm not a local. I don't remember the hurricane of 1972 or the hundred-year storm that hit in the '90s. I never saw that old post office that burned down. I don't understand what an oyster factory is and I certainly don't remember riding my bike on the roof of one. To everyone here, I'm a newcomer, a Brooklynite, a decrepit old hipster looking for a new gig. I always will be. And I let them think that. In fact, I welcome it. I embrace it. I feed into it as much as I possibly can because God help me if they find out the truth.

The truth is, I'm worse than a native. I'm practically a stalker. I know everything there is to know about this place. I've read the entire town code—twice. The natives know that they spent their childhood summers floating down the narrow canal at Mohawk Inlet. That's nice. I know that the canal was created in 1950 after a massive illegal rock jetty was installed to increase the size of the beach in front of the home of the former supervisor. I know that it costs the town $10,000 every year to dredge that canal because it starves the surrounding estuary of oxygen. I know that about every five years the town hires the same outside engineering consultant to do a big expensive study on the canal and the health of the wetlands. I know that those consultants generously contribute to the local politicians every election cycle.

I don't want to be this person. It's important you understand that. Every day, I hope that I will wake up with amnesia and forget why I'm here. I used to be cheerful. I have been told on more than one occasion that I have an infectious laugh, well . . . had. Why do I care about this town? I just don't know. It must be some deep self-hating psychological disorder that stems from a repressed trauma that keeps me interested, keeps me coming back for more. It's a mystery and, by the way, it's contagious. Tom was infected shortly after the late-night living room arson conviction. That was sort of the tipping point for him. Every morning, I make coffee and Tom and I sit on the deck and talk about how we should let it go. "It's not healthy," we say. "Let's not talk about it. We'd be happier if we moved on." But, we don't move on. We stick. We're stuck.

Some things are less about obsessive research and more about time. I've been here a while now. I've learned things–gotten used to things. There's no hustle and bustle. There aren't any distractions. I can recognize the footsteps of my neighbors as they set off for their early-morning walks. Each night, I know which cook is loading the garbage into the restaurant dumpster based on the crash of the lid. These are not things I need to know. They're not useful bits of information, but there they are taking up space in my brain, clogging up every corner and fold. Tom and I stayed in a hotel in the city for a night a few weeks ago. We had an early flight to Seattle the next morning to go visit Hattie. It was a beautiful room. The bed was comfortable. The sheets were Egyptian cotton. Room service delivered a delicious meal. There was a Katharine Hepburn marathon on television. We didn't sleep at all. Neither one of us. We missed home.

And, like it or not, this is my home. I love this town or, at the very least, I love to hate it. I love that I can't walk around my neighborhood without getting into an argument about parking. I love that everyone's favorite insult is "Go back to Brooklyn." I love that they call my house "Henry's house," because a man named Henry lived here eighty years ago. I love that nearly every day someone offers a conspiracy theory about a strange-looking fish that washed ashore a decade ago and that no one will ever truly get over the fact that the old post office burned down in 1992. I love that everyone fancies themselves an undiscovered artistic talent. Everyone is working on a new funky tote bag company or applying for a chunky jewelry peddler's license. I haven't met anyone who hasn't self-published a book. The people here are unique. I love them. But God, I can't stand them.

I don't know how it happened or when, but somewhere along the line, I became one of these people and it's without a doubt the worst thing that's ever happened to me. Hattie tells me every week to sell the house. "You're miserable," she says. Tom and I like to play a game where we pretend someone knocks on the door and makes a cash offer for the house. How much will it take to get us to pack up and leave? We usually land on 1.5 mil. Tom will say something like, "If someone knocks on that door and offers one point five million dollars, we're out of here," and I'll agree. But, no one ever knocks on the door carrying a suitcase filled with cash. So, we stay. We agree that the fighting and the arguing and the deep sense of disempowerment that comes with each interaction with the town board, at the very least keeps us busy. Some people our age have nothing to do. We have a full calendar. We have things to do practically every day and on the days when we don't have something to do, we're planning and plotting our next move. For the first time in years, Tom and I have plenty to talk about. We truly hate the same thing. We hate it with such a burning passion that it has made us fall back in love with each other. That's not nothing. It's definitely something.

If you're confused, well, good, because so am I. It's a very confusing thing. Two years of therapy hasn't gotten to the bottom of it and I doubt it ever will. Here's what it all boils down to: I can't leave, but I can't stay. Tom and I are happy and yet, paradoxically, we're miserable. It's a mess. It's a big mess and to be perfectly honest, ten milligrams isn't doing the trick.

My father always liked to tell a story about the time I was attacked by hundreds of crickets in the Bronx Zoo. (There's a point to this, I promise.) The story was a real crowd-pleaser. He told it every Christmas and Thanksgiving and even worked it into his toast at my wedding. It's a terrible story and it's most likely the only thing a few of my distant relatives know about me. Kathleen, you know, the one who was attacked by the crickets at the zoo. The cricket girl—that's me.

The Bronx Zoo was my favorite place as a child. I loved it. My father took me almost every Saturday morning. I knew it like the back of my hand. I felt safe and free and happy there. One day, I spotted what I thought looked like an extraordinarily beautiful rock just outside the World of Birds. I thought it would make an excellent present for my mother. Well, you know the rest. I lifted the rock and out popped crickets—tons of them, giant ones. They jumped all over me. I was covered. A few got tangled in my hair and had to be plucked out by a zoo security guard who had come running when he heard the tremendous scream I let out. I didn't like the zoo as much after that.

So, what's the lesson? It's very simple. Don't lift the rock. Admire the rock. Say to yourself, *Oh, that's a nice rock,* and move on. Keep walking. For the love of God, don't pick it up. How many times could one person make the same mistake? Apparently, many, because I always pick up the rock. I can't help myself. And I'll tell you this, there's never anything good under there. It's always crickets.

I could have just enjoyed this charming little seaside town and my quaint oyster shack. I could have marveled at the beauty of the water and the peacefulness of the farms and the sailboats and the children on their bicycles. I could have just sat on my deck. I could have said to myself, *Oh, this is a nice place. These are nice people.* But, no. I had to lift the rock. I had to go to the meetings and the hearings and the work sessions. I had to write the emails and make the phone calls and read every law and every code. I had to submit Freedom of Information forms and study open meeting laws. I had to make a friend. I had to get involved. And now, look. Look where it got me.

I'm an accessory to I don't know what. I could have called Agent Hart that night. I could have called him the next day. I could have told him everything that happened with the judge and the arson and the money and the paintings and all the rest of it. But, I didn't, and in the end, it didn't matter. Agent Hart quickly moved on from Operation Seashell. After his gorgeous vineyard wedding at the White family vineyard, he dropped the charges. He transferred to another department and started investigating a new case. I think he said it was a triple homicide, possible serial killer. He said he was much happier now.

So, Josie was right. It all worked out. And I'm sorry to say, I wasn't even mad about it. Whether or not Supervisor White answered my emails, I didn't especially like the idea of him sitting in a jail cell. I didn't think the Bay Mission ladies, at their age, could withstand the stress of a long criminal trial and knowing them, they'd inadvertently admit to crimes they didn't commit. Josie was slippery, but she was good. She was basically good. She just had a tremendous knack for landing on her feet. I rationalized things. I made excuses for everyone.

I said to myself, *Any crime that begins with a Jumbo Jumper is hardly an impressive crime.* And that's when I knew I was truly at home. I was one of them. I could look the other way. I could protect the guilty. I could forgive the unforgivable.

In true Whitbey form, I overlooked the big, blatant federal crimes and instead focused in on the small infractions. To this day, I can't pass a large waterfront home and not wonder about whether or not it violates the eighty-five-foot bulkhead setback. If I get a haircut, I have to ignore the fact that my hairdresser is first cousins with a ZBA expeditor who falsifies building applications. I can't swing by and pick up some vegetables from the local farmer without thinking about the floor plan of his duplex on Central Park South. I get a stomachache every Memorial Day when I remember the beach parking situation. I want to scream when I see every idiot in town selling oysters out of coolers in their front yards. But, I don't. I ignore it. It's all I can do.

The week after Supervisor White was carted to the psychiatric hospital under false pretenses, Josie renewed her vows with Dan in an intimate ceremony on the farm. She wore a floor-length lace vintage bohemian dress with a flower crown. He wore a yellow bow tie that was mocked by the other farmers in attendance. They vowed to love each other unconditionally. Then they listed the conditions, chief among them that Josie would never mention *La Bohème* or stagehand salaries again.

"We should do this," Tom said as we walked to the barn for dinner after the ceremony.

"You want to have a barn wedding?" I said.

"No, you want to know what I was thinking?" he asked.

"Not really," I said as my heels sank into the grass with each step.

"The Cliffs," he said.

"Oh, God," I said. "You love the Cliffs."

"I do," Tom said. "I love it. What's not to love? I bet we could get a good deal too. If we did it in the fall? Halloween wedding! What do you think about that? White pumpkins."

"I am not having a Halloween wedding at a retirement home, Tom," I said. "Have you lost your mind?"

"Well, we should do something," Tom said as we made our way to the buffet line.

"You should get rid of the boat," I said as a chicken thigh landed on my plate.

"I can stay in the house?" he asked.

"You can stay in the house," I said and that was the closest thing we had to our very own vow renewal. We vowed to live together in a two-room oyster shack with a leaking roof and a rotting bulkhead for the rest of our days and if that's not love, I don't know what is.

I'm not sure if the town board had some sort of moral reckoning or if they merely appreciated my newfound criminal discretion, but either way the town settled the case with the Sugar Cube. It's amazing how fast you can rip out an illegal pool when the words *five-year prison term* are thrown around. So, the house was put in order, just like that. And it was glorious. Rosemary and I reveled in the destruction of the waterfall and the collapse of the outdoor shower. We basked in the sound of the jackhammers ripping out impervious stone pavers and we cheered when truckloads of sand arrived to replace the pool. Goodbye, waterfall. Goodbye, wine cellar. Goodbye, unicorn float. Rumor has it that the couple who owned the Sugar Cube got a divorce. I heard the wife moved to Switzerland. A few months later, it was sold for $4 million.

I'd love to tell you something dramatic here. I'd love there to be a hurricane that destroys the whole town or a dead body that washes up on the beach. I'd even settle for the people of Whitbey being mildly interested or surprised about the Bay Mission scandal or their supervisor being arrested and institutionalized overnight. But, I can't. Because nothing happened. Absolutely nothing happened. Everyone heard about the supervisor and the stolen money and the affair and they decided it was none of their business. After all, it's not polite to talk about people who aren't there to defend themselves. And how can anyone be sure of what really transpired? Was the money stolen? Were the paintings bribes? Who can say? There are two sides to every story. It's water under the bridge. There's no sense litigating the past. What happened, happened. Nobody's perfect. People make mistakes. You get the picture. We all moved on. It all worked out. To Rosemary and everyone else's delight, Arthur Quigley was promoted to supervisor. He had weekly listening sessions and made Rosemary the chairwoman of the grievance committee, which had a full agenda every week. The Bay Mission vacant lot is still a vacant lot. We haven't decided what to do with it and it's likely we never will.

Hattie had her baby in the fall and named her Summer. Summer Joy (no comment) came into the world at a whopping ten pounds eight ounces. She was healthy and beautiful and cleared to go home the next morning. Tom and I camped out in Seattle in a little cottage we rented on Bainbridge Island, coincidentally the birthplace of pickleball, where the beaches were rocky and gray and the water was freezing and everyone seemed perfectly happy and nice. A few days into our trip, Rosemary called to offer her congratulations about the new baby and more importantly, gossip about things back home.

"You won't believe the two that moved in across the street," she said.

"Well, they can't be worse," I said.

"That's true," she said. "But they did bring goats and I think a pig. I haven't seen the pig. But, Steve says he saw one."

"When did they move in?" I asked.

"Two days ago," she said.

"Have you talked to them?"

"God, no," she said. "I'm not talking to anyone anymore. I'm not introducing myself. That's my new rule. I'm not meeting anyone new. I've met everyone I plan on meeting in this lifetime."

"That's a good attitude," I said.

"Yeah, well," she said. "How's the baby? How's Hattie?"

"Good," I said. "They're both good."

"And how's the mini crib working out?" she asked.

"Well, as soon as we got here, Tom was handed an Allen wrench to set up the mini crib," I said. "And then, you know the baby is almost eleven pounds."

"Right," Rosemary said.

"So, today we're going over to build the full-size crib that they bought yesterday."

"And you're going to say nothing," she said.

"That's right," I said.

"A package came for you the other day," Rosemary said. "Steve brought it inside for you. He said he left it in the kitchen."

"Package from who?" I asked.

"I don't know," she said. "Fragile. Kansas." I didn't say anything, but I felt a lump rise in my throat. "What?" Rosemary said.

"They're the dishes," I said. "The Limoges dishes."

"Oh, from the lady," Rosemary said.

"Mm-hmm," I said.

"Yikes," Rosemary said.

"Yep," I said.

"Oh, and I ran into Supervisor White," she said. "He was in front of me at Rigger's getting a latte."

"Oh my God," I said. "He's back?"

"Apparently," she said. "I didn't talk to him. But, I heard him tell Julie behind the counter that he was working on a book."

"About what?" I said.

"I guess Whitbey," she said.

"Who would want to read that?" I said.

"Exactly," she said.

We stayed on Bainbridge for a couple of weeks. We built two cribs, a bassinet, and three rockers. We picked up groceries and swaddles and baby nail clippers and blueberry muffins. After the muffins, I stopped in at a jewelry store and bought two gold wedding bands.

"Here," I said when I got back in the car.

"Our rings!" Tom said. "You found the guys?"

"They were hiding in Seattle this whole time," I said.

"Bastards," Tom said and slid the ring on his finger. I did the same.

"What's next?" I asked. Tom fished a crumpled piece of paper out of his anorak.

"Something called a *snot sucker,*" Tom said. "Where would we find that?" And that's about how it went. We'd run errands in the morning. We'd help out during the days and at night we'd go back to our cottage and mostly talk about Hattie and the night she almost killed me. Hattie was born prematurely and delivered in an emergency surgery that landed me a quick stint in the ICU after a series of complications.

She was two months early, had a heart defect, and weighed only three pounds. I wasn't even able to hold her. She stayed in the hospital for months, locked in a little plastic vessel with wires and tubes poking out of her little translucent body. You'll never feel as helpless as you do standing in the NICU. Tom and I spent day after day sticking our fingers through circular plastic cutouts, hoping and praying that Hattie would grow and that her heart would keep beating. Tom read her chart obsessively. Those few months felt like a daze. We were zombies. I never knew what day it was. I just remember feeling terrified, all the time.

After we kissed the new baby a thousand times and reminded Hattie of what she put us through thirty-two years ago, we left Seattle and returned home to Whitbey. We hadn't gotten our suitcases out of the car before the new neighbors introduced themselves.

"Kathleen!" I heard a woman call out from the roof deck of the Sugar Cube. "Hon!" the woman said. "Look! It's Kathleen and Tom! We'll be right down!"

Tom and I looked at each other, bewildered. A few moments later, the couple was standing in front of us in the street. They looked familiar, not extremely familiar, just vaguely.

"Can you believe it?" the woman said, beaming with excitement.

"Surprise!" said the man.

"Oh my God," I said and looked at Tom. "It's Cindy Schwartz." Before I could say another word, Cindy wrapped her arms around me. Tom and I played it very cool. We certainly didn't say, "Cindy, who the hell are you?" But, every piece of Cindy Schwartz–related information suddenly rushed into my mind. Her husband. What was his name? Ben. It was Ben. He was a plumber, but he let his license lapse. He got a DUI, but he finished the community service ahead of time. He cheated on Cindy with his chiropractor's receptionist. They got divorced. What else? She remarried. Ethan. No. Chris. No. Simon. She married Simon. He was a, oh right, a hedge fund manager.

"And this must be Simon," I finally said.

"Nice to meet you," he said and extended his hand. "Coming back from a trip?" he asked, referencing our trunk filled with suitcases.

"Yes," Tom said. "Seattle."

"Oh, I love Seattle," Cindy said.

"Hattie just had a baby," I said.

"Oh, my goodness!" Cindy said. "Oh, that's wonderful. Simon, you wouldn't believe how small Hattie was when she was born. She was such a tiny little thing. Isn't that right, Kathleen?"

"Yes," I said, utterly confused. "She was."

"But she was strong. I prayed for her every night—every single night. And now she has her own baby. You two must be thrilled."

"We'll let you get settled," Simon said.

"See ya later, neighbor!" Cindy said and they both blissfully pranced back into the Sugar Cube.

Before we unpacked or ate or riddled out how exactly we knew Cindy Schwartz, Tom and I opened the package from Kansas that Steve had left on the kitchen counter. We approached it as the time capsule that it was with a sort of reverence and wonder. The sight of the six Limoges dishes immediately transported me back to Kansas, back to the old woman's kitchen, back to the old radios, back to a time when Tom and I would eat breakfast in silence. A small note was taped to the inside of the box.

Dear Kathleen,

The truth is nobody is good enough for the Limoges. Enjoy them anyway.

—Eileen

So, we enjoyed them. Tom and I sat on the couch and ate tuna fish sandwiches off the Limoges dishes as we tried to figure out who in the world was Cindy Schwartz. We practically stayed up all night. Who was she? It started to feel like we were in a horror movie. It took us until the next morning to finally put the pieces together.

"She was a NICU nurse," Tom said. "The young one with the green hair and the tattoos."

"No," I said. "Have you seen this woman?"

"It's her," he said, his eyes crusted over. "That was Cindy Schwartz."

"You're wrong," I said. "That nurse was the meanest girl. You think she was praying every night for Hattie?"

"Yep," Tom said.

"She once told me I should get some sleep because I looked like crap," I said. "On the day Hattie was discharged, she told me she was leaving Kansas City and the hospital because it 'sucked' and she was moving with her boyfriend to . . ."

"Duluth?" Tom said.

"To Duluth," I said and nodded my head. "Well, that's one mystery solved."

"My question is," Tom said, "if they paid four million for the Sugar Cube, then how much is this place worth?"

"I'd say about one point five," I said.

"That's what I was thinking," he said.

"Think we should sell?" he asked.

"Never," I said.

ACKNOWLEDGMENTS

First and foremost, thank you to my agent, Suzanne Gluck, who gave me a chance, pointed me in the right direction, inspired me to be better, and made me laugh along the way. I'm forever grateful.

To Nina Iandolo, one of the earliest readers, who continues to be a reassuring and invaluable lifeline.

To my editor, Caitlin Landuyt, for her keen insights and the vital guidance that helped make this book what it is today. Thanks also to the team at Anchor Books, Suzanne Herz and Edward Kastenmeier, for believing in me.

To my family, for their love, support, and the endless material they provide.

A special thank-you to Elaine Romagnoli, a good friend who is sorely missed.

ABOUT THE AUTHOR

Elizabeth Castellano grew up in a beach town. She lives in New York. *Save What's Left* is her debut novel.